Fractured

A NOVEL

SHAY SIEGEL

FIRST EDITION, 2020
Printed in the United States of America

Cover Design by Murphy Rae

Paperback ISBN: 978-1-7346600-0-5
eBook ISBN: 978-1-7346600-1-2

www.shaysiegel.com

Fractured

A NOVEL

For the fractured

ONE

ine seconds were left on the clock. The stadium lights glared down on my teammates and me as we gathered in our last huddle at the twenty-five-yard line—fourth down. The smell of ripe sweat mixed with turf rubber hung in the air. Trumpets and drums resounded throughout the bleachers. We were down by three, yet the crowd was still chanting, "Mason! Mason!"

"Let's do Play-Action Forty-Three. Get to the corner of the end zone, Garrett, and let's take this game!" I yelled and thrust my hand into the center of the huddle. The other guys piled theirs on top of mine, the weight of their damp palms pushing down on me.

I was only a junior, but I was the starting quarterback, and already in line for a scholarship, even being from little Long Island where football players were mediocre at best. A few college coaches, even one from the ACC conference, were here scouting me because I was by far the best on the team. Best in the county for that matter. That wasn't cockiness, just truth.

"Dude, they've been all over me tonight!" You would've thought my friend Garrett Clemens was a little girl losing a tennis match instead of the tight end he claimed to be. Coach left me to call the last play, and if we wanted any shot at winning, Garrett had to get open.

"Come on, dude! I know we can make the playoffs again. You got this!" My voice carried over the cheering crowd and marching band. I started the count down, and we all shouted "Manhasset" on three.

I'd already played awesome today. My extra training this week had paid off big. I'd proved everything I needed to the coaches here. I probably wouldn't be playing college ball in New York—not competitive enough for me—but maybe they'd spread the word to big-time schools about how good I was. Plus, it would be nice to seal the win with this last play.

I glanced at the sidelines as everyone got into position. My mind was wandering already; usually my eyes were on the field from start to finish. I couldn't help but think about the homecoming dance tonight, though, especially when I spotted my date, Sharon Martin, jumping around in that awesome cheerleading uniform.

School dances were pretty junior high, but girls loved them. And if there was one thing I loved more than football, it was having girls throw themselves at me.

Which they did. A lot.

Sharon was a senior. And not just any senior, the senior every guy in school fantasized about at least once or twice. Blue and orange pleats bounced off her thighs as she flashed me her biggest smile. Her blond hair poured over her shoulders like lemonade. Blue, gold, and orange ribbons flowed from her wavy hair down to her chest where the words *Manhasset High* never looked so good. Then she turned around to shout "O-O-Offense!" at the stands. I wanted to pat myself on the back thinking about how I'd have her under my arm later . . . and my arm probably wouldn't be the only thing she'd be under.

I shook my head and pulled my gaze away from Sharon. *Just nine more seconds to focus. You got this.* I crouched, waiting for the ref's whistle.

Johnson hiked me the ball. I turned and faked the handoff before scanning the end zone for Garrett. He had two guys on him already. Maybe I should've actually listened to his whining instead of losing concentration and studying Sharon Martin's body like *she* was in the game.

Garvey was open and I had to act fast. I dropped a few steps back, planted, and sent the ball to him. The spiral was a thing of beauty, coiling as it left my fingertips. Before I could exhale, a jolt shocked my body and my heart sprang against my chest. Something—apparently a huge defensive lineman—collided against my ribs. I stuck my right arm out as I neared the ground. I should've put it against my side, somehow I knew that, but my brain wouldn't process anything other than "Oh shit!"

A loud snap echoed in my ears between the thick layers of my helmet as I landed sideways on the turf. I turned my head to see my limp, crooked wrist through the small cage in front of my eyes. My spit-filled mouth guard stuck to my cheek. I was pretty sure I heard myself scream, but every sound was so far away now, even the crowd cheering my name.

The band started playing our school fight song. Garvey must've caught the ball for the win. I tried to lift my head, but it wouldn't move, my shoulder pads raised up below my chin. My wrist seared like cleats were stampeding across it.

My eyes blinked open and shut. Hands skimmed my neck, pulling my helmet over my ears. Everything was louder now as more hands lifted me under my shoulders and legs. The bright lights slammed directly into my skull. The ground was no longer beneath me; I was in the air, making contact with a stretcher before being shut into an ambulance. My coach sat beside me, a consoling hand on my shoulder. I couldn't tell if I was knocked out or not. Maybe this was all a stupid dream.

"Your parents will meet us at the ER, Vance," Coach said.

I blinked again, allowing him to come into focus. Definitely not a dream. I would've recognized his burly beard and scratchy voice anywhere.

I nodded, or maybe I didn't. My throat gurgled.

Coach held a Gatorade sport water bottle to my mouth and squirted some inside. I coughed and spat, my eyes fully opening now.

"Is it broken?" I managed, still looking at Coach.

Coach laughed, actually laughed. I gritted my teeth. Was I overreacting? It felt like someone was chiseling away at my arm bones with an icepick. It had to be broken, didn't it?

"If it ain't, then you're a lot more flexible than I thought," he said, the laughter falling away. He clamped his hand on my left shoulder again.

I breathed in, my chest shaking. I coughed and groaned. It was broken. Oh my God, what if I never played again?

My parents were already in the waiting room when the paramedics wheeled me in. My mom rushed over, kissing my head and telling me I'd be okay. Though her frantic breathlessness and shaking hands weren't convincing. Even my little brother, Chad, sat more quietly than usual—his hazel eyes bulging. And he was just a goofy fourteen-year-old who never thought anything was serious other than beating the next level on his video games. My wrist must've been pretty screwed, which only made my heart race more.

My parents and Chad helped me take my gear off. It was pinching and squeezing me in all the worst places now that I wasn't on the field. When Dad pulled my cleats off, the sour stench of my feet probably wafted through every floor of this hospital, waking people in comas, I bet.

The assault on my nose was a cruel momentary distraction from the crushing sensation in my arm. My headache turned into a dull throb—nothing like my wrist.

A nurse cut my jersey down the center and then did the same to the laces on my shoulder pads so Dad could slip them off me. The scissors shredded through the middle of my number one as it split in two. I almost cried . . . almost.

I had to pee real bad after all the Gatorade and water during the game, but I still had my cup on and it was about as uncomfortable as a bunch of pins sticking me now that I was sitting still. Since I was out an arm, my dad had to help me take it off . . .which meant he had to help me take my pants off, too . . . then put them back on since I had nothing else to wear. Seriously, this night was supposed to be the best yet and right now, it couldn't have been any worse.

I had to wait for the ER doctor for hours, but at least the nurse hooked me up to a sweet morphine drip, which faded the pain nicely into the background.

The doctor called me in around the same time that the homecoming dance would've been ending. I'd gotten some texts and Snapchats before putting my phone away altogether. They just reminded me how I wouldn't be getting with Sharon Martin, which of course sucked, but not nearly as much as wondering if my football career was over.

"Will I still be able to play football?" I asked, voicing that overwhelming concern as the doctor gathered all the tools he'd need to set my wrist.

He pulled over some metal thing that looked like a torture

device. "Probably, but you'll be out for a while," he said, parking the contraption next to me. "It depends on how you heal over the next couple weeks. Plus, surgery is still a possibility, so you'll have to see what your doctor says."

"Then how can you be sure I'll be able to play football?"

"Nothing is certain." He strung loops from the top of the metal appliance. "But usually people can resume activity after a break, just with maybe a bit more pain at first . . . and of course, a lot of time and physical therapy."

Great.

He slipped my pointer finger, middle finger, and thumb into those small nooses hanging from the silver coatrack-looking thing, suspending my arm in the air.

"Now, speaking of pain, this is going to hurt a little," he said as he positioned my arm.

Please, dude, nothing could hurt as bad as my bones being cracked and separated all over the place. It couldn't hurt as bad as football being nothing but a distant memory.

"Shit!" I screamed as he slowly moved my arm into place, my fingers ripping right from my hand. My wrist made some disgusting popping noise. I swore flames were burning through my whole body. Okay, it *did* hurt, and not a little—a lot.

I barely noticed my mom squeezing my other hand so tight her fingernails left indents in my palm. Though, for once she didn't scold me for cursing.

After the doctor set my wrist, he molded plaster around it. It was hard and dense and went up to the middle of my bicep.

"Your doctor will probably put you in a smaller cast, but unfortunately this is how we do it in the ER," he said as he went on to bandage the plaster with a roll of ACE wrap. "Better to have it move as little as possible, though, while the break is new."

It would definitely move as little as possible, more like not at all. I was officially restricted. I sighed, hating the feeling of the heavy material squeezing around my arm as it sagged from my shoulder. Hating the feeling of my elbow bent in place. Hating the feeling of everything being different already.

TWO

I woke up in the morning on the living room couch. We'd gotten home from the ER around midnight and I didn't even attempt to climb the stairs to my room. A ton of crust stuck to my lashes as I slowly opened my eyes. Gunshots and cursing came from behind me while I faced the back of the sofa. My husky, Dove, licked my neck while my mom spoke in hushed tones, telling my brother to mute his video game.

I rolled onto my back and Dove licked under my eye, which was gross, but I didn't mind waking up that way. I kissed her ear.

As I sat up, the gigantic cast made my shoulder droop. I had almost forgotten it was there, and a new wave of disappointment, bigger than the cast taking up my entire right arm, washed over me. My lip quivered as I wondered if this was the first day of my life without football.

"Ah!" I groaned as a stab of pain screamed through my wrist when I pushed myself against the arm of the sofa. With my good hand, I tossed the decorative throw pillows aside, realizing they were the reason for the stiffness in my neck right now. The smell of warm toast made my mouth water; I hadn't eaten since before the game last night.

"Mason, easy!"

I looked at my mom, who did nothing to mask the worry on her face. My eyes went to the breakfast tray she was holding, full of buttered toast, blueberries, a mug, and a prescription bottle of pills.

"You look like garbage, Mason," my brother, Chad, chimed in, still furiously punching buttons on his game controller. He wasn't as scared as he'd been last night now that he knew I'd live.

I glanced down at my undershirt and pants, both full of grass stains and brownish-yellow spots. I smelled like rotting milk and didn't know how my mom or brother could stand to be around me right now. But I was still glad they were. My eyes lingered on my football pants, and I tried hard not to think about what a loser I was. How could I be so stupid to break my wrist during a tackle? It was only football fundamentals 101 to not leave your arms out when you went down. God, I was such an amateur, I deserved this.

Mom cleared her throat. I glanced up, forgetting she stood there with food.

"Shit, my arm hurts," I said, shaking feelings of regret from my head.

"Language," Mom said.

"Sorry." I reached out for the plate of toast with my left, mobile hand. Dove moved closer, breathing her dog breath all over my face, hoping for crumbs. "Thanks, Mom."

"This is called Comfrey tea," she said, setting the mug down on the table. "I read that it's good for knitting bones. Make sure you drink all of it."

I raised my eyebrow. Really, tea? I'd try anything if it meant I could get out of this cast faster, but still. Mom was always reading about some new trend or remedy, pushing different vitamins on me.

I picked up the mug and took a sip, nearly spitting it on the floor. "This tastes like it was scooped from the football field," I said, passing it back to her.

"I'll get you some sugar." She popped the prescription pill bottle open and handed me a huge capsule. "You can have one of these every six hours for the pain."

I gulped it down between bites of toast.

"I'll hang on to them," she said, tucking the bottle in her sweatshirt pocket.

I rolled my eyes. She was way too cautious, getting herself worked up every time she heard stories on the news about teens overdosing. I'd never mess around with pills; I had a football career to think about, and that was the one thing I'd always take seriously. Mom already thought I had a drinking problem as it was, no matter how many times I explained to her that this was just what sixteen-year-olds did. I told her maybe she would have a case if I were sitting in my room drinking alone. I wasn't some depressed addict drowning in a whiskey bottle. When I drank, I always did it with friends—or girls.

"I left a message with a recommended orthopedist," Mom said, nudging my legs so she could sit down on the couch. She pulled my feet into her lap. "He's supposed to be one of the best in New York. Can't do anything about it on a Sunday, but I'm hoping we can get in tomorrow when they call back."

An explosion erupted from the TV, and Chad threw his controller on the ground.

"Chad, go play in your room," Mom said, whipping around to glare at him.

He got up and wrapped his arms around my neck, kissing

my forehead with an exaggerated smacking noise. I laughed and shoved him in the shoulder with my left hand, getting butter on his T-shirt. I really loved that kid, he was the only one I'd let mess with me like that, though I'd never admit it to him.

"Mason, you smell. And you have eye black all over your face," he said before disappearing into the hallway. I weakly smiled and rubbed at my face, which was pointless because eye black was nearly impossible to get off without industrial-strength soap and a scrub brush.

"Do you think I'll need surgery?" I asked Mom, my smile fading, as I demolished the rest of the toast. A defeated look registered on Dove's beggar face. She sniffed around and licked my butter-coated fingers.

The doctor last night didn't give me much to work with, but he wasn't an orthopedist. Maybe the orthopedist would tell me I'd be fine. Or maybe . . . he'd say I was done for good. What would I do? Sixteen years old, retired, crippled, no skills not relating to football or sex.

"I guess we'll see what the doctor says." Mom rubbed the arch of my foot. "You'll probably be okay, though." She forced a smile. I knew she was just saying that because it was what I needed to hear.

"Sucks," I said, leaning back against the armrest again. I tried not to give away how worried I was, but my heart was doing flips inside my chest. "Shit, I really wanted to make it to the playoffs." Maybe I was trying to convince myself that it was just this season I was nervous about and I'd be back to normal next year.

"Mason! Do I need to do the bar of soap again?" Mom's sympathy was quickly forgotten as she dropped my foot and stood up.

Mom really hated cursing. When my brother and me were younger and we first learned curses, she'd literally put a bar of soap in our mouths. Chad was a weirdo, though, and liked the taste of soap—especially fruit-scented ones—so her plan kind of failed. He would start cursing just so he could suck on the soap, because if he did it when someone wasn't making him, it'd be questionable at best.

"It's the pain, Mom, I swear. It's getting to my head." I flashed her my best innocent smile while I tried to forget about football. It didn't do any good to keep thinking about it while I had a cast the size of Long Island taking up my right arm. And especially because Mom just didn't get it. She supported us, but she preached about how being a "respectable young man" was way more valuable than any scholarship or pro-sports career. She might not have said that if she and my dad didn't have enough money to send us to college. Accounting may have been a boring job and kept my dad out for long hours, even on some Sundays, but it certainly had its perks money-wise. I was sure they'd like me to get a scholarship, though; they wouldn't turn down fifty grand a year. Plus, it'd just be further proof of my awesomeness. Man, I still hoped I was awesome.

When Mom walked into the kitchen to make her infamous Sunday morning cinnamon buns, I read through my texts from last night. I was in too much agony—physically and mentally—and too out of it from the morphine to bother with my phone in the hospital for more than a couple minutes.

Sharon: *Are u ok?*

Sharon: *Wish u were at the dance w me.*

I smiled a little.

I'd gotten like fifty texts from other people, too, including other girls. I pretty much had some sort of "history" with half the girls in my class, especially Mindy Waters, who I slept with basically every weekend. But Sharon was a new conquest, and I was all about those.

My fingers brushed the screen, ignoring my other texts for now as I typed a reply to Sharon.

Me: *Sorry I missed u last night. Lemme make it up to u.*

She answered immediately.

Sharon: *I was certainly lonely :(*

Sharon: *How's your wrist?*

The smile spread wider across my face and I ran my left hand through my shaggy hair.

Me: *It would be better if I had u to take care of me. I wouldn't want u to be lonely again.*

Sharon: *Can I come over later?*

My lips twitched and I cracked my neck on each side.

I texted my best friend, Chris Garvey, after I made plans with Sharon for later tonight, only after reading through his bazillion texts during the dance.

Chris: *Totally sealing the deal with Hayley later.*

Chris: *Girls love guys who win the football game!*

Chris: *Now I know what it's like to be Mason Vance.*

Chris: *Yo dude. U won homecoming king!*

Chris: *And Sharon won queen. Shit ur missing out!*

All the texts got a lot less coherent after that—probably because whiskey and Hayley took over. Apparently he'd gotten plenty of glory for his catch last night since it gave us the winning touchdown over Syosset High, but it was at the cost of me breaking my freaking bones. He didn't even usually play wide receiver, but a few of the guys on the team were sick this week and he had to step in. He was actually second string QB, which I had almost forgotten about until now. He was going to be replacing me.

More texts from last night filled my inbox. I went to my other friends' next.

Dillon: *You ok bro?*

Freddy: *Mason Vance the homecoming king. Predictable!*

Freddy: *Oh yea, u good?*

Freddy: *Being a drama queen or are u actually fcked up?*

Garrett: *Party at Kelly's after the dance. U be able to come?*

They went on like that. Other girls asked if I'd be at the after party. Other guys asked if my arm was broken. Everyone was having way too good of a time and was too drunk to actually care. For once I wasn't the life of the party.

Coach texted me this morning as some more coherent and hungover messages rolled in from my friends. I told them my wrist was broken, but I'd be fine. Not even my best friends needed to know I worried about anything.

Coach: *Holding up okay, Vance?*

Me: *Yea I'm good Coach*

Lie.

Coach: *Listen, I want you to rest. Don't worry about being at practice. Just be at the game on Friday. I'll catch up with you next week, OK?*

It was pretty obvious he prioritized me given that he came with me to the hospital after our victory, rather than giving the team the post-game spiel. But, still, he didn't need me anymore now that I wasn't king of the team. And reminding me about the fact that we still had games left wasn't necessary—games I couldn't be part of.

Me: *Sounds good.*

No. It didn't.

Chris came over a few hours before I expected Sharon. I'd only moved from the couch a couple times to pee. The morphine IV, Gatorade, water, and nasty tea had all gone straight through me, but I didn't have enough strength for showering or changing. Didn't even have enough strength to wipe the salty sweat marks from my eyebrows.

Chris walked in freshly showered, his sandy blond hair still wet and combed perfectly to the side. He wore jeans and a pink polo. I glanced down at my own dirty clothes. It was the first time I'd ever felt like more of a scrub than him.

"Dude, I hope you're planning on showering and washing that shit off your face before the hottest girl in school comes over," he said, plopping down on the couch next to me.

"Yeah, yeah."

"So, don't you want details on my victory last night? And I don't mean football." He shoved me in the shoulder—my right shoulder. I winced as my cast swayed, the movement sending a subtle, fresh jolt of pain. I held on to my wrist, letting the ache subside.

"Bro, it was about time," I said, turning to face him. "You'd only been on like twenty dates with Hayley already."

"Um, it was five. And I'm sorry, not all of us can be Mason Vance, some of us actually have to put in work first," he said, grabbing the bowl of chips my mom left on the table for us.

Chad came in and took his seat back in the recliner, flipping the Saints game on.

"No way, dude!" Chris and me both yelled. Chris put him in a headlock and I swiped the remote. I wished I hadn't stood up again. This stupid cast made my wrist hurt even more from the extra weight.

"Sorry, Chaddy boy, this is Giants territory," Chris said, sitting back on the couch as I switched the right game on again.

"You don't even live here!" Chad said. "Giants suck."

For some reason my brother had decided a long time ago to disown his home state and pretend he was from New Orleans. I thought it was a phase. Everyone I knew from New York rooted for either the Giants or the Jets (Giants being the more respectable choice, of course). Chad was nothing if not a mystery.

"So what time is Sharon coming over?" Chris said, mussing up Chad's already messy hair.

"Sharon Martin?" Chad perked up. Sure, I'd already told him I was taking her to the dance, but her coming to my house was no homecoming dance.

I winked at him. "Like seven."

"I hope you're planning on showering," Chad said. "She's so hot, wonder what she wants with you."

"Dude, don't you know who your brother is?" Chris said.

"Yeah, yeah. The unstoppable Mason Vance. Too bad he's been stopped." Chad pointed at my cast. He was joking, but I thought about how I'd be missing the rest of the season. I could be missing more than that. I didn't even know how serious the injury was.

I put my head down and fiddled with the string on my pants, scratching at a brown sweat spot.

"It's not a big deal, Mason," Chad said in an attempt to take it back. "You guys suck anyway."

Chris and me both laughed. I stood up. They had a point about my stench and filthiness—a shower was definitely in order. There was still Sharon to look forward to and I intended to take full advantage of my body parts that still worked.

"Little bro is right," Chris said. "Plus, with me as QB we'll suck even more."

I laughed harder. It was kind of annoying that Chris was going to be QB now. It wasn't like it was a competition because he wasn't that good or anything; he didn't take football nearly as seriously or have as much talent as I did, but he'd still be in the spotlight. He was also always trying to be just like me; it was probably the whole reason he joined the team and was good with second string in the first place.

"You're good, man," I said. "And whatever, I'll destroy it next year. Now if you losers would excuse me, I have to get ready to rock Sharon Martin's world."

SHARON CAME OVER after my family and I had eaten dinner. And, of course, after I'd finally washed the eye black off my face and bathed away the day-old sweat. My showers probably wouldn't be happening as often after the ordeal of my mom wrapping a garbage bag around my arm with a whole roll of Scotch tape. It was impossible to get off afterward, all slippery and wet with only one functioning hand. I tried to break free from that plastic prison with my teeth, but it was uncooperative to say the least, and it led to me sweating all over again. I'd just wear more cologne or something.

I convinced my parents to go to the movies, thankfully. They usually went to the movies or out to dinner, just the two of them, on Saturdays. But, since they spent the night with me in the ER, they missed out on that last night. Plus, my dad had been out with a client all day today, so I told them they should totally do something before the weekend was over. My mom didn't want to leave me alone, afraid I'd need her to open jars or something for me. Even though she was usually the one asking me to open things for her. She loved taking care of me, but I told her she'd done plenty for me today. Which wasn't a lie, but I really just wanted them out of the house when Sharon came over.

My parents had been known to hover a bit too much whenever I had a girl over. I really didn't want another talk from my dad that went something like, "It's all fun and games until you're holding a baby at your high school graduation. Try playing football with one of those, son." He didn't think my response, "What kind of father would play football *with* their own baby?" was very funny. Come on, Dad, there were even greater forms of protection than helmets and cups out there.

So, yeah, my wrist didn't slow me down one bit in the girl department (other than the speed at which I could remove my shirt). Sharon was basically all over me the second she closed the door to my room behind her. Having her on top of me, her clothes on my bedroom floor, definitely did the trick in forgetting about my wrist for a bit.

She left an hour after coming over. She helped me re-dress

myself, which was sort of embarrassing, but I didn't care that much. I just scored with the girl every guy hoped to score with and it didn't matter that I couldn't take her to the dance. It was like my arm was my wingman tonight—only, I didn't need a wingman. I needed my throwing arm. I needed football.

THREE

I woke up the next morning—still on a Sharon Martin high—and asked Mom if I had an appointment with the doctor. The pain was in full effect and I came to the conclusion that this cast was designed for ultimate discomfort. The way it took up most of my arm, locking it in a pathetic L-shape. The pressure had my shoulder aching, my elbow cramped, and it had only been a day. Basically, I felt like a little whiny bitch.

The orthopedist was able to fit me in at 11 a.m. My mom let me skip school for the day to take it easy and see how the appointment would go—I liked this sympathy. My mind wandered to Sharon again on the car ride. The way she massaged my shoulders before she leaned in and kissed me, her cinnamon scented neck, her thick blond hair tickling my chin. All a solid memory to distract from whatever news I'd get from the doctor. I shut my eyes and exhaled.

We pulled into the doctor's office parking lot and Mom dropped me in front of the building before attempting to find a spot in this overpopulated, crammed town. She was always worried about being late, and she'd probably have to circle the lot five times before a space opened up.

"I'll meet you inside. Don't go in to see the doctor without me," she said. She loved to treat my brother and me like little kids. Maybe Chad needed it because he couldn't leave the house without forgetting something half the time—like his lacrosse stick when he went to lacrosse practice, or his homework assignments sitting on the kitchen table when he went to school. But my personal favorite was when he forgot Dove when his intention was to take her to the dog park.

I scanned the directory board inside the double doors. North Shore Orthopedics, Dr. Kenneth Kalad—second floor.

There was a girl with short bleached hair and purple streaks standing in front of the elevator. Her sweater with cutouts down the arms gave glimpses of smooth, pale skin, but it covered most of her faded jeans, which were tucked inside a pair of boots with chunky buckles up the sides. She was scribbling in a book with bleeding flowers on the cover. When she saw me out of the corner of her eye, she closed the book and tucked it under her arm, keeping her head pointed at the floor. I stared at her, but she didn't even glance up.

The elevator doors opened and we both stepped inside. She pressed the *3* button with a chewed black fingernail. When she didn't ask which floor I wanted, I pushed *2* with my good arm. I focused on her. She focused on the floor.

"You don't care about my floor needs in this crippled state?" I joked as the doors shut.

She looked up and laughed, like one short exhale. "Sorry," she said, pushing some strands of hair behind her left ear, exposing at least eight hoop earrings.

Her bright green eyes were outlined in heavy black makeup. I traced my gaze down her face to her chest. A cool necklace hung against her collarbone—half of a clock, with the hands pointing to the half that wasn't there. It kind of reminded me of football, waiting for halftime where the game could go in a totally different direction, but that probably wasn't what it meant. My eyes traveled up to the side of her face again.

Yeah, she was definitely hot. But kind of in a surprising way—like an "I don't even know why I'm looking at her" sort of way. I didn't usually go for artsy-emo-type girls. But there was this strange sad look on her face—the corners of her lips turned down, a droopy tiredness in her eyes. You wouldn't think that would draw you to someone, but it made me curious about her. Like, what had her so preoccupied that she couldn't smile or flirt with me?

"I like your necklace," I said, willing her to look at me again.

She glanced up, shoulders tense, and grabbed the chain in her hand, before looking at the floor again and quietly saying, "Thanks."

The doors opened on the second floor. I watched her for a beat longer before stepping out of the elevator. It was like she couldn't wait for me to leave.

Then just as the doors began to shut behind me, she said, "Hope your arm feels better."

"Okay," I said, turning back around. "Take care."

Take care? It was like I couldn't remember who I was or why I was even in this building. Why didn't she have the normal reaction girls had toward me? I couldn't totally blame her—she (and my wrist) had me way off my game.

I stared at myself in the shiny silver doors as she disappeared behind them. I still looked good, despite this gigantic cast blocking the view of my muscles. You could still see the rest of me. I leaned in closer to the elevator doors, running my hand through my bristly brown hair and checking to make sure I didn't have anything on my face. Nope, clear like always. My summer tan was even hanging on nicely.

Mom met me inside the doctor's office after I'd started filling out a mountain of paperwork. I had her take over when it was clear no one would be able to read my left-handed attempt at penmanship.

Before going in to see the doctor, I had more X-rays taken in addition to the ones from the ER the other night. They didn't take my huge cast off for the X-rays either. I expected the doctor to, since I always saw people with broken wrists in little colored casts. Not giant plaster ones wrapped in ACE bandages.

"It's a pretty bad fracture," Dr. Kalad said after introducing himself and asking how I'd gotten injured. He was kind of like a geeky offensive lineman—a big guy in glasses. "Two different places on the same bone. See here?" He pointed to his computer where the inside of my wrist was blown up on the screen. Gray, cracked areas that looked like tree roots showed the two spots where the fractures were. "We may have to do surgery, but it's remained aligned since Saturday, so I'd say let's just keep an eye on it until next week. If we don't have to do surgery then, I'd rather not."

I let out the breath I'd apparently been holding. No surgery was a good thing. I'd heard from all my coaches and trainers over the years that if you got injured and could heal without surgery to always take that option because as you got older, the plates and screws could cause issues.

"But," Dr. Kalad said, "if you don't end up needing surgery, you'll have to be in a cast for around eight weeks total since the bone will have to heal without being literally locked into place."

"When can I play football?" I asked.

He laughed like it was an outrageous question.

"Mase," Mom said. "You need to heal first."

Dr. Kalad nodded. "You'll have to do physical therapy when the cast comes off too, so I'd say it'll be a while."

"But I'll be able to play again, right?" I asked, twisting the fabric of my sweats.

"It's possible you won't be at the same level because a lot of mobility can be lost," he said. "But I'm going to do everything I can to make sure you heal well, and I have plenty of physical therapists to recommend. Just think of this as relaxation time for now."

Relaxation time? Clearly this guy didn't know me. Even in the off-season, I trained six days a week. I only went three months without actual football training during the whole year, but even then I was in the gym and on the track and in the pool. I looked down at my sweatpants, anger and frustration rippling through me.

The second hand on the wall clock drummed in my ears as Dr. Kalad leaned closer to his laptop screen. I glanced up at the clock, smiling a little as the hand moved with each tick. Maybe I could find that girl from the elevator after this. My lips turned down when I realized a girl was making me lose focus again— one of the reasons I was in this mess. Though it wasn't like I had much to focus on in the way of football right now anyway.

I shook my head and stared at the doctor. "Can I still train with the cast on?" I asked. "Like running, and leg and core work?"

He looked at me and pushed his glasses up the bridge of his nose, before sighing. "Give it a few weeks at least. Cardio could cause the bones to move, and if you fell you could end up doing more damage."

I shut my eyes and gritted my teeth hard until pressure built in my jaw.

"Is there anything we can do to make sure the bones stay aligned?" my mom asked. I was thankful she cut in. I'd heard all I could take right now. Maybe I really did need to find that girl to get my mind off things.

"Keep it elevated as much as possible, above the heart," Dr. Kalad said, making a motion with his arm as if I didn't understand what elevation was. "Limit movements and ice it as much as you can around the hand area, which should help with some of the inflammation. Other than that we really just have to wait."

My mom started asking him about her "bone healing tea."

"Sure, you could try it," Dr. Kalad said. "Couldn't hurt."

Ugh, Mom wanted me to drink gross tea. The doctor wanted me to relax. I just wanted to play football.

He went on saying he wasn't going to change my huge cast for two weeks because the break was too new. So, my elbow was going to be locked like this until then.

I looked at the clock on the wall again. I'd been in this place almost an hour already. I wondered if that girl would even still be around. What was on the third floor anyway?

"Well, thank you, Doctor," my mom said. I hopped off the exam table, forgetting that my wrist seared every time I moved too quickly. I said a distracted "thanks" and walked out of the room, clutching my giant cast.

"I've got to piss," I said to Mom after we scheduled a follow-up appointment for the same time next week. "I'll meet you at the car."

"Such a charming boy you are," Mom said, shaking her head as she moved toward the door.

In the bathroom, I splashed cold water on my face and leaned on the sink with my left hand, staring at my hazel eyes in the mirror. "This sucks," I said to my reflection. Looking away, I bit my lip and shook my head. Then I rolled my neck and left shoulder out, before exhaling. "It'll be fine. It has to be," I whispered, pressing back from the sink.

I could at least make one good thing happen today. The bathroom door swung shut behind me and I hit the *Up* button on the elevator outside. I headed to the third floor.

The doors opened and my feet carried me into the hallway. Heavy glass double doors sat right outside the elevator. On the front of them it said: *Plandome Mental Health Services.*

A quick scan of the hall showed there was nothing else up here other than this office and a bathroom. I was about to turn around, feeling kind of guilty for coming up here now. The directory board probably listed the mental health center anyway; I could've just looked at that on the second floor.

As I reached for the elevator button again, the bleached blonde with the purple streaks pushed the frosted glass doors open—and we were face to face. I jabbed at the *Down* button on the elevator a million times like it would get there any faster. It was no use, though, I'd already been discovered as the world's biggest stalker.

Why was I being so pathetic? I was Mason Vance. I just had sex with the hottest senior in school last night—without taking her to the dance and with a broken wrist.

"I'm not stalking you," I blurted, once the girl was standing beside me. The elevator was taking an eternity.

"Didn't say you were," she said, staring at the red numbers above the elevator as they lit up. *Floor one . . . Floor two . . .*

Seriously? She didn't even care I followed her up here?

The elevator doors finally opened. We both got in. "First floor?" she asked. I couldn't tell if she was joking since she didn't ask me earlier.

"Yeah," I said, still staring at her blank face. Then, I straightened up and cracked my neck. "It's a good thing elevators have emergency buttons for fires. Want to know why?"

She laughed without smiling. I'd never seen anyone pull that off before. "In case there's a fire?" She looked down, letting her hair fall in front of her eyes.

"Yup, and I'm burning up just looking at you."

She glanced up at me, her lips pursed. She didn't say anything, didn't even laugh.

"Um"—I cleared my throat—"I'm Mason."

She stared for a second and I wondered if she really wasn't going to respond and tell me her name.

"I'm Lace," she finally said.

"Lace," I repeated. "That's a really pretty name. Which makes sense since you're a pretty girl." I grinned.

She laughed again, still no smile. She crossed her right foot over her left and pushed some stray purple streaks behind her ear. Her round cheeks were bright red.

"Well, it's not like I chose it or anything," she said as the elevator doors opened. We both walked toward the front entrance. I admired the view as she walked in front of me, even though her sweater covered most of her curves. I had an imagination to work with.

I really didn't get why she didn't just say thanks or act flattered or something. Usually pickup lines and compliments worked in my favor, but nothing seemed to work with this girl. "I guess I should be complimenting your parents on it then."

What a lame line. This was a poor display.

She turned to face me. Her eyebrows were scrunched together and she glanced sideways, picking at her fingernails. "Okay then," she said.

I cleared my throat, aware that I was tanking this interaction, but whatever. "So, Lace, this is the part where I get your number, right?"

Out of the corner of my eye, I saw my mom watching me from inside the Suburban. Lace stared at me another minute.

"Nice meeting you," she finally said, before she turned and started walking away.

"Oh, I see how it is," I called after her, trying not to let my pride be totally smashed. "Playing hard to get."

She turned to look at me again once she reached a white Jeep. "Not playing," she said, just loud enough to hear.

She climbed into the car, shut the door, and drove off. No girl had ever turned down the chance to give me her number or had blown me off so completely. What the hell?

I continued to stare at where her car was even though she was gone. My eyes came to rest on my cast, and I felt like even more of a loser than I had in the doctor's office.

The wind blew my hair into my face as I straightened up and pulled my shoulders back. No one rejected Mason Vance. If I couldn't have football right now, then I'd have the only other thing I was good at, and that was girls.

FOUR

All I wanted to do was lie on the couch and watch James Bond movies for the rest of the week. But I had to go back to school on Tuesday. I hated having to do anything while my arm pretty much felt like a diseased growth hanging from my body. Dr. Kalad had given me a sling, which took the pressure off my shoulder, but it pinched the plaster into my elbow. So, it was really a lose-lose and I opted for the feeling that my shoulder was being slowly ripped out of the socket.

I couldn't believe my teachers still expected me to take notes and write so much with my left hand. I pretty much gave up on that and just tried to retain what they said, but I had below average focus even when my wrist was healthy. Every day I panicked at the thought of no more football; there wasn't a ton of room in my head for much else.

My arm didn't get me out of anything other than gym, which was the only class I actually liked. And we were playing flag football in gym right now with the last of the decent outdoor weather. I was pissed I was missing it. And I was more pissed I was missing the rest of the season.

When Friday came around and it was time for our next football game—the game that decided if we made the playoffs—I wanted to crawl under my covers and stay there until my wrist healed.

I stood on the sidelines right between the cheerleaders and the guys playing in the game. Right where everyone didn't matter, next to all the benchwarmers and football rejects—regular kids. Being regular sucked, which I was forced to realize now.

The marching band and cheering crowd was way too loud tonight. I just wanted to head home and watch TV with Chad. He didn't even come to the game since I wasn't playing.

I had never seen Chris Garvey, aka my best friend, play as well as he was playing tonight. Maybe he'd been doing training on his own, which would be weird for him not to mention.

It was the second quarter. I had been standing next to my friend Freddy for most of the night. He was the team's kicker, so other than a few practice kicks here and there, he was relegated to the sidelines like me.

"So, how come you never gave us details about getting with Sharon the other night?" he said, keeping his eyes on the field.

I laughed and shrugged. I had sent out a group text to Chris Garvey, Dillon Saunders, Garrett Clemens, and Freddy Price—otherwise known as my four sidekicks—on Sunday night right after Sharon left my room. It was a picture of my cast that I paired side by side with one of Sharon's Instagram selfies, and a caption that said: *Nothing can stop the Vance man!*

They were definitely all jealous, and they should've been. I thought again about how Sharon's fingers had dug into my chest the other night. The way her lips parted while she leaned over me. I blinked my eyes a few times. Honestly, as awesome as it was, I'd barely thought about her since then. The fact that I didn't even bring it up to my friends other than the one text was evidence enough.

I turned around to see her blond hair hanging behind her in loose curls as she jumped around with the rest of the cheerleaders, chanting to the stands. My eyes traveled down her legs and I smiled. It was still pretty awesome that I got with her.

"You gonna get with her again this weekend?" Freddy said, still watching the field to make sure he didn't miss his cue in case he needed to kick an extra point. Something that had happened a few times already this year.

I'd already ignored Sharon in school all week, which wasn't out of the ordinary or anything, and it also wasn't that hard to do since she was a senior. Manhasset was a small high school— probably like two hundred kids in my grade, but the only way I'd have class with a senior was if I was some brainiac honors student. And, did I really come off as one of those?

"I don't know," I said, turning back to face the field. "I gotta keep my options open." I elbowed him.

Freddy laughed his high-pitched laugh and said, "How could I forget how many of those you have?"

My smile faded as I watched Chris line up behind Johnson, waiting for the snap. I couldn't believe my best friend replaced me as QB, and that he was actually doing a decent job.

I looked at Freddy again, desperate to take my attention from Chris. "I met a new pursuit anyway."

"Who?" Freddy turned to me. "Hey, maybe I should try wearing sweats every day since it seems to be working so well for you."

I shoved him in the shoulder. He wasn't wrong. I *had* resigned to wearing sweats since I broke my wrist. Let's face it, wearing sweats unless you were playing sports pretty much looked like you had given up on life, or at the very least, had given up on getting laid. But there was no way I could work a belt, button, and zipper with one hand. And here I was in sweats again—in our team's "warm up" (meaning benchwarmer) uniform—not playing sports.

"So, who's the new chick?"

"Freddy!" Coach shouted. "Would you quit gossiping and get on the damn field?"

He snapped his head back to the turf and saw that everyone was waiting for him on the field goal. There were five seconds left in the first half.

"Shit," he said, slamming his helmet over his thick staticky brown hair. The kid really needed to invest in a brush, or a razor.

He didn't take long to miss the goal, and for the buzzer to go off. The rest of my team jogged in as the cheerleaders set up for the halftime routine. But not before Garrett ran over to his girlfriend, Vicky, picked her up, and twirled her around. He was attached at the hip—and mouth—with her. He took off his helmet so they could make out in the middle of the field in the two seconds they had to spare before Vicky had to get in forma-tion. If he weren't so awesome I'd have to disown him.

"Whipped," Freddy coughed, glancing at Garrett as he made his way toward us. Freddy wasn't too broken up for a guy who just missed his chance to add to our lead.

Honestly, I couldn't believe we were actually winning this game. I had to give a lot of credit to Dillon, though, blocking Chris's blind side the way he was. He was the best blocker I'd seen in high school. It wasn't his fault I was in this cast at all; he wasn't the one guarding me during that play—it wasn't anyone's fault but mine. It wasn't even a late hit, it was just me being a freaken amateur.

After Coach gave the usual locker room pep talk about not backing off just because we were in the lead, we all headed back to the field's sidelines to watch the rest of the halftime routine.

"So, when you going to the doctor again?" Dillon asked. He was the first to ask how my wrist was on Monday right after my doctor appointment. I told all my friends it was fine and that I was waiting to see if I needed surgery. I wouldn't tell them football wasn't such a certainty anymore unless it was completely necessary.

"Monday," I said, as I watched Mindy Waters do a backflip.

Chris glared sideways at me as he stood next to me. It was no secret that Chris liked Mindy. He told me last year that he wanted to hook up with her and I said he should go for it, then I got drunk at a party one night and she was all over me. I didn't want to turn her down when she'd never shown any interest in Chris. Then, somehow it turned into a regular thing. Chris never brought her up again, but his face pretty much turned to stone every time she came up to me flirting, or if she even looked at me a second too long, which she was right now from the middle of the field—like she was dancing just for me.

I didn't realize that he might've actually liked her and didn't just want to get with her, because none of my friends other than Garrett ever admitted to having actual feelings for girls. And, I never did have actual feelings for a girl, so I wouldn't know what it was like—I enjoyed it that way.

Chris didn't even like Mindy anymore. It was pretty obvious he'd been into Hayley since the end of summer. It was just that Mindy liked me instead of him. That was the way Chris's logic worked. And you'd think he'd be less jealous now since he literally took my football position from me. All the cheerleaders were cheering for *him* tonight—not me. My heart started to race at the thought of them all going back on the field in a few more minutes, leaving me here.

"Who cares about the doctor?" Freddy said, coming over to stand between Chris and me. Garrett was still three feet in front of us, his ridiculously long blond sweaty hair stuck to the back of his neck, as he watched Vicky in the halftime dance. "Your wrist is screwed right now. The real question is, who's your new pursuit?"

I forced a laugh. Thanks, Freddy, for reminding me that my arm was useless, as if this game wasn't doing that enough. And of course, for reminding me that Lace actually shut me down the other day. Why'd I even mention her before? Why was everything in my life a failure right now?

"Who?" Chris said, whipping around to face me.

"Not a big deal." I shrugged, really just wanting to get out of here. I'd been acting like an idiot when I met Lace, my mind on my wrist, my spirits crushed—that had to be why she wasn't into me. Or maybe she somehow knew I had become a loser overnight.

"Ohhh," Chris said as the music ended and the cheerleaders made their way off the turf. "She must be a dog if you won't say who it is."

Freddy let out a high-pitched cackle. He seriously had the worst laugh. I'd never get used to it. Which was unfortunate because he was always laughing.

"Dude, have I ever gotten with an ugly chick?" I said.

Chris opened his mouth, then shut it again, realizing he had no comeback.

The thing about Chris was that he loved to live through me. He basically wanted to be me, which was pretty obvious with his choice of playing second string QB. Why couldn't he just play wide receiver or something like he had the other night? I was a good choice, if he wanted someone else's life, but his jealousy mixed with simultaneous admiration was a little ridiculous at times. He'd want all the details about my hookups, but then clench his jaw and get really quiet when he stopped to think about how it wasn't him that so many great things happened to.

"Who's ugly?" Garrett said from a few feet in front of us. He had been standing as close as possible to the sidelines, watching Vicky. Now, she headed back to the track with the rest of the cheerleaders, not before blowing Garrett a kiss, though. Man, they were lame.

"No one," I said, flashing Chris the finger. "I met this chick at the doctor's office the other day."

"She got a broken wrist, too?" Freddy said, snickering. "How cute, a little crippled couple."

I gave him the finger, too. "No, it's not just an orthopedist office. She sees a shrink there."

"Mental chick?" Chris laughed and smacked his thigh.

"Dude, are you serious?" Dillon glanced up from the play-book he'd been studying. All that kid did was study—football, geography, English, it didn't matter—books were his thing. You wouldn't think the most massive guy in school would be such a goody-goody, but that was Dillon. "Don't call people mental," he said, still looking at Chris. "You sound like an asshole."

"Seriously, Garvey, you stupid?" Garrett added.

Coach blasted the whistle and called for the guys to get on the field and warm back up. He'd barely even said two words to me all night. I couldn't stand much more of this and I had another half to go. Maybe even more than that in the weeks to come if the guys actually won this game.

Mindy came up behind me during the kickoff. She had no idea how thankful I was for her timing. "How's your wrist?" she said.

Not her usual flirtatious self, even if she did come to talk to me on the sidelines. Then I remembered Garrett told me (because Vicky told him) Mindy was pissed I asked Sharon to the dance instead of her. You'd think I'd get a little sympathy since I didn't even get to go to the dance, though.

"Eh, it's fine," I said. "Nothing your party tomorrow can't fix." I winked at her.

She smiled back. "So, you're coming then?"

I put my good arm around her. "When have I ever missed one of your parties?" I raised an eyebrow.

She wrapped her arm around my back.

"Oh, takin' the relationship public, are ya?" Freddy ran over to us after kickoff and smacked the back of my head. "Don't let Chris see!"

I cringed and dropped my arm from Mindy's shoulders.

"Don't forget about your dog girl, Mase." He cackled before continuing on to the water cooler.

"Must be real dehydrated after that big kicking effort," I shot back.

"Who's he talking about? Sharon?" Mindy said, glancing behind her at the rest of the cheer squad to glare at Sharon. She wasn't even looking at us.

I thought about Lace's tired and sad—but pretty—eyes. Her half clock necklace. If only I could have those last nine seconds of the game back. If only *this* half could be over. Then, I wouldn't be watching my best friend get all the glory instead of me right now.

I shook my head. "No one," I said, turning to smile at her again.

"Text me after the game." Mindy jogged back over to the track to join in on the "Rowdy" cheer.

There were only two minutes left in the fourth quarter now, and we were winning by one touchdown. I shut my eyes and exhaled. The crowd chanted, "Garvey! Garvey!" I squeezed my eyes tighter. Less than a week ago that was my name they were shouting.

I opened my eyes and stared at my cast with a new hatred. I shook my head and looked at the field. Chris passed the ball to Garrett. He was running . . . running . . . then he went down— tackled by two guys one after the other, full-on impact. I exhaled, smiling.

Then, the crowd gasped and let out some resounding, "Ohhs."

My eyes widened. I had been rooting for my team to lose? What was wrong with me? I took a step forward, now willing Garrett to stand up. I didn't want my friend to actually be hurt.

I let out a whoosh of breath when he popped back up, totally fine.

The clock kept running, and no one else scored. We won the game. It felt like pebbles were lodged in my chest. Not particularly heavy, just uncomfortable and blocking the air. Would this be my life from now on? Sitting on the sidelines . . . watching?

They were actually in the county playoffs, starting next week. I honestly didn't think they had it in them to do it without me. Could Chris keep this up? Even if he did, there was no way that playing next year and in college and the pros couldn't be in the cards for me anymore.

Staying positive was hard without distractions, so I tried to occupy myself the only way I knew how. The weekend came and I went to the party at Mindy Waters' house.

It wasn't the best idea to get trashed with a broken wrist and stumble into things all night, including the doorways I stumbled into with Mindy, but that was what I did.

All I wanted was to shut everything else out for a little while. But when Sunday came I just ended up feeling worse, not only because of the intense hangover combined with a broken bone, but because I had worried my mom by staying out until 2 a.m. Even though she never actually punished me for anything, I still felt guilty. And I had to face the doctor tomorrow. Had to find out if I was getting closer or further away from football. Or even worse, staying stagnant.

FIVE

I walked through the front doors of the doctor's office on Monday morning and headed to the elevator. Mom was in the midst of the find-a-parking-spot game again.

When I stopped in front of the elevator, my shoulders sank. Lace wasn't there this time. I hadn't even realized I was hoping to see her, mostly thinking about my doctor's appointment, but somewhere in my head I must've been thinking about her, too. It wasn't like all the girl did was wait for elevators or something, though.

I tapped my foot against the tile floor, continually looking around the corner, before looking at the numbers lighting up above the elevator. I swore it went up and down between floors two and three at least four times already. I glanced behind me around the side of the wall again, and it actually worked. Lace rounded the corner.

I stood up straighter and turned to face her, smiling. "It's the lady who completes the elevator ride."

The doors opened and I bowed my head, gesturing with my left arm for her to go in first—which was when I noticed her eyes were red-rimmed and bloodshot like she'd been crying. She wore a baggy sweater and leggings, and her face was totally bare, no black makeup. She sniffled as she walked past me. No smile. No hi.

Well, I was officially blowing it for the second time. I put my head down.

We rode up in silence and I didn't try to hide that I was looking at her flushed face. I could tell that she would have a hint of dimples if she smiled. Her small, curved nose was red on the tip and even though she was clearly upset, she still looked pretty. Especially her bright green eyes, made even brighter against the blond and purple in her hair.

"You okay?" I asked, staring at her lips.

She nodded but didn't look at me. She wiped under her eye with a trembling finger.

The doors opened on floor two, but I lingered for a second.

"Are you upset because you wished you gave me your number?" I asked with a small smile.

She laughed like she was fighting not to. I sighed, glad she got the joke. Her left dimple showed and I smiled a little wider. Then, she pursed her lips and tears streamed down her cheeks; she covered her face with her hair. I stepped back inside the elevator and pushed the *Door Close* button.

"Really, are you okay?" I asked. I reached my hand out to touch her shoulder. She backed away into the corner of the wall.

"I have an appointment," she said in a shaky voice. We were on the third floor now. The doors opened and she walked past me.

I HAD YET another set of X-rays taken. Dr. Kalad said they'd have to X-ray me every week to make sure there were no small shifts in the bone because even the smallest movement could affect the healing.

My plaster cast was propped on the table, a weighted vest covered my chest and abs, and the machine flashed and made robot sounds above me. I shut my eyes and prayed my bones didn't move.

Dr. Kalad walked in the exam room holding his laptop while Mom and me sat quietly. The only sound in the room was the soft whoosh of heat streaming through the wall vent.

"Well, everything looks like it's stayed aligned in the X-rays," Dr. Kalad said. "It would be pretty rare for the bones to shift at this point, but it's still a possibility, so make sure you're careful. No jarring movements or exercising or anything."

I exhaled.

"So," he continued. "As long as everything looks good next week, I'll put you in a smaller cast."

The thought of finally having my elbow back was like a major victory. I wasn't excited about lugging this giant plaster thing around for another week, straining my shoulder, but if it'd protect my bones from moving and keep me away from the surgery table then I'd take it.

"So, I'll be able to play football, right?" He was already closing his laptop and standing up.

"Like I told you last week," he said, "it's a process, and we really need to get further along in the recovery to get answers."

"Just focus on healing, Mase," my mom said, standing up and winding her scarf around her neck.

I shut my eyes and bit down on my lip. Yeah, focus on healing. Who cared if I healed if I couldn't play?

"Time goes faster than you think," Dr. Kalad said. "Believe

me."

I blew a stream of air through my lips and clenched my left fist. The rest of this week couldn't go fast enough.

Mom and me walked out to the parking lot after scheduling another appointment. I stutter-stepped when I saw Lace standing outside, leaning against the building. Her face wasn't red and blotchy anymore, no sign she'd ever been crying at all.

"Weren't you talking to that girl the other day?" Mom whispered as we reached the Suburban. I kept glancing back at Lace, my mind spinning while I wondered what I could say to her. How I could see her again. But I also couldn't tell whether it was worth it. Obviously she had some issues, and I wasn't mocking her or anything, but I also didn't want to be the girl's shoulder to cry on. There were plenty of hot girls to choose from, and plenty who didn't cry in front of me and shut me down. Not exactly my fantasy, and definitely not my elevator fantasy.

"Yeah, for like a second," I said, still gazing at her body while she leaned against the brick.

"She looks like she's waiting. It's freezing out. Ask if she needs a ride somewhere."

My mom, Mother Teresa. And her name really was Teresa, too. Go figure. I turned and walked over to Lace. It wasn't even that cold out, but it was definitely coat weather and Lace wasn't wearing one.

"My mom wants to know if you need a ride," I said. I couldn't bring myself to flirt with her right now, and not just because she was crying an hour ago, but because my wrist was quite the mood killer.

"Oh," she said, glancing down at her phone. "I just ordered an Uber. My car's in the shop."

"No, no," I said, taking a step closer to her. "I can't let you get in a sketchy Uber." I smiled. The mix of feelings from my doctor appointment faded away.

"Yeah, because everyone is so sketchy in this town," she said. Her left dimple showed. "Just as sketchy as strangers in the elevator." She raised her eyebrow, the smile lingering on her lips.

I laughed. Yeah, nothing ever happened in these little sub-urbs. It was the type of place where police officers probably forgot how to shoot their guns and weren't supplied with bul-letproof vests. The biggest crimes were people not picking up after their dogs.

I put my hand over my chest. "I take offense to that. I don't want to be a stranger to you, Lace." I took one step closer and smirked.

She shook her head and rolled her eyes.

"I live in Port Washington," she said. Her eyes were so green, they matched the grass in the planter next to the building. "Is that too far?"

"Come on." I waved my left arm like a cop motioning traffic along. "Cancel that sketch Uber."

She laughed.

"She lives in Port," I said to my mom as I hopped in the passenger seat. "This is Lace."

"Thanks so much for the ride. I hope it's not too much trouble," she said as she climbed into the car.

"Of course not!" my mom said. Great, she was going to become best friends with the girl. "It's getting so cold out, isn't it?" Mom turned onto the main road.

"Yeah, definitely," Lace said. I glanced in the rearview mirror to see her hands shaking.

"Do you like the cold weather or you like summer better?" My mom continued with the small talk.

"Um, I like fall best I guess." She shrugged, her hands still shaking.

"So does Mason." Mom laughed. "Only for football, though, right, hon?" She glanced at me as she made the turn toward Port Washington town.

"Well, football goes until January or February technically," I said. "The pros anyway."

Lace forced a laugh when she saw that my mom chuckled first. I stared at her again as she smoothed her hair a few times, her fingers catching on her many hoop earrings.

Maybe she wasn't totally uninterested like I thought the other day. Maybe she was just shy or something. I didn't get how, though. She drew attention to herself with her looks, like she wanted to be noticed. And now here she was acting like she was so uncomfortable that she wanted to disappear.

The gas light on the car dinged and my mom said, "Oh, shoot. Lace, you don't mind if I stop for gas quick, do you?"

"Not at all," she said.

"Mom, you know you can make it like forty miles when the light comes on. You don't have to stop immediately every time."

Port Washington was probably about eight miles from our house. My mom was the definition of the word *cautious*.

"We aren't all daredevils like you, Mase." She pulled into the gas station around the corner. "You know, I'm going to get another coffee while we're here. Do you guys need anything?"

"No, thank you," Lace said. I shook my head. Whatever, I didn't mind. The more time I spent doing errands with Mom, the less time I had to spend at school after this. I wondered why

44

Lace wasn't in school actually. I glanced at her, trying to assess how old she was. Then, I shrugged and turned around to face her once Mom was out of the car.

"So, are you feeling better?" I asked.

She looked down at her lap and nodded. "Thanks."

"Isn't this better than your creepy Uber?" I tried to lighten the mood.

She laughed. "Yeah. I don't usually take cabs. I don't trust anyone."

"I'm going to take offense to that again." I smiled. "I promise I'm not a serial killer."

"You know a serial killer is actually someone who kills in sequence, usually three people or more, so you're technically not saying you haven't killed two people . . ." She tilted her head to the side, keeping a straight face.

I burst out laughing. "You do have some trust issues, huh?"

"Yeah, being trapped in my head is exhausting sometimes. It's like a reel of worst-case scenarios playing."

"Well, at least you'll be prepared, right?" I kept smiling.

"I don't think I actually would be, though," she said, glancing out the window. "When it comes to fight, flight, or freeze, I definitely freeze." She looked at me again to see that I was staring at her, hanging on her honesty.

I cleared my throat. "Well, you could just call me," I said. "I've got enough fight for you, and I promise to protect you from the killers of three people or more." I winked.

She fought a smile and rolled her eyes. "But not two people or less."

I picked up my phone, still smiling. "So, since Ubers usually give you music privileges." I turned to the radio and switched my phone on the Bluetooth. "Just tell your deejay what you want to hear."

"Hmm." I watched her push her hair behind her ears in the rearview mirror. "Something from the nineties."

"Nineties?" I asked, still looking at the mirror. "Like Backstreet Boys?"

"Definitely not like Backstreet Boys." She laughed. "Though I'd love to know that you actually have that on your phone."

"Hey, no making fun of the deejay." She must've been tired of rolling her eyes by now. She *had* to be into me, though, didn't she?

"My favorite nineties song is 'Lightning Crashes' by Live."

"I don't know that one. I'll have to check it out. Let me find you a Mason Vance owned nineties song." I looked down at my playlists, knowing my gym list had a couple of nineties rock songs on it, because I only listened to that stuff when I worked out. I scrolled until I found Nirvana's "Smells Like Teen Spirit" and figured that would do.

The sound of my mom jiggling the gas pump outside made me jump. I hadn't even realized she'd returned with her coffee and finished pumping the gas.

"Ah, so you went cliché," Lace said. She smiled at me in the mirror. I stared at her eyes again.

"Isn't most nineties music cliché?"

She pursed her lips and looked up at the roof of the car. "Interesting point."

My mom opened the door and immediately reached to turn the volume down. "Come on, Mason. You're probably giving poor Lace a headache with this nonsense."

I put my left hand up. "It was Lace's request." I turned

around to smile at her again. She laughed and shook her head.

"Not quite," she said under her breath.

We reached her house ten minutes later. It was a really sick house, like one of the biggest ones I'd seen in Manhasset or Port, and if you knew these rich towns, you knew that was saying something. It was right on one of the private bays that bordered a handful of houses. I gazed out at the still blue water and tall beach grass before we turned into her driveway.

First, Lace had to give my mom an access code on the gate at the beginning of her driveway. We drove in after it opened to a big round, gravel driveway with lights lining the whole thing. A huge granite fountain sat in the center surrounded by shrubs and exotic flowers and small angel statues. Insanely tall hedges blocked the house in—for the ultimate rich person's privacy, of course. I couldn't see the backyard, but I was willing to bet there was a massive decorated pool and patio out there—probably made of stones and marbles where the water spilled over the edge in majestic blue streams, or some shit like that. And it was all right on the beach.

Most of the people in this area of Long Island had money. It was desirable, close enough to the city, but with just the right touch of suburbia. But not everyone's house looked like this. This was a whole new level of rich.

"Thank you so much for the ride," Lace said to my mom. Then, "Nice seeing you again, Mason. I'll work on my music choices."

I turned around to see her smile. We had inside jokes now? Decent progress. I'd never had inside jokes with a girl before, or had to work so damn hard, period.

My gaze wandered over her chest and for the first time I noticed she had a different necklace on today. It was half of a sword; weird, considering our conversation about "fight." But I wondered what was with the halves.

I looked back up and focused on her lips. Just before she got out of the car, I winked at her once more. She rolled her eyes for the millionth time, her smile lingering a second longer, and then walked to her front door. Her hips swayed as she made her way across the gravel driveway. Yeah, I needed to see her again. I didn't even ask for her number this time. She seemed to like talking to me, but maybe she was just thankful for the ride.

"What a sweet girl," my mom said as I watched Lace close the front door behind her. Like I cared whether she was sweet or not.

I kept staring out the window, wondering if actually maybe I did care. I wrinkled my nose and shrugged.

SIX

Later that night, I searched Lace on Instagram. She wasn't easy to find without knowing her last name or username, but I was determined. I finally found her because a girl I followed from Port Washington (I couldn't remember how or if I even knew her) also followed her. There she was, her account was public: Lace Havern.

I straightened up in my chair like this was a homework assignment I'd actually enjoy. In her thumbnail picture, she sat on the sand at a beach. She wore shorts and a tank top—sadly not a bikini—and she didn't have any purple in her hair, it was just bleached blond. She almost looked more like Sharon Martin (aka my typical type) in the picture. The sun and water reflected off her, making her skin glow. She looked peaceful, but at the same time she didn't really look like herself. Not that I knew what "herself" looked like, but I assumed it was ripped clothes, dyed hair, cracked black nail polish, and nervousness. I liked the way she looked in this picture.

I wasn't sure if it was one of the beaches around here, but it could've been in the Hamptons—aka rich summer paradise. I wouldn't have been surprised if her family had a house out there after seeing her house today.

Her most recent photo was uploaded a few hours ago—right after we dropped her off. It was an image of a lake that said: *Everything was beautiful and nothing hurt* across it. Kurt Vonnegut was credited beneath the quote. I thought I'd heard that before, and we had read a book by him in English class, but I wasn't sure. Probably because I usually just read online summaries for class, and even those I skimmed. There was no caption underneath the image.

I kept scrolling through her pictures. There were tons of scenery shots, usually at night. There were also more images with quotes of depressing song lyrics and poems, some she might've even written herself. One said: *When shadows share this outlook, I'm still alone.* And another: *Dying isn't a nightmare when the dreams are sweet.* My face twisted as I swiped through them.

Then, I got to a whole bunch of uploads of these sketches and paintings. They were kind of eerie and creepy looking—forests, ghosts, and skulls. They were blurred around the edges, which made them look like they were crumbling from the outside in. If she painted them, she was really good. And art was a whole subject I couldn't have cared less about, but yet here I was, thinking about it because of her.

I stopped on a sketch of a hooded man in the forest, holding an axe. He stood above a woman who was cowering away from him on the ground, screaming. I moved closer to the screen, staring hard at where the guy's face should've been. But he didn't have a face, it was an empty blur underneath his hood. My heart beat faster. This was dark. It was so detailed and like, raw or something. I shook my head and clicked back to her other pictures.

Her page was weird, and I wondered if she had another account or something because all the girls I knew posted tons of selfies. Lace didn't have any selfies. Was she even the type of girl who took selfies? I thought they all were. I was also used to seeing group shots in bikinis or mini dresses, or a strategically snapped picture with their backs to the camera. Mindy always uploaded pictures of herself that went along with whatever season or holiday it was. Like on the Fourth of July, Memorial Day, and Labor Day she posed by the pool in her red, white, and blue bikini, holding up an American flag. Christmas she'd wear a slutty Santa outfit while doing the *Mean Girls* pose with a few of her cheerleader friends. And don't even get me started on Halloween—though it was October now and I was kind of looking forward to whenever she'd post a picture in her costume.

I hadn't ever gotten to know girls like Lace before. Usually I didn't have to look much further than Instagram to figure out who a girl was. Talking and joking with her today was fun, but that part of her wasn't in front of me. My foot tapped against the leg of the chair as I continued to scroll.

I finally found a picture of her from June. She hadn't uploaded a single picture of herself in four months, even though she posted other dark stuff at least a few times a week.

The photo was of her in a graduation cap and gown. She was next to a guy who looked older. He had a scruffy beard, long and greasy hair, and part of it in dreadlocks. A silver eyebrow ring circled through his face. His arm was snug around Lace's waist. He looked more like the type of guy she would hang out with, but that just made me want to prove even more that all girls liked me. That *she* liked me. Maybe she had a boyfriend and that was why she didn't give me her number. She wouldn't be the first girl to forget about her boyfriend for a little while when I came into the picture, though.

She must've graduated high school already and that was why she wasn't in school on Monday mornings. She didn't look much older than I did, but I liked the idea of getting with an older girl. It wasn't like Sharon Martin was the first older girl I'd been with—just in our school. I'd had plenty of random hook-ups, courtesy of away games, summer football camps, and fake ID. But I didn't know any of those girls, and I wanted to know more about Lace.

I continued to stare at her face in the picture. Even though she was smiling, she didn't actually look happy, she looked bored almost. And again, there was no caption. She didn't even pretend to let people know how she felt about things—she just left it blank.

Chad busted into my room without knocking and I slammed my laptop shut.

"Were you watching porn or something?" he asked, flopping onto my bed.

"I could've been!" I said. "And what would you do with that image scarring your childhood forever?"

He snorted. "I watch porn all the time, dude."

Chad was a basic fourteen-year-old who tried way too hard to be cool. But as little brothers went, he *was* pretty damn cool. I loved our lazy Sunday football watching binges and getting my ass kicked by him in *Madden*. He was the only person I'd allow to fart in front of my face without beating him until he was unconscious. Even though I got him sent to the hospital once when he was seven. I accidentally nailed him with a cleat when I only meant to *pretend* to hit him. It opened up the skin above his eyebrow, leaving him with a tiny scar. A wave of guilt hit me every time I noticed that little white mark, because the fact was, he was my little bro and I loved him.

"What's up, man?" I asked, swiveling my desk chair around to face him, as I tried to stop obsessing over Lace for a minute.

"Just bored." He picked up a Nerf football next to my bed and tossed it in the air.

"What are you still doing up?" I looked at the clock on my nightstand. It read 12:34 a.m.

"I was texting with this girl," he said. He bit his lip, trying not to smile. He was obviously dying to talk about her.

"Details," I said.

He dropped the football and rolled onto his side to face me, smiling wide now. Wafts of aftershave came off him and I wondered if he knew the girl couldn't smell his powerful aroma through texts. Though, apparently, he took my advice about making sure his hygiene was in check whenever he was with a girl he wanted.

"Okay, she's a year below me, and we made out at the movies on Saturday." His smile grew wider.

"Dude!" I leaned over for a high five. He smacked my hand with his. His fingers were sticky and I really hoped it was just because of his well-known midnight PB&J cravings.

"That stuff you told me totally worked," he said. Last week, I knew he had set his sights on a girl because he kept asking specifically what he should do to make her like him. I told him he should tease her a bunch, mix a few compliments in, and find reasons to touch her. It worked every time. Other than with Lace, apparently.

"Awesome," I said. "Knew you'd be able to lock it down."

"Yeah, so like, how do I—" He looked at his lap, his cheeks pink. "Ya know, do more?"

I laughed and messed up his hair. "Chad, you're fourteen. There is no more."

"Mason, I know you did when you were my age! I thought

you were disgusting!"

"Well, yeah, *I* did. But none of my friends even really did until like last year. They can all count the girls they've slept with on one hand." I shrugged only my left shoulder and adjusted my right arm/cast so it was propped on my desk. Maybe being able to count up to five girls seemed like a lot to a fourteen-year-old virgin, but I had surpassed that a long time ago.

"Okay, so what? Should I like, go under her shirt or something?" Chad was dead serious and I burst out laughing again.

"Dude, I am not going to teach you how to grope a thirteen-year-old." I was proud that Chad wasn't an amateur with girls, and I really didn't think he'd have any problems. He looked a lot like me, was great at lacrosse, and was already growing into his muscles. But I was just protective of him.

I took my shirt off, which was a struggle to get over my cast, and sat down on my bed, forcing him to the edge. My eyelids felt like they were weighted down with lead, my shoulder muscles heavy.

"You are useless!" Chad said, as he stood up.

"I'm a proud brother," I said, stacking a couple pillows on my stomach to prop my arm on top of. "You'll be getting laid in no time. Now be a dear and hit the lights."

He mumbled "jerk" under his breath but continued to laugh as he shut the lights off and walked out of the room.

"Love ya, bro," I said, slurring a bit, my jaw slackening as he shut the door.

Then, I was left to think about Lace again. I closed my eyes and my breathing slowed. I pictured her short, curvy body hidden in her baggy sweaters. Her emerald eyes and mismatched hair. Her face clear, no tearstains. As I drifted to sleep, I watched myself kissing her, running *both* of my functioning hands through her soft hair, tracing my fingers along her pinkened cheeks and heart-shaped chin.

I woke up feeling like the lamest guy in the world. I'd never had a dream about a girl that didn't involve sex.

SEVEN

I went out to eat with Chris and Garrett on Wednesday after school. Garrett had to pick up his sister's lacrosse sticks at a shop in Port Washington, so Chris and me tagged along to go to this pizzeria, Gino's, afterward. They had the most amazing slice of pizza ever invented—a cheese ravioli slice. They put four or five raviolis on top of the pizza and covered the whole thing in vodka sauce and mozzarella. I hadn't had one in a while and was really craving it, even if I'd get sauce all over my cast in the process. It was really a two-hand eating job, but that wasn't stopping me.

After we ordered, we took our slices to the back area behind where the front counter was to sit down. There were four booths along the first wall, a bunch of tables in the center of the floor, and a few booths on the opposite wall. We always headed for the back booth against the window whenever it wasn't taken. Well, it wasn't today, but I nearly slammed into the wall when I realized who was sitting at one of the corner tables across the floor from our booth. It was Lace. With a guy. She was using intense hand gestures and starting to raise her voice. She grabbed at her hair before dropping her hands to the table and looking down at her salad.

The guy had long brown hair with the sides of his head shaved. He wore a few thick hoop earrings and clothes that looked like they hadn't been washed in a month. I squinted at him. Even though I could only see the side of his face, he looked familiar. Then, I realized it was the guy from Lace's only Instagram picture of herself.

"Yo, what're you doing?" Chris said. I was standing there gawking at Lace and taking ages to sit down.

I set my tray down and ducked into the booth. Garrett and Chris both stretched their heads to see what had me preoccupied. Shit.

"Who's that?" Garrett asked, when I glanced at her again to make sure she couldn't see my non-discreet friends staring at her.

"Um, this girl I met at the doctor's office," I said, taking a bite of pizza and hoping they'd drop it.

"Ah, your new pursuit!" Chris said. He looked at Lace over my shoulder again and squinted like he was evaluating. "She's pretty hot I guess." He turned back to me. "But Sharon Martin is still hotter."

"Agreed. But no one is as hot as Vicky," Garrett said, smiling like he had a secret. His girlfriend would flip out if she ever knew her saint of a boyfriend thought anyone other than her was good-looking.

"So, are you going to talk to her or what?" Chris wiggled his eyebrows after taking another bite. He was always busting my balls and I knew he secretly hoped for me to fail or get shut down because he was so jealous. I would've thought maybe my broken wrist and him taking my place on the team would be enough, but of course not. And little did he know that Lace actually *did* shut me down.

"I don't know. I'm not sure who she's with." I shook my hair out of my eyes.

"Looks like he's your competition," Garrett said, glancing behind me again. "And from the looks of it, they ain't going to make it, so here's your chance."

"Not sure you're her type, Mase," Chris said, laughing. "Looks like she goes for guys who have more earrings than her."

I turned around again. The guy didn't have more earrings than her, but that was only because it wasn't possible. Hoops went up her entire left ear. Her face was bright red as she talked to him and gripped the back of her neck. Whoever he was, he was really pissing her off.

"Please, I'm every girl's type," I said, smirking before biting into a soft ravioli.

Garrett's shoulder-length blond hair fell into his pizza and he busied himself with trying to squeeze the tomato and cheese out of it.

Chris rolled his eyes and turned back to me. "You sure about that?" he asked, nodding toward Lace. "When you getting with her then?" He popped the collar of his rugby shirt and laughed before picking up his slice.

"Dude, you seriously think I couldn't get with her?" I gulped some Dr Pepper and looked out the window before looking back at Chris's freckly face as he devoured pizza.

Garrett pushed all his hair out of the way before diving back in. With his mouth full, he said, "I don't know, Mase. Seems like you lost the old touch when you broke your wrist." He smiled. I couldn't blame him for joking around when I didn't tell him that the fracture might've been more serious than I let on.

"Oh yeah?" I said. "How do you explain Sharon Martin then?" I paused. "And Mindy the other night."

Chris chuckled. "Sharon Martin is easy, dude, and Mindy's nothing new. You like this mental chick or something?"

Garrett shoved him. "Don't be an ass."

Chris kept staring at me, smiling. "Someone's gotten soft." He shook crushed red pepper onto his pizza.

I bit my lip before licking my fingers and wiping my mouth with a napkin. I stood up even though I really didn't want to interrupt Lace and that guy. I had to show Garrett and Chris I could make any girl want me, that my wrist didn't have shit to do with anything, and neither did actually caring about this girl. It was like fate that she was here. What if I didn't get another shot to see her?

"Challenge accepted. Watch. And learn, boys."

As I got to their table, I noticed the guy was at least in his early twenties. His silver eyebrow ring came into focus and his hands were calloused and dirty.

Lace finally saw me, and her green eyes widened. The guy turned around to see what she was looking at.

"I guess you're the reason Lace wouldn't give me her number the other day," I said, looking from him to her. I meant to sound cooler and more confident, but I could tell she didn't want me standing there and I wasn't sure what to do now. If I turned around and went back to my table I'd look like the biggest loser in the world.

"Who the fuck are you?" the guy asked just about as aggressively as anyone had ever spoken to a stranger.

Lace didn't say anything, just looked down at the untouched salad in front of her.

"You're unbelievable," the guy said, turning back to face her. "You pretend to be miserable and tell me you want to 'talk about your feelings.'" He put it in air quotes and made his voice high-pitched and nasal as he mocked her. "But you're slutting around with this douche." The guy continued to look straight at her and pointed behind him in my direction, as if we didn't know who the "douche" was.

Her lip quivered as tears collected in her eyes. "I don't even know him, Tyler," she whispered.

I swallowed hard and took a step backward. I didn't glance at Chris and Garrett because I probably looked like a frozen deer in the middle of the street.

"God, just act normal, Lacey!" the guy said as he stood up. Lacey? "We don't have to be best friends anymore." He leaned down and put his hand on the table. He lowered his voice and his eyes softened like maybe he was gaining a conscience. "Sometimes this is what happens when people grow up. They grow apart. You know I'm here for you, but we're just different now."

"Oh is that what happened?" she said, still looking down. "You grew up?" A tear dripped on the table in front of her. Shit, if I'd just sat at my table I could've had the taste of sweet ravioli melting in my mouth. Instead I was standing here, not just making Lace more upset, but also looking like an asshole. I didn't want her to cry and I didn't want this guy to be a dick to her.

"Look, man," I said, surprised to hear myself speak. "Maybe you should leave her alone."

He stared at her a minute longer, before glancing at me with bright red and veiny eyes. I gulped, wondering if he was about to punch me. I was definitely bigger and more muscular, and maybe if my arm wasn't broken I could've taken him, but he was so full of rage that it made him kind of terrifying.

"Screw this," he said, brushing his greasy hair out of his

eyes. He turned and slammed into my shoulder as he walked away, though he was nice enough to choose the left shoulder. "Enjoy my sister," he said, shaking his head.

She tried not to cry while her brother left. What an asshole. I sat down in his chair and smiled at her. It wasn't exactly a smiling type of moment, but I had no idea what to do or say. I was relieved that guy wasn't her boyfriend, but I felt sorry for her. I chewed on my left thumbnail and looked at the wall. I really couldn't win with this girl.

"Cool brother," I finally said.

She laughed. I exhaled loud enough for her to hear. She wiped under her nose. Her hand was shaking so hard it looked like she had a tremor. "Sorry," she said.

"Are you okay?" I asked.

She shrugged. "I think I'm gonna head home."

"Wait," I said a little too loudly. I couldn't let her get away again even if this was terrible timing. "You shouldn't drive while you're upset. I need to make sure you're safe," I joked. "Remember how sketchy this town is?"

She laughed without smiling and dabbed under her eyes with her fingers, still glancing down at the table. She finally looked up at me, pursing her lips. "I'll be safe," she said after a minute.

She didn't even want to joke now. How were you supposed to win a girl over when she was totally miserable? Or, you know, something less selfish than that . . .

"Are you sure?" I said, fumbling for a way to keep her here. She zipped her purse and was about to stand up. "How am I gonna give you the CD I'm making you if I don't have your number? All nineties music, and what's more nineties than a CD?" I smiled.

She looked back at me, not even a hint of a smile. "You're

not making me a CD." It wasn't a question, just a statement.

"Sure I am. That song you told me about that I definitely didn't forget the name of is track number one." I smiled again.

She rolled her eyes. At least one familiar emotion. "See you around."

"Come on, Lace! Don't make me beg. You can let me know anytime you need me to come to your rescue. Serial killers, brothers, I handle them all." I slid my phone toward her as she put her bag over her shoulder. "I promise it'll be just for emergency purposes."

She combed her hand through her hair, the ends slightly damp from her tears. "Yeah, it'd be a real emergency if *you're* the one with *my* number."

I smiled. Damn, she was quick. But she was still here; she was considering it. "Okay, okay, you caught me." I put my left hand up.

She stared at me for a second longer then looked down at my phone, biting her lower lip. The side of her mouth twitched up in a smile like she had just realized something. I squinted at her, wondering why her expression changed so fast. But I didn't care that much because she picked up my phone and tapped the screen.

"There you go," she said, still smiling. She laughed a little as she slid my phone back to me. I had no idea why, but I laughed, too, assuming we were in on some sort of joke together as I put my phone in my pocket.

God, I was good, and what an even better bonus that Chris and Garrett were here to witness this. That I just proved how awesome I was after all of their harassment. Chris didn't get to steal my glory that easily. They didn't need to know that guy was her brother. And they didn't really need any more reasons to praise me, but they were going to get one anyway.

"Well, *Lacey*," I joked, as we both stood up. "Can't wait to see you again."

EIGHT

I was about to text Lace the next morning while I was in history class. I wasn't planning on texting her for at least a few days, but I had another sexless dream about her and figured I really needed to fix whatever lameness was coming over me.

After typing her name in, I sent: *Had a dream about u last night. It's one arm Mason btw.*

My phone buzzed almost instantly and I smiled at how I'd won her over so fast. But the text wasn't from her. It was an error message saying the number I texted was invalid. I arched my eyebrow and scrolled through my contacts to find Lace's name. In the number slot was *123456789* and the label next to it said: *Just kidding.*

She seriously played me? I couldn't help but laugh. That explained why she smiled when she gave my phone back. I stupidly thought that was her way of showing she was into me. Why was she making this so damn hard? I decided to stop caring about coming off as lame and desperate. It wasn't like she went to my school or could talk to my friends, or other girls, about how pathetic I was. I went to her Instagram and messaged her.

Me: *Well played, Lacey.*

She wrote back a few minutes later: *Someone's dedicated.*

I couldn't tell if she was joking or flirting or whatever.

Me: *I always give 110%. That wasn't very nice of u though. Are u gonna make it up to me?*

Lace: *110% isn't a thing. 100% isn't even a thing.*

Lace: *And I'm sure you can find someone else for that.*

Me: *There's only one girl I like, elevators suck without her. Even though she tricked me yesterday, I can't seem to get her outta my head.*

Lace: *Why? She sounds like a real bitch.*

A laugh escaped my mouth. My history teacher, Ms. Garland, whipped around, glared at me, and pointed to my phone. I stuffed it in my pocket. I really couldn't tell whether Lace wanted anything to do with me, and I could literally always tell. I wasn't sure how to show I was actually interested in her.

Then I remembered the song and my joke about making her a CD. When the bell rang, I tried to look up the song she told me about, but I couldn't remember what it was called. Something about thunder? Lightning? I spent most of my next class Googling different weather words with nineties rock. Then, I was pretty sure I found it. "Lightning Crashes" by Live. I looked up the lyrics and bit the inside of my cheek as I read them, having no idea what they meant. I kept scanning, trying to find a line that sounded good, and some way to get her to like me already.

Me: *I feel like rolling thunder chasing the wind, Lacey. Forces are pulling me from the center of the earth. To you.*

I smiled after I sent it, proud of my efforts. Yeah, it was insanely corny, but no one else had to know about it. And it was bound to win me some points with her.

She didn't answer for an hour. I checked my phone at least twenty times, feeling like I was the girl here. Finally, I felt it buzz when I was on my way to lunch.

Lace: *Did your homework I see.*

Me: *When it comes to u, I'm totally willing to work ;) So when do I get to see u again?*

Dillon already had a tray for me when I headed to the lunch line. "I know you can't carry this and all your other stuff in your left hand," he said, piling food onto the tray.

"Damn, man. Sometimes I can't believe you're actually this nice."

We walked to our table to join the other guys. "It comes with the size," Dillon said, setting my tray down. He pointed to his massive body. He was right, people probably would've been terrified of him if he weren't the friendly giant. He was the biggest sixteen-year-old you'd ever meet, which made him pretty damn helpful on the football field. Except that he was blocking for Chris now. I shook football from my head when my phone buzzed again.

I yanked it out of my pocket.

Lace: *Probably in the elevator.*

I laughed, feeling my friends' eyes on me as I continued to chuckle. I kind of liked this banter. But at the same time, I was trying not to let my pride be totally crushed. I was dying to see her again.

"What's so funny, bro?" Freddy asked as I typed a reply.

Me: *U know u wanna go out with me, Lacey.*

Was I overdoing the Lacey thing? I stuffed my phone back in my pocket and took a bite of my burger.

"This girl," I said, with my mouth full.

"The mental chick?" Chris asked. "Probably just using you as a rebound after that older guy we saw her with yesterday." Chris laughed and elbowed Dillon. Freddy cackled, too, even though he wasn't there, but Dillon shook his head. And Garrett kept packing his face with fries like we weren't even here.

"You sound like an asshat," Dillon said to Chris.

Chris turned and stared at Dillon with a raised eyebrow. He was about to say something else, but I cut him off, not wanting to see his jerk comments get directed at Dillon now. Chris would die defending himself even if he was arguing that the sky was green and the grass was blue.

"Yeah, seriously, she's not mental," I said, nodding to Dillon. He pressed his lips together and nodded back.

The rest of my friends stopped eating and looked up at me. They'd never heard me defend a girl before. In fact, I had never defended a girl before. I didn't realize I was defending Lace and Dillon at once.

"Anyway, she can use me all she wants," I said, trying to recover and steer the conversation away from the whole "mental" awkwardness. I took another bite of my burger.

"Do we ever get to meet her?" Freddy asked after they all laughed at my comment. It seemed to distract them from how I was on the verge of being Mr. Sensitive.

"Yeah, he didn't even introduce us," Chris said, smacking his palm down on the table.

My phone buzzed again. I took it out of my pocket.

Lace: *We'll see.*

A smile spread across my lips. I was definitely getting somewhere.

"I'll let you boys know how it goes," I said, tapping my pointer finger on the table a few times. "Someone's got a date."

Okay, maybe I didn't have a date just yet. But I was sure I would soon.

"A date, dude?" Garrett asked in disbelief, finally taking a break from his mountain of fries. He slicked his blond hair back. "Since when does Mason Vance ever go on dates?"

"Hey, Sharon Martin was my date for the homecoming dance," I said, trying to hold in my laughter.

Freddy threw his hands in the air, which somehow made his brown hair look like it was standing up even straighter. "And you didn't have to attend the actual date! Such a lucky bastard."

Him, Chris, and Garrett bowed and waved their hands like a bunch of peasants worshipping their king. Dillon chuckled and shook his head. The rest of us barely noticed when Vicky sat down next to Garrett and shoved her tongue in his mouth. He was still chewing, too. Mindy followed closely behind her and sat next to me. My friends stopped fanning their hands.

"What's so funny?" Mindy asked, scooting over so that our thighs were touching.

Vicky and Garrett pulled apart from their make out session and Garrett said, "Oh, just Mason talking about how much he likes you." He winked at me, and Freddy and Chris burst out laughing again. I grinned, too, and looked at Mindy. Her eyebrows were furrowed like she couldn't figure out whether she was supposed to be angry or happy. I leaned in toward her, pushing her long dark hair over her shoulder. Goose bumps formed on her arms.

I whispered in her ear, "I like you better when we're alone."

It wasn't really a compliment, well, that depended on what you considered a compliment, but she blushed, tracing her fingers along my knee. I swore she was about to lean in and kiss me.

"Unbelievable," Freddy muttered.

Chris narrowed his eyes at me, his freckles more pronounced, and he cracked his knuckles.

I shrugged at him, knowing he didn't even really care about Mindy anymore. He'd just had his arm around Hayley in the hallway right before lunch. Was he always going to want everything I had? It was exhausting.

Mindy looked up. "Oh yeah, you played well the other night, Chris. Hope you can keep it up on Saturday."

He smiled so wide I thought his cheeks might split open. But the smile quickly faded when she turned back to me and asked if I was coming to her Halloween party next week.

It felt good to be praised by my boys for all the girls that lined up for me. It was the main reason I still led Mindy on and made a show of flirting with girls in front of them. I had to say I was a little relieved they didn't all forget about me when I was off the field, because it was bad enough I didn't get any attention during the game.

It still wasn't quite as satisfying as it was a couple weeks ago, though, which was probably because of my worry over my wrist. Or maybe I just wanted to figure out how to get with Lace. She was the only girl really occupying my thoughts at the moment.

NINE

My coach called me into his office after last period while all the other guys got suited up for practice. After coming with me to the ER, Coach waited with my parents for almost an hour, trying to calm my mom down and assure her I'd be fine. Though we both knew that wasn't a guarantee anymore. He'd texted me to check in after my doctor's appointment. He'd made sure I was at the game last Friday and would be again on Saturday. I didn't really get into how nervous I was about this injury since Coach and I hadn't talked much in person yet. He was busy preparing for county playoffs, so he hardly had time for a has-been like me.

"How you holding up, Vance?" he asked as I sat in the chair across from his desk.

"Kind of going crazy, Coach," I admitted. He was a cool, understanding guy and I knew I could confide in him. Not like my friends, who'd just make jokes, or my mom who didn't get how important football was.

"What's the doc been saying? Still no surgery, right?" He took a swig of Diet Pepsi.

I glanced behind his head at the white brick wall of the

tiny office. A signed jersey hung there from the only guy from Manhasset to make All-American in college (in the last fifty years anyway). I tried to forget about how whenever I'd looked at that jersey before, I'd smile, sure that I'd be the first player here to make it to the NFL. Well, other than Jim Brown, but that was like a bazillion years ago. I wanted to be Coach's first real success; he could hang *my* signed jersey up one day.

I cleared my throat and met Coach's eyes again. "He said as long as X-rays are still good next week, he'll put me in a smaller cast. But it'll be for another six weeks. And I'm not even supposed to do cardio or anything for at least a month because it could move the bones." I sighed. "He doesn't know if I'll even be able to play again, Coach." My whole mouth dried up and my eyes stung.

"Come on, Vance." Coach rested his hands on his desk. "You're too damn good to be out of this game. Last year alone you broke three school records. And this year you added two more. Who else has got most completions in a game, most touchdown passes in a game—and in a season, longest pass, highest scoring game, and longest run down the field?"

I half-smiled. Usually he didn't blow me up like this, saying I should be more humble or whatever.

"Plus," he added, "you won MVP the past two years, along with All-League, All-County, and last year, All-Island and All-State. Even though you can't play the whole season, you'll still win awards at the athletic banquet in May."

My smile faltered, because I realized all he was doing was trying to make me feel better. The wrinkles on his forehead grew deeper and he gripped the edge of the desk. Maybe he was listing all my accomplishments because I'd never be able to add to that list again. I was his one shot at a state championship. Next year I would've gotten stronger and improved more over the summer.

Now I'd be lucky to even hold a football by then, if ever.

"But what if I really can't play?" I asked, wanting his reassurance but wanting him to be straight with me at the same time.

"Then I guess you'll be a better student," he said. He reached for his soda and took another gulp.

As much as it annoyed me sometimes, he actually did care about our grades. Which was kind of a good thing because even though I ruled at football (and hopefully still would), I needed to do well enough in school to get those scholarships.

I rubbed my palm on my sweatpants, fixing my stare on the tiled floor.

"Come on, Vance. What will worrying do right now?" Coach said. "Just focus on school and healing. Everything will work out."

I nodded, having thought he was the one person who wouldn't bullshit me. But what were you supposed to say to someone who had one dream in the whole world and right now that dream might've been gone?

"The SATs next semester will be a good distraction." He stood up and walked over to me, clamping his hand on my left shoulder. I let out a half-hearted laugh.

"You really know how to make a guy feel better, Coach."

"That's what I'm here for. I'll even put your name down for SAT tutoring myself." He leaned against the side of his desk, jingling the keys around his belt loop.

Chris knocked on his office door while I chuckled again.

"Hey, Coach, can I get started on some drills after the warm-up?" Chris asked, before looking at me. "Oh, hey, Mase. Sup?" He glanced at my cast like he was making sure my wrist was still broken.

It wasn't his fault he finally had the chance to be QB1, but I still gritted my teeth. He'd been waiting to take my place, not just in football, for as long as I could remember. Even though I was a lot more talented than him, it didn't matter right now. Since when was he such a go-getter anyway?

"I'll be right out, Garvey," Coach said to him. "Just start the warm-up."

Chris nodded at both of us and shut the door.

"Between you and me." Coach leaned in. "I miss you out there, Vance. And not just because you're the best player I've ever had. You may be a cocky little bastard, but at least you've never kissed my ass."

"No offense, Coach, but there aren't enough beers in the world for me to kiss your ass."

He laughed again before hacking and coughing the diet soda in his lungs. "Vance, stay out of trouble." He took another sip to offset the coughing attack. "Believe that you'll bounce back from this and don't do anything stupid just because you're frustrated."

I faked being insulted and pointed at myself like I was saying, "Who, me?" Then I forced a laugh and said, "I'll try to stay positive."

I shook his hand with my left and walked out past the field to meet my mom. Watching my team do jumping jacks and push-ups out on the turf, without me, kind of killed me inside. I needed a distraction. And I needed one now. I took my phone out to message Lace again.

Me: *Come on. What do you say, tomorrow night?*

My feet tapped against the floor the whole ride home, as I kept glancing at my phone, waiting for Lace to reply. She still hadn't answered when I headed into the house and grabbed a bag of Cheetos. I sat on the couch with Dove and flipped an action movie on. Mom went back out to pick Chad up from tutoring and bring him to off-season lacrosse training. My phone lit up, as I stuffed my mouth with a handful. Let's face it; I was staring at it, waiting.

I tossed the Cheetos on the table and picked up my phone with orange-coated fingers, smearing grease on the screen. I didn't even try to stop Dove when she stuck her head in the bag and started eating.

Lace: *Ok, but only because I fear more lame pickup lines.*

"Touchdown!" I pretended to spike the football with my left hand. I shimmied my shoulders from side to side and fist pumped like I usually did when one of my teammates or I found the end zone. Lace finally flirting, and agreeing to go out with me, was totally worthy of my victory dance. Though I had to cut it short when my movements jostled my right arm.

Me: *Oh but I will be picking u up…at 7 for dinner. Have I earned your number yet?*

I couldn't stop smiling as I took the Cheetos away from Dove and scratched behind her ears. "Someone's got a date, Dovey." She licked my face, which I took to mean she was happy for me, or maybe I had cheese dust on it.

Lace said she'd see me then and gave me her number. Surely my mom would let me borrow the car for this. Of course she'd be cautious since my whole right arm was out of commission, but I'd just be going into town.

The smile was permanently plastered on my face while I half paid attention to the battle scene on TV. I was already planning some flattering lines and picturing kissing her at the end of the night . . . and then continuing the night in the back of the car. Damn, I hoped I could make that happen. But then my mind drifted back to talking to her, making more jokes about music and serial killers and stuff. I tried to push that from my head. Even if I badly wanted to hook up with her, I couldn't deny that I liked talking to her too. In the few conversations we'd had she'd seemed funny, honest, and smart, like if she said something, it was something that would matter.

TEN

My dad knocked on my bedroom door the next night, as I was getting ready to pick up Lace.

"Your mom told me about your big date," he said.

"It's not a big deal, Dad. Just dinner." I adjusted the collar of my polo in the mirror. It was nearly freezing out and I could only wear short-sleeves over this cast since it went past my elbow. The weather report already showed a chance of snow this weekend. Hello to frozen fingers.

I pulled the waistband of my jeans higher. It had been like two weeks since I put a pair on; they were a bitch to maneuver with one hand. But Lace was definitely getting a better presentation than sweats from me. Let's just hope I didn't have to pee.

I spritzed some cologne on my neck and ran my hand through my perfectly messed up hair, smiling at my reflection. At least I'd look good while I froze. I had my lucky polo on, not that I ever needed luck, but I had been told on more than one occasion that this one brought out the hues of green in my hazel eyes. Which led to it being taken off me and crumpled on the floor—my favorite way to wear it. Hopefully the same results would come tonight.

"It's okay to treat a girl right, you know, Mason. I'm just glad all hope hasn't been lost on you." My dad laughed. I shut my eyes and sighed.

If I could only count the lectures from Mom and Dad about respecting girls. Mom went on my computer once and found a group message between me and my friends the day after I hooked up with this girl Lexi last year, and let's just say I'd said a lot more than rhyme her name with sexy. Like, pretty explicit details. It was the closest my mom had ever come to actually hitting me. She preached about respect and how it wasn't impressive to degrade women—that I shouldn't think it's cool to use girls and brag about them to my friends. She made me call Lexi and apologize for "compromising my values" especially when we weren't in a "devoted relationship," which incidentally only made Lexi want me more. Mom deserved thanks for that one, but she didn't need to know that. She also made my dad take me to get tested for STDs. I was clean and all, but she did *not* deserve thanks for that.

Just when I thought they might've given up, I had to go and ask a girl on a real date.

"Well, don't wait up," I said as I walked with my dad out to the living room. Dove ran up and put her paws on my shirt. I rubbed my knuckles on her head and checked to make sure she didn't get any dirt on me. She licked my shirt herself. Now I smelled like a mixture of drool and Armani.

"If by that you mean we'll see you home by midnight, then good."

I snorted and rubbed at my polo. It would dry.

I grabbed the keys for Mom's Suburban. They wouldn't get me a car of my own until I was a senior. Only seniors were allowed to park in the school lot, and I didn't get my full license until I turned seventeen anyway, which was in a couple months.

They also rarely let me drive their cars unless one of them was with me, but I always had a way of sweet-talking it out of them. I doubted they really liked chauffeuring me around.. Whenever I wanted to borrow the car I'd just like, empty the dishwasher, reload it, maybe do some laundry, take out the trash. My mom would be touched by my thoughtfulness and reward me with the car.

It took some extra convincing for the car now that my arm prevented me from driving "safely." But just like I knew she would, my mom finally folded.

I kissed her on the cheek before snagging one of the roses out of the vase on the kitchen table. I shook the water onto the floor; Dove lapped it up.

"Oh, big spender," my dad said as I headed for the door.

"Sell out!" Chad called from the living room sofa.

"Yeah yeah. Who's gonna get action from a real girl tonight instead of some girl on their computer screen?" I was just messing with Chad. It wasn't like I really meant it. Well, I did, but I was also looking forward to the actual date part of the date.

Mom and Dad both shot me disapproving glares. "Mason Daniel!" Mom said. "You better learn some respect."

"Just messing around, Mom." I gave her my sweetest smile, held up the rose, and patted my cast. "Like I said, it's the pain. It's gotten to my head."

I walked over and hugged her, grinning at Chad over her shoulder.

"Respect, please," she said, pulling back and holding my shoulders tight.

I nodded. "Don't worry, Mom." I smiled again, and then was on my way.

LACE WALKED OUT to the car a few minutes after I pulled up to her house. I would've gotten out and rang the doorbell, maybe even opened her car door for her like the fine gentleman I was, but she texted saying she'd meet me outside.

Her black jeans were ripped at the knees. A tight sweater with a denim jacket over it left a small strip of skin showing around her hips. She wasn't exactly skinny; she had a really curvy waist. All the halfway gentlemanly feelings I'd been having about her earlier went out the passenger window. I forgot to even look at her face until after she shut the car door behind her, totally distracted by her boobs pressing against her sweater. It wasn't even low-cut or anything, but it looked good.

"Hey," she said, smoothing her hands over her hair a few times.

Her green eyes were rimmed in heavy black with purple on the lids. It matched the streaks in her hair that grazed her shimmery cheeks.

"You look really nice," I said. "I like your sweater." I took the opportunity to scan her chest again.

She laughed and rolled her eyes. Then she looked down, letting a few strands of hair fall in front of her face. "Thanks," she said, almost too quiet to hear.

I smiled and held the rose out to her. "For you."

She stared at it for a minute before reaching for it, like it might be poisonous or something. "Thanks," she said again. "It's pretty." She didn't smile.

I thought she would've gushed over it. Maybe kissed me, hugged me, shown some can't-keep-her-hands-off-me appreciation.

"I award you music privileges." I handed her my phone.

Her expression didn't change as she took it and started

scrolling through my playlists.

I tried not to show any disappointment over her lack of enthusiasm.

"All your playlists have really weird names," she said, still looking down. "I like it."

I bit the inside of my cheek. Yeah, she was totally into me even if she was trying to act too cool for roses and compliments.

"Why's this one called 'Saints are Sinners'?" She kept scrolling.

"It's mostly songs my brother likes. His favorite football team is the Saints. All the playlists are named after something to do with football."

She looked up at me and nodded before scrolling through the songs on the list. She pursed her lips, probably realizing hers and Chad's music tastes didn't match up. Unless she liked hardcore rap, which I doubted she did.

"I think you'll like the one called 'Hailing Mary.'"

"Okay." She put the playlist on shuffle and "Scar Tissue" by Red Hot Chili Peppers played through the speaker.

"So, no dietary restrictions, right?" I said after she set my phone down in the cup holder.

She laughed without smiling. "Um, I'm a vegetarian."

"Oh," I said. "But you like Italian?"

"Doesn't everyone?"

WE SAT AT a small table in the back of DiMaggio's. It was pretty packed, but then most places were in this small, overpopulated town, especially on a Friday. It only took like five minutes to get here from her house, but she asked twice if I wanted her to drive since I was basically crippled. This was my first time driving since I broke my wrist and I might've underestimated how difficult it would be. It wasn't like I was going to ask her to pick me up, though, or that (God forbid) I'd meet her at the restaurant after *my mom* dropped me off. As far as she knew, I was invincible Mason, even if it did take me almost ten minutes to park—crookedly.

"So what's your real hair color?" I asked, taking a piece of bread from the basket and soaking it in oil.

"That's rude," she said. I was pretty sure she was joking, but it was hard to tell with her deadpan manner.

"Well, I know it's not purple." I raised an eyebrow.

"It's like light brown, dirty-blond maybe." She shrugged. She stared at the bread but didn't take a piece.

"I like the purple," I said, even though I wasn't really sure I did.

She pursed her lips and nodded. I scooted my chair closer to hers; she looked away.

"What happened to your arm anyway?" she asked, tucking a strand of hair behind her ear. The earrings up her left ear were studs tonight, not hoops. "Football?"

"Yeah. Fractured my wrist during the homecoming game. I might not be able to play anymore. I don't know what the hell I'll do if I can't."

My heart surged and sweat collected above my lip. A heaviness pressed down on my chest. I hadn't told anyone that not playing was a possibility, and definitely not that I was upset about it. I didn't even talk about it much with my parents or brother. Why did I admit it to Lace without thinking twice?

"Wow," she said. "That's tough."

I shrugged, trying to show I didn't care or something. Even though I just admitted I did. And I could tell she knew I did by the way her eyes lingered on me.

"What position do you play?" she asked, like she was letting me pretend I was still the football star I wanted to be.

"QB." I smiled, taking the opportunity to steer the conversation away from my possibly ended football career. "Is that your favorite position?" I smirked.

She laughed without smiling again and ignored what I implied. "I don't know anything about football."

"Well, we'll just have to change that then." I moved closer to her, catching the scent of flowers and honey, practically able to hear her heart pounding. I really wanted to kiss her. I wasn't used to waiting an entire evening—totally alcohol-less. I leaned in toward her anyway, ignoring the fact that we hadn't gotten our entrées yet.

"No, thanks," she said, moving a few inches backward. At first I thought she was saying "no, thanks" to the idea of kissing me. Then she said, "I don't really like sports anyway."

"Oh." That caught me off guard. Usually girls didn't call me out on what were supposed to just be lines or meaningless banter. "That's cool, too."

"Yeah, I'm mostly into art," she said.

I exhaled and leaned back in my chair. "What type of art do you do?" I asked, even though I had already seen a bunch of her drawings and paintings on Instagram. She probably knew that too since it was how I messaged her yesterday.

"I draw and paint mostly," she said. "Usually darker stuff, kind of like nightmares."

I'd gathered that. Most of her uploads were blurry horror scenes. You just got the feeling that something was wrong when you looked at the drawings. And *feelings* and *art*, especially when they went hand in hand, were a couple notions I wasn't familiar with. I couldn't even say what was hanging on the walls in my own house, other than the Giants stuff and *Sports Illustrated* models in my room.

"Why nightmares?"

"Um, I just like dark themes for some reason. I guess it helps calm me." She smoothed her hair.

I raised an eyebrow. "You might be the only person who's calmed by horror."

She laughed and then shrugged. "I don't know, it's like I can put how I feel on the inside onto paper. Get it out of me in a way, I guess."

I nodded, not really sure I had a clue what she was saying. "Can I see some of your art sometime?"

She shifted in her seat. "I guess. I actually get to have my stuff featured at this one art gallery sometimes in the city. My parents' friend owns it."

"That's sick," I said, resting my cast on the table. "You'll have to let me know when the next time is."

"Sure," she said.

The conversation died after that. I was relieved when our food arrived, since we seemed to have run out of things to talk about.

I asked her a bunch of questions about herself throughout the rest of dinner, all of which she gave one or two-word answers to. She didn't even ask me anything back. I was completely floundering, probing her for things I didn't care about.

She'd gone to Schreiber High School in Port Washington, and just like her Instagram implied, she graduated last spring.

She was still seventeen and going to Hofstra part-time while she lived at home. She said she wasn't ready to go away to college. That was weird, like who wouldn't want that freedom? Hofstra was a really good school, though, so it wasn't that strange of a choice. Their lacrosse program was pretty good, which I knew because Long Island as a whole was way more into lacrosse. Even at my school most of the guys on the football team were more serious about playing lacrosse. And there was really no future in it other than to play college. You could be the best player in all of division one sports and you'd never make any money in the pros. It was pretty awesome that the sport I happened to be incredible at was the biggest sport in America. Well, it *had been* awesome.

Hofstra didn't have a football team anymore, though, and I didn't want to go to college in New York anyway. I *definitely* wanted to live away from home. But I'd go wherever the football program was biggest.

The waiter cleared our plates and we sat in silence again. My eyes wandered down to her neckline where I noticed her three layered necklaces. One was a half moon. One was a half of a peace sign. And the last one was half a stick figure person—a guy chopped down the middle.

"What's with all your necklaces?" I asked and realized I must've been staring at her chest with a confused look. Not how I usually stared at a girl's chest, but this was the third time I'd noticed the half objects around her neck, and they were always something different.

"Oh." She scratched the back of her neck. "I'm into halves."

I didn't know that was a thing people were ever into.

"Why?"

"I just don't think anything is whole," she said, like it made perfect sense.

"What?" I said. "We don't have our bodies chopped in half like that unfortunate guy around your neck."

She laughed without smiling and shifted in her seat. "It's more of a metaphor."

I nodded. "So I guess you're a glass half empty kind of girl then, huh?"

"Actually, no." She sat up straighter. "Because either way you look at it, the glass is either *half* full or *half* empty. It's not whole."

That was sort of a good point.

"Sounds like glass half empty mentality to me." I nudged her foot under the table. It honestly did sound like she was taking the whole pessimistic thing to a new level; it made sense, but I couldn't help but think of the day she cried in the elevator. Of all her sad quotes and lyrics on Instagram, and now her thinking nothing was whole.

She laughed as she leaned forward and shoved me in the shoulder. I stared at the spot her hand touched.

"I really do hate that expression, though," she said, getting serious again and glancing away at the wall. "It's such a cliché, and you can't always see the glass as half full or half empty." She shrugged and looked down at her lap, picking at her nails.

"Why not?" I moved in closer, wanting her to touch me again.

She looked up and our eyes met. "Every situation is different, and no one sees the world the same every day."

I leaned back and put my hands behind my head. "True. But you always see it as half, don't you?"

She smiled enough to show her left dimple. "I guess I just

think the idea of being whole means being perfect, and that's not possible. Not with anything."

I stared at her, my eyebrows furrowed. I liked that she thought about stuff; it was refreshing. I didn't really know if other girls I'd hung out with thought about stuff like this too; I didn't talk to them long enough to find out. I was glad I was talking to Lace, even if her views were making my chest feel heavy.

"You're very deep, you know." I smiled, trying not to think about how her words were affecting me. I moved closer again, but she pulled away and her cheeks flushed red. Couldn't she just let me kiss her already?

We left the restaurant, after I paid, and headed back to the car. I gave her my phone again to play music. I wasn't even listening to the alternative rock song she chose, too busy thinking about how it could be possible that I actually liked a girl. She didn't throw herself at me or want attention and validation. She was kind of lost in herself, and it sort of made me want to get lost there, too. It knocked me off my game, but in an interesting way. Sure, it would've been nice if she'd accepted my offer to drive down to the bay for a little while. I would've liked to end this date more "my style," but it didn't matter as much as I thought it did.

"Can I ask you something?" I said, after I pulled through the gate at the end of her driveway.

"I guess," she said.

"What happened with your brother the other day?"

She pressed her shoulder into the window, creating a cloud of frost against the glass. "Um, I just wanted to talk to him about something that happened over the summer. We haven't talked much since then and we used to be pretty close. But he wasn't really sober when I asked him to talk, so we both got upset and it was kind of pointless."

"Is that why you were crying the other day? In the elevator?"

She moved her legs back and forth.

"I was just upset," she said. No shit. Award for most vague player went to Lace Havern.

I laughed, but quickly stopped when she turned to look at me with no smile.

"It's just—you seemed happier when my mom drove you home, so I don't know, thought maybe I could help."

She didn't say anything. She turned and looked out the window, her seat belt already unbuckled. I hoped she wasn't ready to sprint away from me and never talk to me again. I pulled in front of her house and put the car in park.

"You can't," she finally said. For some reason, it stung.

"I just think you're really cool," I said. "And I don't usually think girls are cool." I shut my eyes and bit my lip as soon as I said it. *Way to go, Mase.*

She snorted. "Whatever."

"I'm sorry." My heart raced. "I'm just—I like you."

She opened the door and turned to face me, about to get out. "You don't know me enough to like me."

"No, wait, come on." I reached across the steering wheel with my left hand, grabbing her arm with more force than I meant to. I loosened my grip before letting my hand drop into my lap. "I want to know you," I said, almost whispering.

She stared at her arm before looking up at my face and shaking her head. "Thanks for dinner." She forced a smile that looked more like she was in pain. Then, she stepped out of the car before making her way up to her house. She left the rose on the center console, already wilting.

ELEVEN

I kept waking up in the middle of the night, tossing the sheets off me, boiling hot. Only to wake up later and be freezing. Every time I drifted off I had a new terrible dream.

I stood on the field, getting ready to release the ball and send it soaring right to Chris in the end zone. Then, bam. My wrist snapped.

I gasped and tossed the blanket off me again. When I fell asleep next, Lace was standing in front of me with her arms crossed. She said, "You're just a pathetic has-been." Then, she smiled and walked away. I was in that strange state where I knew I was dreaming but couldn't wake myself up. My team all ganged up on me in gym class and shouted, "Vance isn't getting a football scholarship anymore!"

I rolled onto my stomach. I could hear my own breathing. Then, my wrist crunched again, and just before I woke up, Lace stood over my crumpled, broken body and shrugged.

Needless to say, I wasn't looking forward to the next football game tonight. The first playoff game.

I lay around watching the Notre Dame game with Chad and my dad, while eating snack after snack. Mom's chocolate chip pancakes kicked off my morning. She even cut them up for me like I was six years old again. It was a sad display when I ate anything that went beyond the capabilities of one hand these days. I couldn't even balance the fork between the fingers of my right hand; this cast wouldn't let my arm bend that way. So, every meal usually resulted in getting some sort of sauce all over myself and giving the ACE bandages around my cast a little dirty, sticky character. Just another reason I couldn't wait to get a smaller cast already.

I was practically crawling in my skin. I sat around being a fat ass with a bag of chips, pining after the only girl who didn't want my attention, when I should've been getting ready for my biggest high school game yet.

Mindy's Halloween party was tonight, but I couldn't bring myself to care. I just wanted this day to be over by the time I left to go stand on the sidelines again.

MY COAT WAS pulled partway around me in the frigid air. Time was moving so slow I may as well have been sitting in history class.

One of our running backs stood next to Chris in a shotgun formation. I held my breath. He was doing the last play I did— Play-Action 43. The one that landed me here on the sidelines. Maybe the last play I'd ever call.

Johnson hiked the ball to Chris; he faked a handoff to the running back. Then, he threw it downfield to Garrett. Only, the ball went nowhere near Garrett—and he didn't have anyone on him this time either. Chris sent it sailing straight into open field for an incomplete pass.

I exhaled, smiling a little. If I were the one faking that play-action pass, I would've actually finished it. Maybe Chris had the fake down, but he had no passing skills. Still, it wasn't me. And the way I finished it last time wasn't exactly my idea of a good play either. My smile faded.

"So, you give up on that chick after last night?" Freddy asked, snapping me out of the deep trance I was in where everything revolved around my inability to play football.

I had group texted him, Chris, Garrett, and Dillon after my date with Lace. They were going to ask about her anyway and I may as well have gotten ahead of any ball busting. I started it out with: *This is why I don't date.* Then, I went on to tell them Lace didn't even kiss me. I wasn't one to lie about getting with girls—there was no need since I hooked up with plenty, pretty much whenever I wanted.

Chris loved that Lace shut me down, and my friends made jokes about the world coming to an end.

"I don't know," I said, turning to Freddy. It was hard to focus on anything other than Chris standing in my spot on the field.

"Not like you to walk away from a challenge, Mase." Freddy cackled and nudged me in the left shoulder.

I forced a laugh and shrugged. "Yeah, I guess."

I didn't really think of Lace as a challenge anymore. I more just thought of her because she was her. The end of our date kind of pissed me off. It wasn't fair for her to write me off for not liking her because I didn't know her well enough when she didn't *let* me know her well enough. But then I wondered if maybe I was pissed because somehow, she saw through me, like she knew I never wanted to know a girl before.

I barely even looked behind me at Mindy or the other cheerleaders throwing seductive glances my way whenever they turned around to face the field. I tried to be glad I wasn't totally irrelevant to everyone, but all I could do was just keep staring at the scoreboard, waiting for a few more seconds to pass. I found new reasons every minute to hate standing here freezing instead of sweating on the field.

The guys ran off the field at halftime and we all headed to the locker room. After Coach's typical motivational pep talk, we went back to the sidelines and I sat down on the bench next to Chris. He looked like he was fighting the urge to slam his helmet into the Gatorade cooler. So much for Coach's speech about starting this half new.

I softened a little, deciding to stop feeling sorry for myself. Chris was just doing his job, it was his position now and he needed help. I put my hand on his shoulder. "It's all good, man," I said. "You got another half to go. Look, you're telegraphing too much. It's obvious who you're going to before you release the ball."

Chris snorted. "Yeah, I get it, I suck."

"Dude, that's not what I said. I'm trying to help you with what you might not be seeing." I took my hand away from his shoulder and ran it through my hair. Whatever, if he was going to be a dick it wasn't up to me to fix his mistakes.

"Sorry," Chris mumbled. "This game is just shit." He threw his helmet in front of him on the turf.

"You can get it back, trust me, just take your time and don't give away who you're going to." I stood up, about to walk over to Garrett, Dillon, and Freddy.

"Thanks, Mase," Chris finally said, standing up with me. "Can't wait to be done with this game and party tonight."

We walked back to the other guys. "Don't lose focus yet," I said. If only he knew how disastrous that was for me two weeks ago. "I promise you'll get your shitty Miller Lite." I laughed.

"You coming to party too, right?" Garrett asked me as we

all stood together, watching the same halftime routine the cheer-leaders did last week.

"Why wouldn't he?" Chris asked, narrowing his eyes at me.

"I don't know." Garrett shrugged. "Thought you might have another date with that girl or something."

Freddy laughed his high-pitched laugh. "He already told us that one was a dud. But don't give up, Mase, you'll just have to keep taking her on dates if you want any chance at getting laid."

Dillon took a gulp of Gatorade and then crossed his arms. All he'd said in response to my group text last night was: *At least you had a date.* His jokes were pretty tame, especially because it wasn't like girls didn't like him. He was just surprisingly low-key and "good" for someone who looked like him.

I ground my teeth together and popped my knuckles. But it wasn't like I'd say anything to Freddy for talking about Lace that way. Even if I did like her, I didn't really know what that meant or if I actually wanted more from her than to hook up. I was pretty sure I did, but at the same time, I didn't know how to talk to her again after she left me so abruptly last night.

"Yeah, you definitely won't let it go without nailing her." Chris laughed, but his jaw was clenched. "You'll even give up getting with girls like Sharon Martin, Mindy Waters, and Emma Litsky-Titsky for her."

Emma was a girl I hooked up with once over the summer. The guys just liked that her last name rhymed with Titsky, be-cause truthfully her tits weren't even that big—and I should know. My eyes drifted in her direction on the field, swaying her hips. I inhaled and looked away.

Freddy cackled and high-fived Chris. "That just ain't right, man," he said to me. "You need to come party tonight and get her out of your system with someone more willing." He glanced back at the field to watch Emma and another handful of girls I'd been with.

Maybe they were right. Maybe I should just forget about Lace, hook up with some of the other girls who were actually interested. Maybe it would make it feel like less time until my wrist was healed. I should've been having fun right now, not getting myself even more depressed.

In the next half, Chris seemed to be taking my advice a little too well. He set up for one of the plays I came up with myself last year next—Hook and Ladder 42. I sucked in a sharp breath while the guys got in formation. That was my play; I was supposed to be standing there waiting for the snap. There had to be some sort of rule that you shouldn't do another guy's play while he stood next to the benchwarmers like a loser. I was all for helping him, but that didn't mean he got to actually *be* me.

Johnson hiked Chris the ball. He turned, getting ready for the pass to Lewis. He took his time like I told him to; he wasn't giving himself away. But he took way too much time. He got sacked. I laughed, then clamped my left hand over my mouth when Freddy turned to look at me with raised eyebrows. I shrugged.

If that were me setting up for Hook and Ladder 42, Lewis would've had the ball about three seconds before then. I smiled underneath my hand, but it faded because it wasn't me setting up for my own plays. Apparently my advice to him wasn't as heartfelt as I'd thought. What was wrong with me that I actually wanted to see him fail? It didn't matter how bad Chris was, he was the one playing . . . and I was just here, not part of it.

He continued to get sacked two more times and threw three interceptions by the start of the fourth quarter. He wasn't giving away his passes anymore, but he had a whole new set of problems. He looked over at me on the sidelines like it was my fault—like I had somehow given him bad coaching. It wasn't up to me to fix him anyway.

We were close to being done for the season, barring a miracle—no county or Island championship. I shouldn't have wished my team out early or have gotten so much satisfaction out of my best friend's misery, but I wanted to be a part of the playoff glory. I wanted to be the only football player people talked about. I wanted the chance to break more school records.

I bit my lip and pressed down hard on my knuckles, so I didn't even notice that my phone was vibrating in my pocket. I nearly leapt in the air when Lace's name flashed on the screen. I quickly accepted the call; Coach was too preoccupied with our demise to notice.

"Hey," I answered.

"Mason?" Her voice broke as she said my name.

"What's wrong?"

"Um, no, sorry, never mind." She sniffled and her voice wavered. She was crying. "I just—I'm gonna go."

"No," I said quickly. "Where are you?"

I turned to walk across the track.

"Yo, Vance, where the hell are you going?" Freddy called after me.

I waved over my shoulder, not caring that I was supposed to be here for the whole game. If my coach said anything, I'd just tell him an emergency came up. Not that I had any clue if that was true right now. I continued to hold the phone to my ear while Lace told me where she was. I hopped in the Suburban, thankful Mom let me drive again tonight, and put the address in my phone.

Lace actually needed me. And I needed this.

TWELVE

I pulled up near the seafood restaurant by the bay. Lace was sitting on the curb, just like she told me she would be. There was nothing else around and the street was totally dark. She stood up and opened the passenger door, climbing into the car.

She swiped under her eye with her palm. "Thanks for coming," she said. "You really didn't have to. Sorry for ruining your night."

"You didn't ruin it." I reached across myself to touch her shoulder with my left hand. "What happened?"

"I just—" She inhaled sharply. "I walked down here from my house. Sometimes I sit on the dock to draw." She gestured toward the boating dock next to the restaurant, secluded in moonlit darkness. "And I don't know really. I hardly even re-member calling you. I just started freaking out."

She stared straight ahead, not looking me in the eye.

"Does that happen a lot?" I asked, still looking at the side of her face.

"Sometimes. Not in a while, though." She turned to face me and took a jagged inhale that seemed to get stuck in her throat.

"When I realized you were the only person to call, I felt even worse. My heart is still pounding." She pressed her palm against her chest.

I gripped her shoulder harder, like I could will her to calm down. "Where are your parents?"

She shrugged. "I can't tell my parents about this. They don't get it."

I wasn't sure I got it either, and I hated feeling so helpless. "Well, don't worry about it," I said, giving her shoulder one last squeeze before turning and sitting back in my seat. "Let's just go somewhere and hang."

She nodded, shutting her eyes, and whispered, "Thank you."

I DROVE TO a bay in Port a little farther down from where I picked up Lace. It was already 8 p.m. I knew the game was over by now because my phone kept buzzing with texts in my pocket. It was probably the guys telling me they had lost, wondering where I'd gone, asking about how we were getting to Mindy's party in a couple hours. Mindy probably texted me, making sure my leaving early didn't mean I wasn't coming to her party, too. I honestly didn't care about that right now. I didn't even take my phone out as it buzzed one after the other.

I put the car in park by the waterfront and opened my door to get out. The wind blew across the surface of the water, making small ripples, and it cut through the car like sharp ice as soon as my door was opened a crack. Welcome to freaken Long Island where it went from a nice fall afternoon to straight up winter in a day's time.

"It's kind of cold out," Lace said.

I shut the door, relieved that she wasn't too proud to say it. I looked over at her, opened my mouth, then shut it again.

After a few minutes of me looking at her and her looking at the water, I turned all the way to the right and put my left hand over her arm. She twisted to face me, then quickly looked away again. She had taken her coat off before I drove us here, her hand still resting against her heart like she was trying to slow it down. The sleeves of her sweater ended at her elbows.

I rubbed my fingers over the inside of her arm, hoping she would relax more.

Her arms went rigid and her shoulders caved in on themselves. She started to move her arm away from me, but I kept stroking it, hoping to achieve . . . I didn't know what. Then, I realized why she was pulling it away. I felt the raised skin on the inside of her forearm. I turned it over to see small, straight white scars—maybe ten of them. They were thin, faded slices that looked too perfectly aligned and spaced out to be accidental. I looked up at her, but she still wasn't meeting my eyes. I swallowed hard.

"What's your favorite sound in the world?" she asked, finally turning to face me.

"Um." My mind went blank. All I could picture was her crying and bleeding, hating her life. I shut my eyes and shook my head. "Your voice?" I finally said, forcing a smile. My heart was pounding in my throat—my ears.

"You and your pickup lines," she said. I laughed and wiped the beads of nervous sweat from my upper lip. "Come on, think about it."

"Okay," I said, inhaling. "The sound of the football leaving my fingertips."

My stomach twisted into tiny knots as I realized I might not hear that sound again.

Lace tilted her head to the side like she was weighing the

answer, then she nodded a few times. "That was oddly poetic."

"Why, thank you." I mimicked taking a bow, careful to avoid bumping my head on the steering wheel. "What's yours?"

I hoped it wasn't the sound of a razorblade slicing through her skin. Not that she'd tell me if it was.

"Complete silence," she said.

I raised my eyebrow. "I guess you win when it comes to being poetic."

I reached for her arm again and took her hand in mine. She turned to look at me. "There's no one like you," I said. She squinted, searching my eyes, and I added, "That's not a pickup line, I promise."

She smiled and shook her head.

"No, really." I cleared my throat. "I do use a lot of lines, but, like, I mean them with you." Ugh, I had definitely used that as a line before, too. I seriously didn't blame her for calling me out.

A slow smile spread across her small lips and she burst out laughing. I laughed, too, thankful she seemed happy, even if it was at my expense.

After she stopped laughing she said, "No one is exactly the same, but there are plenty of people like each other."

"I guess." I shrugged. "Maybe you just have to find the people who see the tiny differences."

She turned and stared at me; it was the longest amount of time she'd ever looked at me without nervously glancing away or letting her hair drop in front of her face or touching her ears. I hoped I hadn't offended her or something, but she finally opened her mouth and said, "If only everyone could be so lucky."

She looked back out at the dark bay. I gulped, not know-ing exactly what she meant. But it gave me too much time to think about those scars again. To think about how she called me, crying, in the first place.

"So," I said as I watched her green eyes gazing straight out the windshield. The water was almost eerie, surrounded by the woods at night. "You really didn't seem okay before, and I'm glad you called me. But why can't you talk to your parents? They know you're in therapy, right?"

She snorted. "Yes, they pay for it. Anything to get me talking to someone other than them. That's why I don't go to them when I have panic attacks or drown in depression." She paused and turned to face me. "Usually I don't go to anyone. I don't like to give more people the chance to hurt me, so I just keep hurting myself."

I coughed, figuring she meant hurting herself emotionally, but I glanced at her arm again, which she was holding against her stomach now. Here I was thinking only she'd been having an effect on me, but now she was admitting it was mutual. It caused my breath to hitch, in both a good and bad way.

"So, that's why you see a therapist then?" I asked.

A seabird landed on a branch above the car, letting out one sharp *squawk* and shaking drops of water onto the roof.

"Yeah. I struggle with depression and anxiety." She stared at the bird overhead. "I don't know why. Nothing specific happened to me. Well, not when I first started becoming aware of it. I just . . . I don't know." She took a deep breath like she was frustrated she couldn't explain it the way she wanted to. She rested her fingers on her temples and shut her eyes. "It's like, your wrist is fractured, right?" she asked, turning to me.

I nodded, not sure if I understood where she was going with this.

"Well, I'm fractured, too. But you can't see it on an X-ray.

No one sees it, there's no proof I should be in pain, but it's there. People just assume I'm fine, they assume everyone is when they can't see something wrong. But with your wrist, no one is telling you to get out on the football field already, right? People act like that's what I should be doing every day."

"That you should get out on the football field?" I asked, suppressing a smile.

She turned to look at me and started laughing. A real laugh. I smiled wider. "The football field of life, I guess," she said.

"I can get on board with that."

We sat in silence for a few minutes as my attempt to lighten the mood passed. Lace stared out at the water again.

"The hardest part is that I used to be a lot worse. Especially when my brother was kind of falling apart. And then, I just made things worse for myself, like I didn't know how to fix it, so I just let it overtake me." She glanced at me. "Tyler, my brother, takes painkillers—even after he went to rehab. And I always tried to keep it together, convinced myself there was no reason for me to be tired or stressed out or sad all the time. Then, I started having panic attacks. And I didn't want to try and keep it together anymore."

I reached for her hand, not really knowing what else to do. I remembered how worried my mom had been with my prescribed pain medication. She had no reason to be, but clearly some people struggled with those drugs. What was so great about getting high all the time? Even with drinking, like yeah, I liked it, but I couldn't see myself sitting in my room getting drunk every night while watching TV.

"Sometimes," she said, turning all the way away from me. "I wish something truly horrible had happened to me so at least I'd have an excuse to feel this way." Her shoulders shook as she breathed in. She sat there for a minute, looking out the frosty window, her chest rising and falling, before saying, "I've never said that out loud before."

She turned back to face me and we stared at each other. I didn't blame her or judge her for feeling that way even though I might've before I really knew her. I swallowed, not glancing away from her.

"I decided to work harder to be better," she finally said, running her hand through her hair. "I try to remind myself that everything is more rewarding when it isn't easy."

"No pain, no gain, right?" I asked.

"Cliché, but yeah." She smiled before turning away. "I know I've made progress, but no one sees it unless it's perfect," she talked into the glass again.

I stared at the side of her face, glad she trusted me enough now. I was starting to understand why she held back so much last night, why she wanted to push me away after our date. It would've been easier to forget all about me, but she didn't have anyone else, and that part wasn't easy.

"I know you don't like clichés," I said. "But no one is perfect. That's what your necklaces are about, right?" I gestured toward the half star against the base of her neck. "I mean, even *I've* thrown interceptions before."

She faced me and laughed. "You really love football, don't you?"

"More than anything." I glanced down for a second, knowing I could open up to her about how screwed my football career might be, but I didn't want it to be so real. And even though she was laying out her deepest feelings, I didn't think I could do the same. "You could be the best QB in the world, but you always have to focus and work hard—in every practice, in every play.

Otherwise you might get clobbered, and it'll be on you."

It was corny explaining it that way, but it was true. And I had proven that just a couple weeks ago. Usually, I liked to lead people to believe I was born awesome and always would be. But Lace saw through that and I actually appreciated it.

"You get it," she said, nodding.

I nodded back, even though I wasn't sure I did get it. I couldn't relate to what she was going through, but I wanted to understand.

"To be honest," she said, still looking at me. "I always thought of football as pretty violent or bringing out the worst in people. But, I guess, there's more to it."

"Oh, there's plenty to it." I smiled.

Then, my throat bobbed as I swallowed hard, because I didn't know if anything related to football even mattered anymore. I couldn't really say Lace was wrong either. I'd smashed many helmets, ripped apart plenty of jerseys, cursed guys out (on my team and the opposing team) and let everyone tell me how amazing I was all because I was good at throwing a weird shaped ball. A lot of people said that sports taught people life skills, and I wanted to believe that—they instilled values, we had to make hard choices, do what was best for the team. Lace might've been right that it brought out the worst in people, but I thought also, it could bring out the best. That definitely wasn't the case for me earlier, though, when I was forced to realize I'd been hoping for my team to lose, and that I didn't care whether Chris blew the game or not.

I shook my head, not really wanting to question everything I had worked for in my life. Nothing was going to make me stop loving football, but I didn't want to confront my behavior or "team player attitude." I didn't want to think about it, even though I thought about it more than ever with the state of my wrist these days. I had to draw the attention away from me—and my fracture.

"I want you to call me whenever you feel like you did tonight," I finally said, after a long stretch of silence, pushing everything football-related from my head.

Lace's eyes widened like it was the most shocking thing I could've said, and in a way it was. It wasn't a line. It was real.

She smiled, but was she ever actually happy? Was there some pit of darkness constantly waiting to suck her in? And something wrong with her that I'd never understand? She worked at it and said she didn't want to be sad anymore. She wanted to heal. But she might be battling the "fracture" for the rest of her life, in the same way that my wrist might never be one hundred percent. It was kind of depressing that she had to push herself to just feel normal. It didn't scare me away from liking her, just like I wasn't giving up my football dreams yet. It made me feel like I got her a little more. I only hoped I wouldn't make it worse.

THIRTEEN

I lay in my bed on Sunday morning Googling cutting. I was hoping to find out why people did it, but apparently it could've been any number of things. A cry for attention. Communicating their depression to the outside world. Suicidal thoughts but afraid to go through with it. To feel something—anything. Provide a distraction. I found one recurring reason, though—a lack of control.

Apparently, cutting could make people feel more in control of their lives, because it was the one form of pain they could dictate. I hated to say it, but it almost made sense. And it made even more sense when I thought about Lace's explanation in the car. No one understood her and she couldn't control that. She thought about things in a different way. She couldn't do anything about her brother. She also couldn't control the way she felt when apparently nothing obvious happened to make her feel that way.

It was pouring outside the window. Rain pounded the glass and a crack of thunder made my shoulders jump. I glanced back at my phone. The picture at the top of the article was a girl's white and red-scarred arm. Thunder boomed again.

Lace was kind of like a thunderstorm. She was intense and dark. She wanted to be heard and felt. Only, most people didn't like the rain unless they were curled up inside—away from its force. They didn't want to be right in it, getting drenched; they wanted sun. I shut my eyes while the rain continued to splatter the window. Maybe it was just what I needed. Nice, sunny days on the football field weren't an option right now. Maybe *she* was what I needed.

My phone vibrated with a text from Chris asking how my period cramps were. I rolled my eyes. I never went to the party at Mindy's last night and my friends had already been asking why the hell I left the game early before that. Chris was also bitter because he blew our shot at the playoffs, and he knew if I were the one playing we would've won that game. He also blamed me for the advice I gave him at halftime. Well, he didn't outright say that, but it was obvious from his first text: *Guess telegraphing my passes wasn't the biggest problem, huh?*

After I dropped Lace off at home I read through their other texts.

Chris: *Did u ditch the game for that girl? u better at least be getting some.*

Chris: *Guess I'm no Mason Vance at QB. Come help me drown my sorrows.*

Dillon: *Should I pick u up for Mindy's? Everything good?*

Freddy: *Vance! Why'd u leave?? Couldn't stand watching us novices try to play?*

Garrett: *I thought you were coming to the party?*

I told them that something came up and my mom was mad at me so I couldn't make the party. That got a lot of harassment, especially since I never missed parties, and they knew my mom never punished me either. I was too shaken up by the weird and intense night I'd had with Lace and all I wanted to do was chill with Chad and Dove after that.

I ignored Chris's ball busting and went back to scrolling through self-harm articles. It wasn't like I was going to accomplish anything, and I didn't know how the hell to bring it up to Lace, or if I should say anything at all.

My phone vibrated again with a text from Mindy this time. I clicked on it and my throat went dry. It was a picture of her in her bra and underwear, with a text that said: *Since u missed my Halloween costume last night thought I'd show u what else u missed.*

I stared for a few minutes, wishing I wasn't as turned on as I was. I had just been researching cutting because of the girl I liked, and now all I could think about was removing those last layers Mindy had on.

It wasn't like I hadn't seen this view a bunch of times in person, but she hadn't ever sent me pictures of herself like this, other than Snapchat. This picture she knew I'd save.

I took a screen shot of the picture and text and sent it in a group message to my four friends and said: *Still questioning my manhood Chris?*

I knew I was being an asshole and that Mindy probably didn't want me sending her picture around, but I was so tired of Chris's comments. He had his chance to take my place and he couldn't. I was also sick of being worried about my wrist, and Lace. I could still be me. Plus, Mindy probably expected that I'd show it to people. She knew I'd told my friends plenty of details about our hookups, and like, she looked really hot in that pic, so no big deal, right?

I turned on my side, still looking at the pic. I wished it were Lace. That she could forget about all her problems and thoughts for a little while and let me see her like that. I shut my eyes, trying to fight the feelings, but I was losing the battle.

I DIDN'T SEE Lace by the elevator on Monday morning at the doctor's office. We'd already texted a little yesterday (and I felt guilty every time I thought about how I wished they were texts like Mindy's), but I still liked seeing her at the elevator, like our own little place. Yeah, it was lame.

After getting more X-rays, I headed into one of the exam rooms. Me, that machine, and weighted vest were way too acquainted with each other. I was so ready to finally be able to move my elbow again. Today was the day I'd get the smaller cast. It had only been two weeks, and I already forgot what life with mobility of both arms was like.

Dr. Kalad walked into the room with his computer. "Well," he said like he was trying to figure out how to tell me something. "Ready for the smaller cast?"

He set his laptop down and leaned against the counter, looking up at me.

I furrowed my eyebrows. "Is there something wrong with the X-ray?" I had almost forgotten that was a possibility, too distracted by Lace, and wondering if I'd play again. I didn't think about the fact that this could get worse.

"The bones are still aligned," he said. He walked over to the cabinet above the sink and took medical materials down. He leaned against the counter again. "But you have what we call a delayed union, which means that you're producing new tissue, it's just happening very slowly."

"So what'll happen?" I asked.

"It's not totally uncommon, and everything is still aligned, so that's great. But it could take longer in the cast."

My heart constricted inside my chest. It felt like the weighted vest from the X-ray room was still draped over me.

"You just have to keep being careful," Dr. Kalad said. "And I'll put you in the smaller cast, because since you'll probably be in it longer, then that means the tendons and ligaments will get tighter from the restriction."

I still didn't get it. I figured this would take a long time to heal, but Kalad was acting like it was something uncommon, even if he said it wasn't. If you kept an arm in a cast long enough, how could the bones not mend together?

"Do you think you'll have to do surgery because of this?" my mom asked.

"Sometimes when the tissue is produced this slowly then it can cause the bone to heal in a way that isn't straight," Kalad said, taking a seat in the rolling chair next to the exam table. "So, if it starts to happen then we'd probably want to do surgery. But let's try the small cast for a week." He glanced up from his computer screen where he was studying the X-ray. "And we'll see how it looks next week, sound good?"

"But would surgery make a difference?" I asked. "I mean, if we don't do it then will my arm be all fu—" I glanced at Mom and stopped myself. "Screwed up?"

Mom stood up and rested her hand on my shoulder, giving a small squeeze. Neither of us understood anything about healing and medicine. All we understood was that my life might never be the same.

"No, not for right now anyway. Some people heal quicker than others depending on blood flow and nutrition and factors like that. Let's give it a week and see. It doesn't hurt any worse, does it?"

The realization that I didn't heal as fast as everyone else was a blow to the ego. I looked down and thought about Lace on Saturday night. How I felt more like her than ever right now.

"It feels like you'd expect a broken bone to feel." I glanced up again. That wasn't really true. It felt way worse, just not physically.

Dr. Kalad nodded. "I recommend you start taking vitamin C and D. And make sure you get plenty of calcium. Let me get my assistant to put you in a smaller cast."

Apparently that disgusting "magical bone healing" tea that Mom had me drink wasn't enough. It tasted like dirt and leaves, even with mountains of sugar, and it didn't fix me. I'd take whatever vitamins were thrown at me if it meant my arm would be normal and I could play football again.

I'd always thought I had such good luck. Everything had been easy for me. I never broke a bone before this. I had two concussions over the course of my football career and those healed within days—no stitches, no sprains, nothing hard. And now everything was.

But I was stronger than this.

Dr. Kalad's assistant came in, smiling too wide for my mood. He unwrapped the ACE bandages and pulled the heavy plaster apart on my cast. My usually muscular arm looked smaller and paler already and I shuddered at the thought of what it'd look like whenever this injury was over. The skin was flaking, too. Nasty.

I chose black for the new cast, which pretty much symbolized how I felt right now. Normally I might've chosen blue or orange for our school colors, or blue or red for the Giants, but I couldn't have been further away from football spirit.

The assistant slipped an open-ended sock-like thing around my arm with a hole cut out for my thumb. Then he wrapped the bandage around it between my thumb and index finger and across the top of my hand. He kept winding it up my arm until he stopped at the middle of my forearm. When he was done looping the bandages, he squeezed it all together, holding it in place while it hardened into a regular, normal sized cast. I barely cared about having the freedom to move my elbow again, which was what I had been wanting for the last two weeks.

Mom and me walked out to the car after scheduling yet another appointment. An appointment I'd be worried about all week. I was starting to feel like this place was my second home. A shitty home.

I held the door open for the person I heard walking behind me, but I was staring out at the parking lot, lost in thoughts about my injury, about Lace's injury. Why was everything so difficult?

"Thanks," Lace said as she walked through the door. That snapped me out of it. Despite everything, my mouth lifted into a smile.

"Was looking for you at the elevator," I said.

"I guess you'll have to settle for the front door." She shrugged; her left dimple barely showed. "So, you got a different cast, I see." She nodded at my arm.

I glanced toward the parking lot again; my mom was already sitting inside the Suburban. She gave me all the privacy I wanted when I paid attention to a girl for the "right reasons."

"Want to be the first to sign it?" I asked, still smiling.

She stuffed her hands in her coat pockets. My gaze drifted to her arms. "I hate to break it to you, but I don't have a marker that would show up on a black cast."

"Damn, you're right." I forced a laugh, shoving the intensity of Saturday from my head.

"Well, I'll text you later," she said and turned to walk toward her Jeep. It was so abrupt; I didn't realize we were done joking around.

"You better, *Lacey*," I called after her. "Otherwise I'll have to hunt you down for our next date."

She turned back around, still smiling, and kept walking backward. "Bye, Mason."

My jaw almost hurt from smiling so wide. Whatever she was dealing with I could deal with, too. Her problems and mine. Just like that, things didn't seem so bad anymore.

FOURTEEN

It was strangely deserted in the diner for early Saturday afternoon, other than the usual guys who sat at the counter, either reading the paper or watching the football games while drinking coffee. A lot of kids still had fall sports, even if football was done for, so maybe that was the cause of emptiness.

Lace and I slid into one of the cracked, red leather booths and the waitress handed us gigantic plastic menus. I probably knew the menu by heart, so I set it down. I used to come to this diner all the time with my family, and now it was pretty much a regular hangout for my friends and me during the winters—not during football season—but I didn't tell any of them I was coming here today. Chris had asked what I was doing and said we should hang. I kind of blew them all off to be with Lace today, though, which Chris probably knew. We were used to it with Garrett ditching us for Vicky, but when it was me . . . I didn't think my friends would get used to it or be okay with that.

"You know what's weird?" Lace said, snapping me out of wondering what my friends thought of me now.

"What's weird?" I said, putting my left hand on the table and smiling at her.

"It must take giraffes such a long time to swallow. Like the food has to travel all the way down their necks."

I started laughing. If I had a list of the least likely things I thought she'd say, that would be on it. Actually it probably wouldn't be because I couldn't even imagine someone coming up with something so weird out of nowhere.

"That was a bizarre thought," I finally said. "Maybe it gives their food a chance to cool down, though." I liked joking with her. It was actually becoming one of my favorite things even if I had no clue when we were supposed to joke and when things were going to get intense. When she was sad or when she was okay.

She finally smiled. "I think they just eat leaves and stuff."

The waitress showed up, interrupting us by setting glasses of water on the table. Then she took her notepad out, deciding for us that we were ready to order. I went with a buffalo chicken wrap and onion rings. Lace ordered a salad.

"So, I guess you're like a giraffe then . . . ordering a salad," I said after the waitress left. "Only much cuter."

Lace rolled her eyes, but she still smiled. I traced my gaze down her neck where a half circle necklace rested against her collarbone. Her necklaces were always there—always half—whenever I saw her in person, even a few were posted on her Instagram account. Half butterflies, half skulls, half smiley faces, half ribcages, half stars and suns and moons.

"So, where do you get all these half necklaces?" I asked. The gold shined against her pale, smooth skin.

"I make them." She glanced down at her chest.

"You make them?" I'd assumed she had just found some weird half objects website that she ordered them off of or something. Maybe they'd even have some slogan like: *Halves Half Off.* She was seriously good at everything, and she didn't seem to believe it at all. She came up with weird, witty remarks. She painted and took photos. She made intricate necklaces. She was . . . affecting me. I bit down on my lip.

"It's pretty easy once you know how to do it," she said, picking up her straw wrapper and rolling it between her fingers. The waitress came back with our food and set it on the table.

"What're you up to the rest of the weekend?" she said. I smiled wide, hoping her question meant that she wanted to see me again soon. Even when I was with her I was thinking of when I could see her next.

"Nothing else today," I said, even though I had plans with the guys to go to a party tonight. "Going to the Giants game tomorrow."

"Is it hard for you watching football now that you might not be able to play again?" She glanced behind us at the TV where a college game was on. I kept my eyes on the side of her face.

"No, I'll play again." I swallowed hard, wishing I hadn't mentioned how afraid I was, even if Lace was the one person I could tell.

"Oh, the doctor told you that?" She mixed her salad around with her fork.

"Well, no." I twirled an onion ring between my fingers. "I just—I'll be able to."

She shrugged. "Okay."

"You'll be able to watch me play before you know it," I said, like if I convinced her then I could convince myself, too.

"Sure," she said, stabbing at a piece of lettuce. She looked up and smiled. "You know what else is weird?"

I laughed, knowing she was about to say something totally random, and I was glad that she seemed to get exactly what I needed right now. "What?"

"If you see an eagle at the zoo, you're technically looking at America's symbol of freedom in captivity." She took a bite of salad.

"Do you have some book of weird observations?" I asked, still smiling.

"Maybe I'll write one." She smiled back.

"You seem good today," I blurted, then bit the inside of my cheek. I didn't want to draw attention to the fact that I was kind of analyzing Lace's mood whenever I talked to her. Wondering how happy she was, if she could somehow be set off. I stared at her arms as she paused to stare back at me. She wore long sleeves.

"Yeah, I'm okay," she said. "The dark times come in phases, it's not like constant."

I wanted to ask her more. Wanted to know what could have been so bad, but I didn't know how. So, I half-smiled and picked up my wrap again. "Good."

WE WALKED TO the park around the corner after leaving the diner. It was pretty cold, but the weather could have been worse for early November. We sat on a bench in the middle of the grass—pretty much the only people out here other than a few little kids with their parents by the playground.

"I found out I'll have an art show in the city the day before New Year's Eve if you want to come," Lace said. "I know you said to let you know, so . . ."

"Definitely." I smiled. I kind of liked the idea that we'd still be . . . whatever we were . . . almost two months from now. We hadn't kissed or anything, or even really hung out much, and I didn't know what she thought about our relationship, but I still liked that it was a relationship at all. Even if I wasn't sure I had much more than this in me, maybe that was okay.

I leaned back and put my arm around her. She didn't move away.

"Oh, and speaking of art." She rummaged around in her purse for a minute. Her bright hair fell against her cheeks. She finally pulled out a Sharpie.

I tilted my head to the side and stared at her.

"It's silver," she said. "It'll show up on your cast."

"Oh!" I pulled my right arm away from her shoulders and rolled up the sleeve of my fleece, forcing it over the length of my cast. "Have at it." I held it out to her.

She placed my arm in her lap and leaned over it with the Sharpie. I tried not to think about how good it felt, even with the barrier of my cast between us. Tried not to think about how good she smelled as I inhaled the scent of lemon and flowers on her neck and hair. I wanted to lean in toward her so bad, my heart was pumping fast, but instead I watched her intent and focused face as she drew on me. I didn't even care what she was drawing. If it were Chris or one of the guys, I might've been concerned that they were drawing a dick or boobs or something, but that humor probably wasn't Lace's style.

"Do you ever get really mad that you broke your wrist?" she asked, still looking down as she drew, distracting me from the jolt of warmth that passed through me every time her fingers brushed mine, every time her legs moved underneath me. I would've given anything for us to be in my bedroom, for her to be willing to do that sort of thing.

I swallowed hard. "Um, yeah, pretty constantly," I said,

barely paying attention to what I was supposed to be focusing on, which were her words.

"You don't think it happened for a reason?" she asked.

I forced myself to look away from her thighs and stared back across the park at the oak trees. The leaves were turning from red to brown, some breaking away and falling to the grass.

"That seems like what people say when something shitty happens, so I don't know." I shrugged. Her cold fingers brushed my hand again.

"I guess I know what you mean."

"Did something ever happen to you that you think must have been for a reason, even if it sucked?" I asked.

She stopped drawing and stared at me. I couldn't tell if she was mad or just thinking about it. I couldn't get her words out of my head—how sometimes she had "dark times." And I remembered she kind of hinted at something happening over the summer that she wanted to talk to her brother about—that she thought had made her depression worse even if it wasn't the cause of it in the first place. And suddenly I really wanted to know what it was, if maybe it was something so bad that of course she would be depressed and anxious.

She glanced back down, took hold of my arm again, and kept drawing.

"I just remember you saying something happened . . ." I continued. It seemed like she didn't want to talk about it, but she had been so honest about everything else up until now and I wanted her to trust me.

"Yeah," she said, still looking at my cast but letting the Sharpie hover above the material. "It's a little weird for me to talk to you about it."

I leaned back against the bench and shut my eyes. "You can

tell me," I said.

"Um." She colored in areas of the cast. "I hooked up with my brother's friend over the summer."

I opened my eyes again and stared at her. That was it? I had to stop the urge to laugh. I'd hooked up with so many girls—older, younger, whatever. It hardly seemed like anything worth mentioning and yet Lace acted like it was somehow troubling her.

"Well," she went on. "I feel like hooked up is the wrong way to put it. I'd never been with anyone before. And I was really, really drunk." She left my hand in her lap but wasn't drawing at the moment. She grazed the edge of my cast with her fingers.

I still didn't get the big deal. I hooked up with girls when both of us were drunk all the time. And I'd taken plenty of girls' virginities, too. I wasn't going to say anything and dig myself into a hole, though.

"I feel like I'm doing a shitty job explaining this," she said, glancing up at me. "I'll start at the beginning if you really want to know."

I cleared my throat. I actually really did want to know why she thought of this as important now that I knew what it was about, but I just nodded and said, "If you want to tell me."

She looked down at her lap again. "Okay, my friend, Lea, who isn't really my friend anymore, has been obsessed with my brother for years and she wanted me to convince him to let us come out with him, and some of his friends, to that bar on Port Boulevard."

She didn't seem like she was particularly upset by what she was getting at, it was more like she was telling a story that hardly involved her.

"So, my brother let Lea hang all over him all night. And I

felt really awkward with just his friends. Tyler and I hadn't been as close for a while, which I was down about because he was really there for me before. He talked me into going to therapy, but this night was right after he got out of rehab." She paused and looked at me before going back to half-drawing on my cast. "So, anyway, that night I started drinking a lot to feel more comfortable. I'd been drunk before, but never out at a bar. The only time I drank was alone in my room, which I know is pathetic, but it made me feel better sometimes."

I shut my eyes again. I had always thought about the people who did that as pathetic, but Lace wasn't pathetic. I reached for her hand that wasn't holding the Sharpie and grasped it. I felt so sorry for her. I felt sorry for anyone who used getting drunk to dull their pain instead of to actually have fun.

She pulled her hand away after another second and picked my cast up again, flipping it over to keep drawing on the other side as she continued, "I remember most of the night, but it was almost like my mind and body wasn't connected anymore. I tried pulling my brother aside and telling him Lea was really drunk and to please take us home. He asked me why I couldn't just 'act normal.' I couldn't believe he was the same person who used to be so understanding, but ever since he started taking painkillers, he's been such an asshole. I can't even tell him I'm worried about him, he'll just lash out."

I swallowed hard and looked away. I probably would've thought a girl trying to cock-block me was a loser, too. But when I thought about that girl being Lace, everything she struggled with . . . I looked down at my lap. Her legs shifted underneath my hand.

"Tyler is four years older than me. And he didn't care that he was twenty-one, hooking up with a seventeen-year-old." She kept scratching the Sharpie against the rough surface of my cast.

"He's the reason Lea stopped talking to me. She was pretty much my only friend and she came over a few times after, but got so upset when he ignored her. I mean, ideally my brother wouldn't blow her off, but sadly that's what usually happens . . . to all girls. I don't know, I guess she wasn't that good of a friend, after all." She exhaled.

"They left and went back to my house, but I didn't remember. So, I was alone with all his friends, no ride home or anything. I just kept drinking. Eventually, my brother's friend Aiden offered to take me home."

She leaned back for a minute, not touching my arm anymore, and stared up at the sky. "I felt nauseous. Everything was so hazy. I remember telling him it was okay . . . but it wasn't. I just wanted to feel better. I was so depressed all the time; I wanted to feel like I mattered to someone even if it was for a little while. Like I had power over someone else, I guess, because I had none over anything else. I realize how dumb that sounds."

It wasn't dumb; I was starting to get it. Her brother and best friend ditched her and it wasn't just for one night. She was alone and she was sick of it. This wasn't about that guy—it was about the weakness and loneliness he brought out of her.

"I mean, I know I was drunk," she continued. "But I always thought I was better than that and more logical; I had to realize I was just like everyone else when I spent my whole life trying to be different. One of the things I hate most is that I'm constantly torn between wanting to be someone and no one at all. I wish I could just turn it all off."

I shook my head, staring at the side of her face.

"I'd think that's why most girls let guys use them. To feel like they're someone. Like they're actually important, when they never are. Then, they're left emptier."

I looked down, hating that I had to face what she was saying.

She capped the Sharpie. I didn't know if I should take my arm out of her lap. It was starting to tingle from being in one place for so long, but I didn't want to lose my connection to her.

"My brother knows what happened and he doesn't care. A couple weeks ago when you saw me with him I wanted to tell him how much I'd thought about it and regretted it, that I wished I could take it back and I was so drunk that honestly, it was technically . . ." She trailed off. "But he was high when I asked to talk about it. I just wanted to know what he thought—if it bothered him at all what happened with Aiden and me. What happened with him and Lea. It doesn't seem like he cares about anything."

"What a dick," I said, trying to deflect onto someone else and hoping she couldn't see right through me. I tried to imagine what it would be like to have a sister; if I found out she lost her virginity to one of my friends like Chris or Freddy and they treated her like she was nothing. Would I care? I hoped I would, but I'd never know for sure.

"I'm not traumatized or anything," she said. "I just don't like the way I felt and I don't like that I thought someone could take the emptiness from me—fill me with life or whatever." She waved her hand at the air. "After that night, I swore I would remember that empty feeling and not let it happen again. To find the right people to get close to, because being alone is better than being with the wrong people. And it wasn't even really him that made me feel bad, like yeah, he made me feel like I could be anyone. And I didn't like that. But it's up to me to not let that happen."

She stared at me and I felt like she could see straight into my brain. Like she was telling me she didn't keep her promise to herself, that she let me get close enough to hurt her in the same way. That she was looking for temporary relief and to feel less lonely when she agreed to go out with me, to give me chances. Like she was hoping I wouldn't be like everyone else, that she couldn't have been so wrong to let me in.

"If that guy thought you were just anyone, he's an idiot," I said. I was so full of shit. Like I had really never treated a girl exactly like that? Like I had never treated them worse? She had to have known that, and yet she was still here. Maybe she saw something in me that I didn't see in myself.

She uncapped the Sharpie again and went back to drawing in silence. I stared out at the maple and oak leaves rustling on the ground, trying to make sense of everything. Trying not to be aware of my hand still resting on Lace's leg—how I really didn't ever want to move it.

After a few more minutes she finally said, "There."

My eyebrows knitted together, before I realized she was talking about being done with the drawing she'd taken many breaks from. I looked down at the rough surface of my cast to see that Lace had drawn an elaborate football field on the inside of it, and on the part that went onto my hand she drew a perfectly shaped football with all the detail of the stitching.

"Damn," I said. "That's awesome."

"Just some encouragement," she said.

I looked at her, trying to ignore the pressure pushing against my ribs. As discouraged as I was about football and the last doctor visit and everything, and however much I hadn't wanted to think about it lately because it was too upsetting, this was what I needed. I hoped it was what she needed too—to tell me everything that she just did. Maybe she was encouraged, too.

"Want the Sharpie so other people can sign your non-ideal colored cast?" Lace asked. Her dimple showed as she held the marker out to me.

I shook my head and smiled back. "I like my one signature just fine."

FIFTEEN

Dad got Giants tickets from one of his clients last week, so he, Chad, Chris, and me were on our way to the game. It was understood that Chris had first dibs on the fourth ticket. He basically tried to adopt himself into my family. He called my mom "Mom" as a joke sometimes and gave Chad an abundance of "brotherly" advice, plus plenty of noogies and wet willies. I didn't really enjoy being around him lately, but he was still my best friend. At least he wasn't my quarterback replacement anymore, but he gave me way too much shit about how I'd been hanging out with Lace. And the fact that I hadn't slept with her yet.

We got to the stadium around 11 a.m. and pulled out the portable grill to make burgers and hotdogs. Chris poured rum into each of our Coke bottles when my dad went to the bathroom. I didn't feel the need to drink today, especially since I went to a party with the guys last night—after my day with Lace. I got drunker than I thought; her whole story about her brother's friend kind of freaked me out because I could relate too much. And it wasn't Lace that I was relating to.

I hoped the rum would help with the nagging hangover in my skull, even after I drank a gallon of water. It was too bad a splash of rum didn't give me the slightest buzz, because I was still feeling weird about how much I liked Lace after everything. Chad, on the other hand, was definitely buzzed after the drink. He didn't want it at first, but Chris pressured him to "be a man."

"Dude, he doesn't have to drink if he doesn't want to," I said, leaning against the trunk.

"Give me it," Chad said, grabbing the rum and pouring it into his bottle.

"Yo, did you show your brother that pic of Mindy?" Chris said, pointing to my pocket.

I glanced at Chad and took a bigger gulp of my drink. I shook my head.

"What picture?" Chad asked.

I shrugged, but was too slow to stop Chris with my cast on one hand and my drink in the other. He grabbed my phone out of my pocket. Predictably, I had saved the picture, which he already knew. Before I could stop him, he was giving Chad an eyeful.

Chad swallowed hard and his eyes got about two sizes bigger. "She s-sent you that?" he finally asked, tripping on his words.

"No big deal." I took another sip.

"But . . ." He furrowed his eyebrows. "She's not even your girlfriend."

Chris cracked up. "Man, sometimes I forget what life was like before seeing a naked girl." He put Chad in a headlock and ruffled his hair.

"Wasn't that long ago, dude," I said under my breath.

Chad turned to look at me, keeping his eyes on my face a few seconds too long. "Did she tell you not to show anyone else?"

I glanced away.

Chris was hysterically laughing again. "If she didn't want it flashed around then maybe she should've used Snapchat or something." He smiled wide. "And maybe she shouldn't have sent it to the world's biggest man whore." He shoved me. I rolled my eyes and was glad for Dad's return from the never-ending porta potty line.

Chris was really trying to get me to stop hanging out with Lace. He nearly pissed his pants, he was laughing so hard, when I told him we hadn't had sex yet. I didn't point out that I hadn't known her that long and he'd said himself that sometimes you had to "put in work first." I also didn't know if that was what this was even about, especially after what she told me yesterday. But our relationship was nothing like her relationship with that guy, so it barely seemed comparable.

My four friends—even Dillon—were floored when I didn't hook up with anyone the night before at the party. Especially when Mindy was sitting on my lap on the couch, slurring her words. Sure, it might've been like the second time in my life I went to a party and didn't, at the very least, make out with someone, but I was kind of trashed and pretty much only thinking of Lace.

Chad was halfway done with his drink when he started babbling to my dad about the girl he liked—the one he made out with at the movies. Thankfully he left that part out while exclaiming about her to Dad. I hoped he wouldn't catch on to the fact that Chad wasn't sober because, of course, I'd get the blame.

"She's so pretty. And her name is Aurora. Isn't that such a cool name?"

Chris and me were cracking up at Chad, leaning against the trunk of the car. I wondered if I was ever like that when I was fourteen. Maybe I should've been. Girls hadn't had as much power over me as they did over Chad. They kind of consumed my brain in one way, but I never really saw them as people who mattered that much. Other than Lace . . .

I checked my phone. I hadn't talked to Lace since we said bye at the park yesterday, but I wanted to. After everything she'd opened up to me about, but I was also unsure whether I could be a decent enough guy, it was all really confusing.

"Okay, are both of my sons girl crazy?" Dad said, cracking open a beer and gesturing to my preoccupation with my phone.

"Are they?" Chris raised his eyebrow. He still thought my quest for Lace was to sleep with her—not actual feelings.

"Sounds like just Chad to me." I started on a second burger. "He wants to be Mr. Aurora."

"Sure," Chris said, pursing his lips. He stared at the part of my cast, with the football drawing, peeking out from under my Giants hoodie. "What's that on your cast?"

I looked at my arm like I didn't know what he was talking about and was discovering the drawing for the first time. He reached out and pushed up my sweatshirt sleeve.

"Wow, I didn't see that, Mase," my dad said, leaning closer to Lace's drawing. "That's amazing."

"So, that girl did this?" Chris asked, his forehead creased.

"Lace, yeah," I said.

Chris smirked and pulled his phone out. Obviously he was going to text the guys about what a lame loser I was. I wasn't embarrassed about actually liking Lace, but it was kind of hard to navigate given my past, and Chris was a jealous jerk. He'd had his chance to be me, to build his success with football and popularity and girls on top of mine, and it was short-lived. Now he was going to text the guys making fun of me and leave me out?

We packed up the tailgate stuff a little while later and headed into the stadium. I hadn't been to a game in almost two years, and I totally missed the smell of filth and the gigantic, packed stadium where you couldn't walk two feet without getting shoved. I hoped someday all these people would be here to watch me. A pang stabbed my chest, and I wiped at my forehead, wondering if that would ever actually happen. As much as I loved coming to NFL games, it was different today. It made my heart race and my throat dry. It made me want to cry because all my dreams might've been over. I could be sitting in the stands for the rest of my life, just another spectator.

The game was going in the Giants' favor. We watched a bunch of awesome plays, and they were up by two touchdowns at the end of the first half. My dad got up to go to the bathroom and get us more food.

"Yo, how hot are the cheerleaders?" Chris asked, looking out to the sidelines where the Gotham City Cheerleaders were still jumping around. They started to head off the field for a local band to play the halftime show.

"It must be the best job ever to be in the NFL," Chad said, gazing at them, too. His rum haze had worn off a little while ago and he had been mostly quiet other than cheering and booing along with the rest of us, though I was surprised he wasn't rooting against the Giants today. I never understood how his team preference line up went. "You get paid millions to play football, *and* you get those girls around you all the time."

"Yeah, and can you believe this ass is probably going to make that a reality?" Chris said, shoving me in the shoulder. Maybe I'd been reading too much into his ball busting earlier.

"I don't know," I said. "It's a long way away. What if my wrist doesn't heal right or I get hurt again in college?"

It was the first time I let on that my wrist might not have

been as sure to heal as I told everyone. Chris didn't notice.

"Yeah right, pussy." Chris turned to face me now that the cheerleaders were out of sight. "You're going to get drafted someday and you know it."

"Yeah, Mase," Chad added. "You know it."

I squinted at Chad. He knew the doctor hadn't given me a guarantee that I'd heal. He knew that my bones weren't mending as fast as possible. He knew that Dr. Kalad said sometimes people were never at the same level after breaking a bone.

Chad shrugged and glanced back at the field.

Usually I loved talking about how awesome I was or taking bets on what team I'd play for in five or six years. But now all I could do was panic about my wrist and check my phone again, wanting to talk to Lace.

The Giants won, but they didn't score another touchdown in the second half. Chris, Chad, and me were reenacting a sick play by one of the new wide receivers in the car on the way home. Chad was using his water bottle as the football, leaning over the headrest to catch it, but he fumbled and it hit Chris in the thigh. My bro was no NFL All-Star. I was cracking up, while Chris dramatically acted like the bottle hit him in the nuts and he was paralyzed, when my phone buzzed in my pocket. It wasn't Dillon, Garrett, Freddy, Mindy, or any of my other friends that had texted me today. Most of which I gave minimal replies to. It was Lace. It had only been like twenty-four hours since I talked to her and it felt like too long.

Lace: *Hey*

My fingers moved rapidly as I typed a reply, realizing how much happier I suddenly was. It wasn't like I couldn't have texted her sooner, but I just wanted to know she still wanted to talk to me. I didn't necessarily like caring, but I had to face facts—I *did* care.

Me: *Hey*

"Who's that?" Chris asked, pointing to my phone.

I didn't say anything.

He stared at me as we pulled into his neighborhood. He already knew.

"By the way," he whispered, "I got with Hayley again last night, and you will never believe what she let me do."

"I can hear you, Christopher," my dad said from the driver's seat. "How about some respect back there, boys?"

Chris smiled and rolled his eyes. I gave a weak smile back, but I didn't like being lumped in with Chris about learning respect. I knew I was usually the biggest offender, at least in my parents' eyes. But I didn't say anything about Hayley or ask Chris to elaborate. I didn't have to, though, because he mimed what Hayley let him do by moving his fisted hand up and down and opening it over his chest.

I laughed, more at his silent acting than at the actual act. I didn't really want to think about my best friend ejaculating. Not that we hadn't discussed it a million times before, but for some reason, it felt wrong today. Maybe because I felt bad for Hayley that Chris was talking about her behind her back. My smile faded. She didn't deserve people gossiping about her all because Chris wanted to look like "the man." I chewed my thumbnail and shook my head, relieved when Chris got out of the car.

SIXTEEN

Lace invited me to her house on Monday after school. After everything she'd told me, and the way she shut me out in the beginning, now she was doing the total opposite. I'd be lying if I said it didn't freak me out a little, but I wouldn't let that get in the way.

I missed morning classes for my doctor appointment again, and I felt slightly better this week because Dr. Kalad said the bones were knitting together more. He also said I'd probably heal fine without surgery and that it would just be more difficult once I started physical therapy since the tendons and ligaments would be restricted for so long. It was annoying, but I tried to just forget about it for now and enjoy the afternoon with Lace.

I couldn't wait to finally see the inside of her massive house when I pulled up the driveway. It wasn't like a few of my friends didn't have houses like hers, they made for some epic parties, especially in summer, but it was always cool to check them out. It looked exactly like I thought it would on the inside—huge open rooms, marble countertops, dark wood floors, expensive art and crystal vases. Paintings hung on the walls that were abstract and weird, but probably cost as much as a Bentley. An elaborate gas fireplace with an accompanying machine that made crackling noises and smelled like burning wood, under a dark mantle that looked like a tree.

And her mom was home. I'd thought she had been keeping me some big secret from her parents, which I didn't really blame her for. There was no point in meeting them unless we were in a serious relationship. Though, I kind of hoped her mom being there didn't mean she thought we were *that* serious. I could only take so much change at once.

"So, this is Mason," her mom said, offering her hand for me to shake. She looked exactly like the Port Washington housewife I pictured. She wore a tight fitting dress and heels, her golden wavy hair frozen in place, and her makeup made her look more like a mannequin than a real life person. My mom wasn't some bag lady or anything, but she pretty much never wore heels, only wore enough makeup to look "natural"—whatever that meant— and she was a firm believer in jeans. She wasn't a housewife since she worked in real estate part-time, but even though we had our fair share of money, the differences were noticeable.

"You're absolutely adorable," Lace's mom said, taking my left hand. "Aw, poor thing." She waved at my cast.

"And you're Lace's sister?" I said, smiling. I was basically just messing with Lace because of her hatred of clichés and pickup lines, but I had definitely said that to plenty of moms before.

She laughed. "Oh God, even more adorable now. I didn't know he was your type, Lacey."

Lace didn't smile. She stood in the foyer, her shoulders tense, tapping her foot on the wood floor.

"Well, I'm meeting Dad in the city. I'll be back late." She

hugged Lace, then said, "Very nice to meet you, Mason." She fluttered her fingers before heading out the front door.

Lace's room was nothing like the pretentious, expensiveness of the rest of the house. It was like an explosion inside, but not because it was messy, it was actually disturbingly neat. But because of all the crap she had on her walls. There was so much artwork and posters, I thought the place would combust. There were even sections of her walls that she'd painted quotes or images directly on. A huge, circular window was lined in shapes of half hearts made out of tons of different materials—metal scraps, glass, paper, string, rubber, plastic, marbles.

We sat on her bed for a while watching *Friends*. I wasn't really paying attention; I was busy thinking about my doctor appointment and the possibility of damage to my ligaments and muscles. I wondered if it were possible I'd need surgery for that still. I should've asked Dr. Kalad, but I honestly didn't even think of it as a possibility anymore. I knew a lot of athletes had gotten surgery and were able to play again, even won major championships again, so if I had to have an operation, I bet I'd be all right. But I wasn't even seventeen. I hadn't even played college ball yet. I bit my lip hard, wishing I could go back to the moment I got tackled and put my arm against my body before hitting the ground.

My mind was spinning so much, I almost didn't notice when Lace sank into the crook of my arm. But after a minute I was aware of her head against my shoulder, her lavender-scented hair underneath my chin. She wasn't any other girl who had done this before. I wasn't thinking about taking her clothes off or plotting my next move. But now I was aware this was the first time we were alone in a room together—on a bed.

I swallowed hard. She was comfortable with me. It should've made me feel good, but all I felt were knots in my throat, a thumping against my chest, and shaking hands.

"Your mom seems nice," I said, needing to take attention away from this coupley position we were sitting in.

"Yeah, I guess." Lace shifted her legs on top of the blanket. "I don't know, my parents are fine, but it's kind of like they gave up on the whole parenting thing once my brother and I were old enough to do things for ourselves. Like, they're somewhat interested in our lives, but it's more out of obligation and appearances." She shrugged.

"What do you mean by appearances?" I asked, turning to face her. My movement forced her to take her head away from my shoulder.

She straightened up, still staring at the TV. "Like, they made my brother go to rehab, but they never even tried to understand why he was using in the first place. They don't really want to believe Tyler's and my problems exist because that would mean there was something wrong with us." She turned to look at me now. "So as long as it doesn't look like anything is wrong, then to them it isn't. As long as we get our college degrees, I sell my paintings, Tyler releases songs on iTunes. Something they can show to other people."

I nodded and swallowed hard. I got annoyed when my parents hovered too much or babied me. They definitely gave me more freedom than some of the crazy strict parents I'd seen, but when I put it into perspective, it was nice to have people care about you and worry that you were okay. All this time I thought I'd just wanted to be praised for my football accomplishments, but when I thought about it, my parents not putting all that pressure on me or bragging about me to other people was right. They wanted me to be a good person.

I stared at a section of the wall Lace had painted a quote on: *make the darkness, drown the roses.* Black roses engulfed the words, and I remembered the first day I saw her, writing in that notebook with bleeding flowers on the cover.

"That painting is cool," I said, pointing to it. Her eyes followed my finger.

"Thanks." She sat up straighter again. "It's about facing fears, even when they swallow you."

I continued to stare at it and nodded.

"What's your biggest fear?" she asked as I looked at the drops of black around the roses.

"My wrist not healing," I said without even thinking about it.

"Hmm," she said. "That just happened to you, though. Didn't you worry about anything before that?"

"What's the use in worrying?"

She laughed and sank back down into my arm. I took a deep breath, holding it in, as her head pressed into my shoulder again.

Maybe I was trying to convince myself, because no one else knew how much I worried these days. I knew she always did, though, and she didn't just worry, she literally dissected every single mundane detail about the world, probably more than I even knew. Sometimes she would get this far away look and I could tell she was thinking about something so obscure that no one would have ever realized before she pointed it out. She had already proved that many times. The giraffe thing, the eagles in captivity, the way she described her depression and panic attacks. It was like nothing was ever simple to her; everything was more than what it was. I didn't come close to thinking about the things she did. It must've driven her crazy. Actually, that I even thought about how much she thought about things was more thought than I was used to.

"There's no use in worrying," Lace said. "It isn't like people enjoy it, but I can't exactly reason with my fears and tell them they're irrational. It's just inevitable. Unless you're you, I guess."

"I feel like that was an insult, but I'll forgive you."

She laughed again and started to say that wasn't what she meant, but I cut her off and tickled her. She squirmed around her bed, cracking up and gasping for air, but I kept working my fingers into her sides. I couldn't pin her back very well with my lack of arm, but it didn't matter, she was laughing too hard to fight me off.

I kneeled above her as she wriggled, enjoying her laugh. It was so free and uncalculated for once. Then, I stopped to stare at her. Different colored streaks of hair were splayed out behind her on the black pillowcase. Her green eyes shined as she opened them, watering at the corners. Her chest rose and fell as she recovered beneath me, her gaze locked on mine, both of our smiles disappearing now.

I leaned down, a few inches from her face, giving her a second to stop me if she wanted to. She didn't move or look away. I kissed her, easing my body onto hers, propped up on my elbows, my cast resting by the side of her face. It grew deeper and longer. She held on to my back and linked her left leg around my right. We kept kissing for a few minutes, and I was starting to sweat and anticipate what came next. I groaned against her jaw and made myself pull back.

I got up to go to the bathroom, shutting the door, and exhaled as I gripped the side of the sink with my left hand. I looked up into the mirror and ran my hand through my shaggy, brown hair that had been flattened by lying in Lace's bed. I splashed some cold water on my face and tried to calm down. My heart was still hammering and I was waiting for the tent I had been pitching in my pants to deflate. I couldn't be alone in her bedroom with her; I was going to screw it all up. I knew she probably didn't want to have sex—however badly I did, I wanted more badly not to chase her away. It was just a couple days ago that she told me about that guy over the summer—I didn't want her to think of me like that. I didn't want to do anything she wasn't into.

I looked around for a towel or paper towel to dry my hand and face with, but couldn't find one. I opened up the medicine cabinet and forgot all about my damp hand when I saw two prescription bottles inside. I picked them up one by one. Prozac. Xanax. Both of them stamped with *Lace Havern* on the label. Next to them were a bunch of different types of hemp oils and anti-anxiety drops and sprays. That was definitely enough to make me lose my excitement. I realized they were common enough medications, but I never stopped to think about Lace taking them. I knew she was depressed—she told me that. I knew she had cut herself—I saw that. But this? It was like the confirmation of how fragile she was, and I didn't like it.

I walked back into her room, trying to forget what I saw in the cabinet just like I had been trying to forget her scarred arm. It didn't seem like there was a good way to bring any of it up. I sat back down and kissed her softly.

I was about to pull back again, let us keep watching the show or whatever, but she held the kiss, picking up from where we left off.

After a few minutes of contemplation, I shifted my weight on top of her. Eventually, my confused thoughts left me, and I eased back into the moment, enjoying my tongue against her tongue and her body under mine. I moved my left hand to her hip, slowly inching it up her side under her shirt.

She reached down and pulled my shirt off, totally surprising me. Did she want this to happen? Maybe I'd been reading into everything else too much.

She ran her hand up along the lines of my abs once my T-shirt was on the ground. I reached for the button of my jeans, but she grabbed my hand to stop me, still kissing me.

I moved my hand back to her side, trailing it up, but she grasped my hand again. I sat up on my knees. "You okay?" I asked, kind of confused about the mixed signals.

Her face was flushed and she swallowed. "I'm just—sorry— I know it's what you want, but . . ."

"No," I said, shaking my head. "It's cool if you're not ready." I reached for my shirt on the ground, losing my balance and knocking my knee against the bed frame. My cheeks heated up and sweat pierced through the skin on the back of my neck. "I didn't mean to pressure you."

"Thanks," she said, sitting on the edge of her bed. "Sorry."

I kind of felt like a jerk. I didn't know why she was apologizing.

"Can I ask you something?" I finally said, wrapping my arm around her.

She looked at the floor, like she was still embarrassed, but nodded.

"Will you be my girlfriend?"

She swiveled to stare at me, before tilting her neck to the side. I smiled, still rubbing her shoulder.

She didn't say anything for what felt like ten minutes. There was so much silence that I was about to take it back. Then she finally said, "You want . . . a girlfriend?" like she didn't believe it.

I brushed her hair behind her ear and kissed her cheek. "If that girlfriend is you . . . yes." I hadn't realized just how much I wanted it until now. Just how much I liked her.

"Okay," she said, her lips curling into a small smile, just enough to show her left dimple.

I pushed her onto the bed and started tickling her again. And somehow I felt closer to her than I had to anyone else before.

SEVENTEEN

Lace and I did all the coupley things I imagined most boring couples did for the next week. We went to eat, Starbucks, to the movies, for walks (even along the beach), we hung out and watched TV. And we still didn't do anything other than kiss.

Sometimes I would get the feeling she was retreating from me, she'd be so quiet and wouldn't smile at all. Other times she was more in a joking mood, giving plenty of glimpses of her left dimple. I didn't know if I should say anything on the days she was down—not sure if her mood ever had to do with me, because sometimes she didn't even want to hang out at all, she'd just say she'd talk to me tomorrow and shut her phone off.

I liked her a lot, but I didn't know if this was what a relationship was supposed to be, especially since I'd never been in one before.

It was already Thanksgiving, so I hadn't seen Lace for a couple days and probably wouldn't until at least Saturday. I ate more than anyone ever should. My mom always went overboard with her ridiculously elaborate meals for only four people. The turkey she got probably could've lasted us until Christmas, and I made an impressive dent in it. Since I broke my wrist, I had been even hungrier than I was when training three or four hours a day.

Chris came over with his parents for dessert, and I got a second wind when the pumpkin and chocolate pies hit the table. Chris seemed like he'd barely eaten all day, shoveling down three slices of apple pie in a matter of minutes.

"So, did you boys sign up for SAT prep yet?" Chris's mom asked.

"Mom, it's Thanksgiving," Chris said with his mouth completely stuffed. He was grossing me out.

"Signups aren't until after winter break," I said. I wasn't sure if that was true, but it sounded familiar from the handout Coach had given me on the courses last month, pleading for me to make his life easier and do well on the test in the spring. Neither of us admitted that his life might not be easier anyway, because I might not get back on the field.

"Yeah, Mom, listen to Mason," Chris said, laughing. "He is the academic here, after all."

I punched him in the arm.

"Ow, dick!" He shoved me back.

"Christopher!" his mom and my mom said in unison.

"My bad." He kept on shoveling pie. "So, Mase, how's that girl you've been keeping a huge secret?"

Ugh, I knew I wasn't fooling my friends into thinking I was just busy, or that my mom was mad at me for some reason or another and it was why I was around less. Of course they knew I'd been hanging out with Lace. I wouldn't have cared about telling them if Chris wasn't such an asshole. He'd never accept me having a girlfriend.

"Oh yeah," my mom said. Then she leaned into Chris's mom

and said, "He met this adorable girl at the doctor's office. Lace, right?"

I nodded and glanced at Chris. He took a break from his pie to clench his jaw and narrow his eyes at me. If he was actually jealous that I met a cool girl then why couldn't he just admit that instead of acting like the world's hugest dick? Was he still mad about blowing the playoffs, too? Everyone knew he wasn't nearly as good at football as I was, but he got to play at least.

He snorted and repeated, "Lace." Yet another thing the guys (Chris and Freddy, and kind of Garrett) bugged me about, saying "how cute" it was that Lace and Mase rhymed.

I glared at him before dropping my fork to the table, then glanced back at my mom and said, "Yeah. Lace. My girlfriend." I tilted my head at Chris.

His eyes widened, and his mouth dropped open, before he quickly jutted his chin out and tried to look uninterested.

"Girlfriend?" my mom said, like she prayed someone wasn't messing with her.

I nodded, keeping my eyes on Chris.

My mom and dad stared at me like they didn't recognize me. Chad dropped his forkful of pumpkin pie onto his plate. Dove barked from her barricade in the kitchen—though I didn't think that was because I was some foreign family member, she just wanted food.

"Probably some scheme so you can finally nail her," Chris said under his breath. Not quiet enough, though, because his mom heard him.

"What's wrong with you?" She raised her voice and leaned in closer to him. "That's unacceptable."

"Sorry," he mumbled, before taking another bite of pie and smiling through his mouthful.

"Yeah, anyway," I said, turning away from Chris. "She's awesome." I tried to keep my voice steady, tried to keep the confidence I started with when declaring she was my girlfriend two minutes ago, but Chris was already under the layers of my skin. He and Freddy would probably talk shit about me now. Call me a pansy ass. Say I'd gotten soft since I broke my wrist. I squeezed my eyes shut before taking a deep breath and opening them again.

Chris sniffed and pulled his shoulders back, hitching the side of his lip up.

"You know," he said louder. I scowled at him, knowing he was going to further piss me off, but I'd already lost the nerve I started this conversation with. "Me and the guys have never even met her. You should invite her to Mark's party this weekend."

"Oh, that's a good idea," my mom said. Since when did she think that a party was ever a good idea? She probably just hoped that if Lace were there I wouldn't drink as much or "use" other girls.

"Maybe." I shrugged. I knew Chris wasn't going to let this go. He'd hound me saying if she were really my girlfriend then she'd come around and hang with my friends. He'd say I was whipped if I only did what she wanted. He'd ask if I needed some tampons while I sat cuddled on the couch weeping at *Titanic* and my feelings. It shouldn't have bothered me, I shouldn't have cared. But I wanted to show that I wasn't a completely different person after everything this year.

SO, YEAH, CHRIS had gotten to me. I sat in my room on Thanksgiving night, watching *Fast and Furious* instead of the football game. I had the world's largest stomachache. Just thinking about turkey and pie made me want to crap my pants.

While I was groaning, scratching under Dove's chin, and watching unrealistic car races, I picked up my phone and texted Lace.

Me: *Did my girl have a good Thanksgiving?*

Lace: *Pumpkin pie is the meaning of life.*

Me: *Haha. I don't think I'll need to eat until next Thanksgiving.*

Lace: *Yup, a day of being grateful for what we have by massively overindulging. Irony at its finest.*

I laughed, which turned into groaning. I clutched my stomach.

Me: *So Chris came over and he said the guys wanna meet u. Can I talk u into a party Saturday night?*

I knew Chris and the guys didn't want to get to know her. I doubted even Garrett did. It wasn't like I'd ever shown much interest in hanging out with Vicky. Lace probably knew that, since I'd never bothered to introduce her before. It might've been a terrible idea for her to come to a party with me. Drinking, other girls, guys being assholes. I knew that and yet I wanted to be the same old me. The me I was before everything got so complicated. Lace and I could do that together, couldn't we?

Lace: *Um. Maybe . . .*

Me: *No pressure. But if u decide u will maybe u can come over for dinner w my fam first?*

My mom would be overjoyed about having Lace over, and

I'd like it, too. I wanted her to be part of my life—like everything about it. I was fantasizing about Saturday already. A laidback dinner with my family, then a fun night out with my friends. They'd be able to see what I saw in her.

Lace: *Ok, that sounds nice*

Me: *The party too? I promise if it sucks we'll leave.*

Lace: *Ok.*

I exhaled. She was actually coming to a party with me. I needed some sort of plan so this didn't all blow up in my face.

I'd just stick by her the whole night. I'd defend her if any of the guys (aka Chris) said anything jerkish. And I wouldn't talk to any girls while I was there. And if she wanted to leave, we'd just leave.

That all seemed totally doable. This would be fine.

EIGHTEEN

Lace's relatives, who came in for Thanksgiving, had left on Saturday morning. Her grandparents went back to Florida—all old people from Long Island eventually moved there. My grandparents lived in Florida, too. We ate Thanksgiving leftovers for the third day in a row when Lace came for dinner. My mom even went out and got Tofurky especially for Lace when I told her she was a vegetarian.

"So, Lace, Mason told us you're going to Hofstra. What are you majoring in?" my dad asked as my mom finished setting everything down on the table.

Chad stared at Lace's chest, not even paying attention to my mom piling turkey on his plate. You would've thought he had X-ray vision or something. I could hardly blame him, though; I was trying not to be too affected by how good she looked myself.

Her black jeans, ripped down the thighs, were hidden underneath the table, but when she first showed up, my eyes were all over her legs. Her loose green sweater draped open in the back and I caught a glimpse of her bare skin after I took her coat and led her to the dining room to meet everyone.

Now, I sat staring at her straight, bright hair, dark makeup that made her green eyes more vibrant than a freshly cut football field. Her stud earrings shined all the way up her left ear, and she had two choker necklaces at the base of her neck. Then, as expected, one long chain with a half heart shape.

"Um. I'm not really sure yet, maybe psychology," Lace said, snapping me out of my ogling. I was just as bad as Chad. She shifted in her seat. My eyes landed on her lips before I looked up at her.

I never knew she thought about majoring in psychology. I wondered if it was because of her own mental health. That pulled me out of my other shameful thoughts.

"How come?" I asked, only recognizing after I said it that I was probably making her more uncomfortable.

"I'm just interested in it. I'm taking a weird variety of classes right now, though."

I realized I had no clue what classes she was taking either, forgetting that people even got to choose their own classes in college and weren't forced to sit through chemistry, math, and Spanish.

"What are you taking?" my mom asked, continuing to serve everyone.

"Psychology, creative writing, and Economics," Lace said, thanking my mom as she handed her plate back to her.

"Creative writing sounds cool," I said, then I pursed my lips, wondering when it was that I started thinking anything related to school was cool.

"Yeah, it's fun." She smiled. "I've written some poetry, but I mostly like visual art. Painting and stuff."

"Mason, you should definitely take creative writing," my mom said, sitting in her chair. "He used to write stories about football," she said to Lace, a proud smile on her face.

"No, I didn't." I narrowed my eyes at her. "When have I ever written a story?"

"You used to sit in front of the football games and write religiously in your notebook!"

"Mom, I was taking notes on how to improve and coming up with plays. I'm not some poet." I shook my head.

Lace laughed. "That's really good dedication, though."

I smiled at her and winked. She smiled back and rolled her eyes.

"Lace paints professionally already," I said, glancing back at my parents.

"Wow," my mom said. "That's fantastic. Are your parents artists, too?"

She laughed like she didn't mean to. "No." She brushed her hair off her face and took a sip of water, her hand trembling. "My mom is more of an 'art collector.'" She put it in air quotes. "And my dad works on Wall Street, pretty much the opposite of art."

My dad laughed. "Hey now, don't pick on us business guys."

Lace forced a laugh and shifted.

"Maybe he can give me some investment advice," my dad joked. Or maybe he was serious. He was always researching new investment opportunities, hoping to strike gold.

"Boring, Dad," Chad said, scooping up a forkful of mashed potatoes.

Lace laughed again and smiled at him. "I'd have to agree," she said. Chad smiled back at her like they were in on some secret joke.

"Well, your parents must be proud of you," my mom cut back in. "It's always nice to see your kids find something they care deeply about." Mom glanced at me and nodded. I looked down at my cast, wishing I could just forget about my wrist for one day.

"Yeah, I guess." Lace shrugged, turning to face me, but not smiling. I wasn't sure what her expression meant. "They're leaving tomorrow for a vacation in Mexico."

"Aw, how nice," my mom said, taking a bite of peas. "Will you be at home alone?" The concern in her voice was unnecessary. Didn't she realize Lace was seventeen?

"No, my brother will be with me." She pushed some corn around her plate.

"Oh, good," Mom said. I wasn't sure if it was good or not after everything Lace told me about her brother. It was like she still couldn't work out her feelings toward him. Maybe if they were home alone for a week they'd spend more time together. I could tell how much she wanted to be close with him again. I totally got it. Having a brother for a friend was awesome. I glanced at Chad and smiled while he spilled a bunch of peas into his lap. Dove was a reliable vacuum cleaner and made sure none were left behind.

It was probably more than I learned about Lace—on the surface—in all the weeks I'd known her, but somehow none of it seemed that important. The important stuff was that she dyed her hair purple, that she fidgeted and blushed when she was uncomfortable, that she didn't like to get close to anyone but she got close to me, that she thought about the world so much it almost drove her insane. That she was coping with pain no one could see. But I saw her. That she was weirdly perfect and I couldn't explain how I felt around her.

My mom drove us to Mark's house after dinner. She'd been letting me drive since I broke my wrist obviously, even though she reminded me every time not to text, change the radio station, take a sip of water, basically anything that required my one hand from leaving the wheel. She would've never let me drive to a party, though, which I actually liked (though she didn't know that). Even though there had been many nights where I couldn't remember anything other than the girl next to me, and sometimes not even that, I'd never drink and drive.

"Hey," I said to Lace after we got out of the car. We started up the gravel driveway to Mark's house where there was already loud music and voices inside. "If you're not having fun, we can leave. My friends just want to hang with you, they feel bad they haven't gotten to know you." Maybe that wasn't entirely true— or true at all.

"Thanks." She leaned into my arm around her. "I'm sure it'll be fine."

I squeezed her shoulder, thankful she was cool about it. I didn't want to miss out on parties. No matter how much I liked her and wanted to be with her, I still wanted to be me.

After walking around the party, having a couple beers from the cooler, Lace getting scowled at by a few girls I'd hooked up with and some that I hadn't, we found Chris and Freddy by the keg. They stood with some girls from our class. I put my arm around Lace's waist and walked over to them. Mindy and a few of her friends stood just outside the kitchen, but I didn't want to look at her. I knew she was pissed, especially since I had ignored her texts this week.

"Hey, boys!" I called over the blaring music in the kitchen. "Finally, the real reason I'm here." I pointed to the keg and grabbed two plastic red cups. I filled them with some difficulty, but since getting used to the smaller cast, my right arm wasn't completely useless. I handed one to Lace.

She looked at it for a second.

"Shit, sorry, did you not want another one?" I asked, pulling the cup back. She'd already had one beer and I remembered her confession the other day—about how much she drank that night. How much she didn't like it.

"No, it's okay." She reached out to take the cup.

I wasn't sure she really wanted it, but she wasn't one to try and fit in or anything. I handed it back to her before looking at the guys.

"Guys, this is Lace," I said and widened my eyes at Chris.

"How's it going, Lace?" Freddy asked, stepping forward. He took her hand and kissed it. Seriously? What a tool. Lace cringed when his lips touched her knuckles.

I downed my beer and filled it again. "Dude, you're a creep," I said, putting my arm back around Lace.

"Sup?" Chris nodded at her. This was his big effort to get to know her?

Lace gave a tight smile back. Then she looked up at me as I took another gulp. I smiled at her and wrapped my arm tighter around her waist.

I was drinking fast because I was excited to be out with her, but there was something else, too. Something I didn't want to dwell on—that dating her scared me for at least ten different reasons. And that also, she looked really hot tonight and all I could think other than being scared by her was how much I wanted to sleep with her. I hadn't thought about that much since the day in her room, not wanting to let my mind go there when I knew she wasn't ready. But looking at her now, her outfit in full view, my eyes drifting to the bits of skin exposed in the rips of her jeans. My mind gave up trying to control those thoughts. It was okay to at least think about it . . .

"What?" she asked, blushing. She looked down when I

didn't stop staring at her.

"Just glad to be here with you." I winked and pulled her against my legs. She laughed, shaking a little, and backed away, taking a bigger swallow of her drink. Cigarette and weed smoke filtered throughout the kitchen. A bunch of lacrosse guys stumbled through the back door, shouting so loud the music was drowned out until they were outside.

"Are you guys dating?" one of the girls Chris and Freddy were talking to asked, after the rowdy seniors shut the door. Her name was Lena and she was one of Mindy Waters' friends. Well, really, most of these girls were Mindy's friends. There was a certain crowd at our school who came to these parties.

"Yup," I said, rubbing my fingers over Lace's soft sweater.

"I know, who would've seen the damn day where man whore Vance would settle down, right?" Chris snorted.

I swallowed hard, not able to think of a comeback. Why was Chris being a drunk idiot and being so mean to Lace in the process? I glanced at Lace and shook my head. "He's a dumbass," I whispered, forcing a smile.

"And apparently Mason doesn't know what he's doing because his girlfriend looks miserable." Chris kept going, gesturing toward Lace. She tipped her cup back again. Ugh, my hope that Chris wouldn't ruin this was shot. Lace didn't look miserable, did she? "Lace, I'll be a way better boyfriend than Mason. Wanna come upstairs with me?" He cracked up and Freddy high-fived him, his high-pitched laugh drowning out every other sound. The cheerleaders giggled along with them. Lace swallowed the rest of her beer and filled it again herself.

"Dude, why are you being such a dick?" I asked, stepping closer to Chris so I could lower my voice. The bass picked up, vibrating the floor, and the room swirled around my head.

"Just letting your fine little girlfriend know I'm available if she needs someone to satisfy her needs." He winked at me. "You know, since you haven't been able to do that." He cackled again.

Lace glanced up at me. She drank another quarter of her beer.

"Are you trying to win a 'who's the biggest asshole' competition?" I kept my feet planted in front of him, wishing he'd realize it was time to stop acting like this. He had it in him to be a decent guy, didn't he?

"Except you're always the one winning," Chris said. He clenched his fist. He was the one pissed off? Being jealous didn't give him the right to say that stuff, and yet I didn't know how to respond. He kept talking anyway. "At least you finally found a girl who won't—"

"Why is it that everyone is so obsessed with sex?" Lace cut him off. I was thankful for her interruption, but wished she had chosen a different topic. I realized she just had three beers in a matter of a half hour. She was probably a lightweight. I also remembered the prescription bottles in her medicine cabinet—I bet those didn't mix well with alcohol. At least, that was what I read online.

"Oh, Lace," Chris said, welcoming the interruption. "We all know about Mason's newfound celibacy."

Lace laughed, like she was part of a joke that went straight over Chris's head. I was really drunk and confused. I filled my cup again, wanting this conversation to be over.

"Seriously," she said, ignoring Chris. "It's really sad how shallow our culture is, like it's all based around something that ants can do." She slurred a bit. I took her cup and set it down. "Doesn't anyone care about anything a bit deeper?"

The cheerleaders giggled and whispered to each other—undeniably about Mason Vance's freak of a girlfriend.

"Oh, you want deeper, do you?" Chris said, moving toward her.

Freddy's earsplitting cackle filled the space again. "Yeah, she won't get that from you," he said, laughing harder.

"Oh my God, Chris!" Lena shoved him in the shoulder.

"Exactly my point," Lace said, looking at me like I was the only one who understood.

I half-smiled at her, but then had to look at the floor, feeling like a fraud. I stepped forward to fill my cup a fifth time. Chris looked back and forth between us, and then grinned. "Guess Vance has been feeding you some lies if you think he doesn't want to fu—"

"Dude, shut up!" I took Lace by the arm and walked with her out to the living room. I hated him. He said he wanted to hang out with her. I knew he wasn't being sincere, but I wanted to believe it. I wanted to believe that if he saw us together he'd accept it and stop being an asshole. That maybe if he accepted it, I could accept it, too. I probably could've predicted this disaster, but my C average in school already proved I wasn't the brightest. You didn't get to be Albert Einstein and Tom Brady all at once. Thankfully Lace didn't seem bothered by it.

"I like that you think about things," I said, sitting down on the couch next to her.

She nodded, looking at the floor. Her cheeks were flushed. "Can you get me another drink?" she asked. "Maybe something stronger?"

Stronger might not have been a good idea. I looked at her for a second, kind of wanting to tell her she didn't need it. "Are you sure you don't want to leave? We don't have to stay."

"No, I'm good," she said, leaning back. "Just want another drink."

I pressed my lips together, then shrugged. I was no buzzkill. "Sure, be right back."

I walked back into the kitchen where there were a bunch of liquor bottles and mixers on the counter. I couldn't deal with Chris right now. At least he had a distraction now that Hayley found him, and he could be consumed by his horniness the rest of the night. If only she'd found him a few minutes earlier he wouldn't have said all that shit to Lace. Mindy wasted no time in waiting until I was alone.

"Hey, Mase," she said, leaning against the counter next to me.

"Not now, Mindy." I spilled some vodka on the counter and searched for a dishtowel to wipe it up, stumbling into her as I opened the kitchen drawer.

"Aw, am I gonna have to take care of your drunk ass tonight?" she asked, grabbing my waist to steady me. "Because I don't mind," she whispered, her lips brushing against my ear.

"Why do you even like me?" I snapped. She stepped back, looking like I'd slapped her. I didn't know why I was mad. Maybe I was mad at Chris and taking it out on her. Maybe I was kind of mad I brought Lace here at all. I was mad she didn't seem that happy and that she wanted to keep drinking. I was mad about my wrist, about everything. That nothing was the same—not even me.

I pushed past Mindy, spilling some more of Lace's drink, and headed back to the living room.

When I walked over to the couch, Lace's eyes were fluttering open and shut. Shit, she was wasted. More than I thought. And I wasn't in much better shape. I swayed as I walked, the edges of my vision blurry.

"Hey." I tapped her. Her eyes snapped open and she smiled

wide.

"Oh, hey!" she said, like she had just seen me for the first time tonight.

I laughed and set the drink on the coffee table. She definitely didn't need it. I lifted her up underneath her arm with only my left hand. "Let's get you out of here."

She stood facing me; I steadied her shoulder. "Mason," she said like she was saying it just for fun.

Then she held on to my shirt collar and started making out with me. I didn't care how drunk either of us was anymore. Suddenly, all I could think about was sleeping with her. I wished I could forget about that, but it was now the only thought circling around in my hazy head.

"Guess someone cares about what ants can do after all!" Chris shouted from the doorway in the kitchen. I pulled back and wrapped my arm around her, leading her to the front door.

"Later, Chris," I called over my shoulder as we made our way through the mob of kids, smoke, and puke stench.

Once we were outside, I realized I didn't have a plan on how to get home. Usually, I got an Uber or something after parties, sometimes I dared to call my mom and have her pick me up.

"Uber?" I asked Lace, taking my phone out of my pocket.

"Can we walk a little?" she asked.

I glanced down the street. Mark's house was five miles from mine and it was the end of November, snow already coating the blades of grass. Well, we didn't have to walk all the way home. Maybe the cold air would help sober us up. It was pretty refreshing on my face right now.

We started in the direction of my house for a few minutes until we got to the park near the diner—the same one where I sat with Lace and she drew on my cast. I opened the gate, which predictably wasn't locked because, like I said, nothing ever happened in these little suburbs.

"Why're you going in there?" Lace said, laughing and following behind me.

I held the gate open for her and she walked through.

"Let's sit," I said. "This is way too long of a walk." I was tired and wobbly and just wanted to sit in the iciness. We trekked across the grass and were all the way around the side of the jungle gym now where there was one bench. It was complete darkness other than a streetlamp fifty yards away. There were no cars, or anyone, in sight.

I pulled Lace onto my lap and kissed her. She laughed as she kissed me back.

After a minute, I picked her up with one arm and pulled her on top of me on the grass behind the bench. The moist ground shocked my skin as my clothes stuck to me. We kissed longer; the intention for more was building. She slid her hand down my chest to my belt and ran her hand along the buckle, but she stopped and said, "What's with your friends?"

I was panting, silently begging her hand to continue. I slipped my left hand underneath her sweater and ran my fingers along the outside of her bra. She grabbed my hand and pushed it out of her shirt, looking at me like she actually expected an answer.

I groaned and pulled her toward me again, kissing her neck. She relaxed, her warm breath skimming my ear. Then, she pushed back against my chest.

"Seriously," she said. "You seem different from them. They don't want to know anything about me, just that we slept together. Like is that really what makes people interesting?" She was getting deep again and I was wasted with her on top of me.

I really didn't care about her rant. I wasn't different from them, and I didn't know why she thought I was.

"They're just a bunch of assholes," I said, pressing my lips against her collarbone. "I don't even like them anymore." I had no idea if that was true. I hated Chris right now actually, but my words weren't connected to any specific thoughts. The only thoughts I had were about her legs on either side of me, her boobs pressing against my chest. I grabbed her hands and tried to bring them back toward my pants. She didn't resist me at first. She undid my buckle and ran her fingers along the edge of my boxers. It was finally going to happen. I never needed to worry about her not being ready. This was nothing like that night she told me about. I could hardly wait anymore.

"I want you so bad," I said. I tried to guide her hands lower.

"Don't do that," she whispered, pulling her hands away and resting them on my shoulders. She was leaning over me, her knees pressing into my hips, and we continued to kiss. I unhooked her bra, letting my left hand roam all over her chest, and then I grabbed her around her lower back and pressed her against me. I unbuttoned her pants and tried to pull them off.

"Mason, stop," she whispered. She kept kissing me, though. I slid my hand inside her pants, just enough to notice she wasn't wearing underwear, which only turned me on more. "I don't—" She tried to take my hand out of her jeans.

I barely noticed both of her hands tugging at mine. I rolled on top of her and slid my hand farther down her pants, grinding my hips against hers. I pushed her sweater up inside her coat, kissing her everywhere.

"Mason, don't," she said. I ran my fingers all over inside her jeans and pushed them down as much as I could with one hand, and her weight on top of them. I finished unbuttoning my pants. Then, I pressed my mouth to hers again, my tongue forcing its way inside.

Suddenly, she hit me hard in the chest. "Stop!"

It sobered me right up. I pulled my hand away from her and rolled onto my side, breathing so hard I thought my heart would rip through my chest. I fumbled with my belt buckle. She scrambled off the ground, buttoned her pants, and pulled her coat tighter around her. Tears streamed down her cheeks.

"Shit, I'm sorry," I said, not fully realizing what had happened. "It's just—it seemed like—" I hung my head, feeling like crap, and not just because the beer was swimming through my brain or because my pants were cold and stuck to my skin.

"I'm going to get an Uber," she said, sniffling.

"I'll come with you to make sure you get home okay, then I'll take it back to my house."

"No." Her voice was sharp. Tears glimmered in her glossy, green eyes while the streetlamp reflected off her face.

"Lace, please. I just—I don't know what happened."

"Don't—" she said, as I reached out to hug her.

"Why are you so upset? I thought—it seemed like—"

"Seemed like I wanted to screw you in some park?" she asked, her shoulders shaking. "We're both so drunk, I would've never—it's not how I wanted it to happen. I didn't even want it to happen. After what I told you?" She dropped her head into her hands. "I trusted you," she whispered.

"You can trust me!" I was short of breath. I put my hand over my heart.

"I told you to stop." She shook her head, tears streaming down her wind-burned face as her teeth chattered. "You wouldn't stop."

"Please, don't be upset. It's not a big deal, we stopped. It won't ever happen again." I reached for her arm, but she put her hand up so I wouldn't come any closer.

"I have to go home. I don't want to be around you." She opened the Uber app in her phone and walked back toward the gate, away from me. She sat on the curb outside.

I whispered, "I'm sorry" again, before I turned away from her and started toward the other side of the fence across the park. My fingers were numb and my nose was about to snap off. How did I just screw up so badly? I pulled my coat tight, trying to fit my right arm in it. I looked at her again; she was sobbing, sitting on the sidewalk. And those tears were my fault.

I kept walking home after making sure the car picked her up. She must've known I was standing there, forty yards away by the tire swing at the opposite end, but she didn't look up. I didn't get home until over an hour later. I took my phone out. I had one text from Chris, two from Dillon, two from Mindy, two from Garrett, one from Chad, one from this girl Megan, one from Freddy, one from Mom, and none from Lace.

I ignored all of them and texted Lace: *I'm so sorry. I've never felt so bad in my life.*

I passed out in my jeans and shoes with my coat halfway around me, and as I drifted to sleep, I noticed I was crying.

NINETEEN

Someone opened my bedroom door in the morning. I was curled on my side, my eyes glazed over, while I stared out the window. The sky was gray and gloomy, and I continued to think about what a screwup I was. People always said things looked better in the morning—they didn't. Lace never texted me back. I had scrolled through the texts from my friends.

Garrett: *I can't believe u left so early, dude.*

Garrett: *Hope it's going good w ur girl.*

Dillon: *Yo, we didn't even see u. I was third wheeling w Garrett and Vicky. Was Chris a dick?*

Dillon: *Let's chill tomorrow*

Chad: *I just beat the last level of call of duty! Suck it!*

Megan: *Hey Mase. Wanna hang later?*

Freddy: *Yooooo, Vance! Come back, man. U know it's just*

jokes. Emma Titsky just got here!

Chris: *She seems kinda cool. U getting lucky like always?*

Mindy: *Ur an ass.*

Mindy: *Let's meet up*

Mom: *Please let me know when you get home.*

I threw my phone at the wall.

"Mase?" It was Chad who opened my door. Thank God, he was probably the only person I'd be able to deal with right now.

I grunted to let him know I was awake, alive, whatever. He sat down on the edge of my bed and stared at me.

"You okay?"

I rolled onto my back and glanced at the clock. It was already almost noon.

"Not really." I sighed and pushed myself up to a sitting position. I cradled my head between my knees and thought I might start crying again. My hangover and the desperate need for water were totally secondary right now.

"Well, Mom and Dad went to the city for that play. She said to smack you for not letting her know when you got in last night. I think she was joking, but I'll tell her I did anyway."

I cracked a smile, but it quickly turned into a frown because all I ever did was screw up.

"Come to the living room," Chad said. "We can watch the Giants game. I'll try to make Mom's pancakes."

I laughed. Chad nearly burned the house down last time he tried to cook anything. He also never wanted to watch the

Giants when the Saints were on at the same time. I felt a little better, knowing however badly I messed up, I'd always have one person on my side.

I got out of bed and brushed all the nasty beer taste out of my mouth, losing the taste of Lace along the way. I pissed for like ten minutes straight, washed the crusty, salty tearstains from my cheeks, and went out to the living room.

"Let's just order pizza," I said to Chad. "We don't need the fire department to be called again."

He blushed at the memory. He was home alone last year and you would've thought it was some massive, ripping house fire with all the trucks and sirens plowing through our neighborhood. But nope, just Chad smoking the place out while trying to toast a Pop-Tart.

He called the pizzeria and ordered us a buffalo chicken pie.

"What happened?" he finally asked as we sat mindlessly in front of the pre-game on TV. "Usually you're like in a good mood after you go out with your friends. Aside from the hangover," he joked.

"I screwed up," I said, picking at my right fingernails that dangled from my cast. I stared at Lace's drawing on the underside of the hard material, biting my lip and fighting to keep the tears back.

"Your girlfriend?" he asked, and there was no mocking of the word "girlfriend" like I had come to expect from Chris or Freddy. They texted me stuff over the last few days like: *Lil Miss Vancey and his girlfriendddd.* Or: *You bringing your GIRLFRIEND to the party? You gonna hold hands all night? Maybe Garrett can teach you how.* And: *hahahaha.* And apparently they were right. Apparently the idea that I could have a girlfriend was a joke— but probably not for the reasons they thought.

"Yeah." I sighed, still looking at the TV.

"So, she broke up with you?" Chad asked.

"I don't know, but I'm sure she never wants to see me again, so I guess."

"What'd you do that was so bad? Did you like hook up with someone else at the party or something?" He kept staring at me. I watched the TV, too ashamed to make eye contact with him.

"No." I took a deep breath. "It was just—I don't know, I went too far."

He squinted at me, waiting for me to explain.

"It was like I couldn't control myself. I really fucked up."

"You mean with sex?" he asked. "Hadn't you guys done it before?" He probably wouldn't have been the first one to assume that. Chris and my friends had assumed it until I admitted it to them. Why did I have to let everyone get in my head?

"No, we hadn't," I said, shutting my eyes and exhaling. Not that it should've mattered anyway. "She was like scared of me last night. She kept telling me to stop and I didn't." I finally turned to look at him.

He stared back and swallowed hard. The little white scar that I put above his eyebrow all those years ago stretched across his skin. My lip quivered as I fixated on it. All I did was hurt everyone around me. I glanced back at the TV, trying to keep my legs from shaking.

"Did you—" He gulped again. "Did you force her?"

"No!" My eyes bulged. "I mean—" I shook my head, grabbing at my shaggy hair. "No," I whispered to myself. I turned to face Chad again. "It never went that far. I didn't, right? If I had realized how upset she was I would've stopped right away!"

He shrugged one shoulder, but didn't mask his concern. His

big, hazel eyes—my eyes—were wide with worry.

"Fuck!" I shouted so loudly, the ceiling fan shook. "How could I let this happen, Chad? How could I be so stupid?"

Dove jerked her head up, lying at Chad's feet. When she saw it was just me who'd yelled, she rested back down on her paws and shut her eyes.

"Mase," Chad said, leaning over to pet her. "I think it'll be okay. You said you stopped. She'll understand. I mean, at least you feel bad about it. A real rapist wouldn't feel bad." He hitched one side of his lips up, like the world's most unconvincing smile. But that word: *rape.* How could I ever be associated with that word? I wanted him to be right. But either way, I crossed a line. And I knew it. It didn't matter that we stopped, I should've stopped the first time she said it—and I didn't.

I called her like ten times throughout the afternoon and she never answered, not that I expected her to. Every time the ringing stopped and her voice message came on, I hung up. I couldn't even put anything into words. What was I supposed to say?

As much as I wanted her to forgive me and forget about this whole thing, I didn't care as much as just knowing she was okay. After seeing the scars on her arm, the prescription bottles in her medicine cabinet, how upset she was about the night with her brother's friend—I just felt sicker and sicker with myself.

Then, around 8 p.m., I decided I had to do something. I hung up the phone when her voicemail came on for about the four-teenth time. My chest hadn't stopped pounding and my feet had been tapping against the floor pretty much all day.

Mom and Dad were still out; they wouldn't be getting the train home for a while. Chad retreated to his room to play video games after we watched a very silent Giants game together. He didn't know what else to say to me and I didn't know how or if I was supposed to explain myself further. We ate our pizza (he had four slices, I couldn't even stomach one), we drank our Coke, and we pretended to care that the Giants beat San Francisco. Any other day, that victory would've been huge.

I didn't bother calling out to Chad that I'd be back in a bit when I took the keys for Mom's car and drove to Lace's house. Her parents had already left for the week on their vacation. I just hoped she'd talk to me.

I rang the doorbell, and her brother answered. His eyes lingered on my maroon polo shirt; I forgot to even grab my coat, too lost in thoughts of shame when I left my house. I stood on the front steps shivering, and Tyler looked like he couldn't believe someone like me was standing at his door. He snorted before laughing and walking away.

"Lacey! Some douche is here to see you!" he called out as he disappeared down the hall. Great, I really needed him to reinforce that right now. I wondered if he was always like that or if he was high. Or maybe Lace told him about last night. Probably not, though, because he would've punched me in the face rather than walk away if he *actually* knew what a douche I was.

She walked up to the door, her face red and blotchy. Her hair was in a knot on the top of her head. She wore baggy, ripped sweatpants, and a T-shirt without a bra underneath. I wanted to punch *myself* in the face for noticing that.

"I'm so sorry, can we talk?" I asked.

She left the door open and turned around to walk back down the hallway to her room. I took a hesitant step forward, assuming she was letting me follow her. I closed the door carefully behind me and walked to her room where she was already sitting on her bed.

"Can I sit?" I asked.

She waved her hand at the bed, staring ahead at the TV, which was off. Mellow rock music played softly from the speakers on her desk.

"Look," I said. "All I can do is tell you how sorry I am and I wish I could take it back. I just wanted to know that you were okay." I stared at her for a minute. "Are you . . . okay?"

She sat cross-legged and looked at me without saying anything. I faced her, sitting across her bed.

She pushed the sleeve of her shirt up and held her arm out to me, presenting those straight white scars for me to look at— really look at. I swallowed and touched one with my finger, my hand shaking. I traced the line of raised skin.

"I know you saw that day in the car," she said, watching me as I stared at the scars. "Maybe, on some level, I wanted you to see. When you never said anything, even after what I told you about my family and that night, I felt like maybe you got me. That you understood I just needed things to feel a little lighter, and you helped with that." She paused. "You accepted that even though stuff happened that I don't like, there's no big reason for why I feel like this. And you never treated me like I was fragile, but you also didn't dismiss me."

"I—" My voice cracked. I cleared my throat. "I didn't think it was my business."

"That's why I liked your reaction," she said, rolling onto her back and causing my hand to fall away from her arm. I lay back, too, hoping it was okay to lie beside her. I stared up at the ceiling at a quote that said: *If all you want is to dream, stay sleeping.* "Other people act differently if they see, like there's something wrong with me. They're either overly cautious or go out of their way to ignore it. Or else, they think I just want attention. They don't want to get to know me because I hold back and am sad and quiet—it's not convenient. I'm not easy to get through to.

But you were just you."

I stayed silent, moving my gaze to a poster of a gothic fairy, dressed in black, with black tearstains on her face beneath a half moon. Did I really ever understand Lace? Maybe all the signals I had given her were just luck. I did think about her differently after seeing the scars, at least I thought I did.

"The first time I did it," she said, still staring at the ceiling; her fingers brushed mine. My hand twitched and I moved it farther away from her. "It was over a year ago. I couldn't stand feeling so sad all the time and not even knowing why. I just wanted to be in control of something, feel something different for once. Everything was so heavy and I was desperate. I felt like no one would ever understand. I didn't even have anyone in my life who would try to understand."

She peered out of the corner of her eye at me. I was on my side watching her again as she spoke. I glanced at her hand, wanting to take it in mine, to comfort her, but . . . I couldn't. Maybe last night scared her because she didn't have control. She thought I understood her and what she wanted, but I didn't. I let my own selfishness get in the way of making her feel safe.

"So," she continued. "I cut myself. And for once, it was something I wasn't afraid to do."

Tears streamed down her face now, but she wasn't actually crying and sniffling. I reached over, about to wipe them away, but I dropped my hand back on the mattress instead.

"It didn't help me feel better. I kept doing it, though, obviously." She let out a nervous laugh, gesturing toward her arm, her fingers fidgeted. "Then I just felt worse about myself, like a coward. I mean, my life seems pretty easy. I'm a spoiled, rich girl; I feel like I'm not allowed to feel bad because other people have it worse than I do. And that just makes me feel even worse—like a never-ending cycle. I felt like there was something seriously wrong with me. And I would've never guessed my brother would be the one to get it. He saw the cuts on my arm and he didn't make a big deal of it. He just said, 'I get it, Lacey.' He suggested therapy and said maybe someone could prescribe me something. I mean, I wish he didn't think pills were the answer to everything, but in my case they did help. I've been on antidepressants for like a year. They make me a little more comfortable sometimes, and I'm not as shy as I used to be, but it's almost like I'm a fraud. I wish I didn't need help, and admitting that I do is unbearable."

"Everyone needs help," I finally said, startled to hear my own voice after listening to hers for so long.

"You don't," she said, turning over so we were facing each other again. How could she even suggest that after last night? There was something wrong with me if I could do that to her after everything I knew about her. I felt lost. "I already told you I feel a lot better now than I used to, but sometimes I wish it wasn't such hard work to feel okay. I would've never gone out with you if we'd met a year ago. So, the fact that I felt comfortable with you quicker than pretty much anyone else told me I was doing a lot better, but it also scared me because I didn't think you felt the same. I didn't think you got it at first that it was hard for me to be with you, but then I thought maybe you did, and I realized it was just as hard for you to be with me."

She shut her eyes. I focused on her bare eyelids, her thin, wispy eyelashes. She kept talking without opening them. "I didn't want to care about you." She opened her eyes. "But I do."

I swallowed, realizing the enormity of last night. I finally reached for her hand, barely brushing her fingers with mine, feeling like I might set her on fire if I took hold of it.

"I couldn't tell if it was real or not, if I was blowing you up in my head because you were the first person to actually show interest in me and want to know me even if I don't make it that easy. But . . . it was real."

"It's real for me, too," I whispered, pulling my fingers back from her again.

"But last night you didn't care about me," she said, like she didn't even hear me.

I sucked in a sharp breath and sat up. I faced the wall, sitting on the edge of the bed, and dropped my head into my hands. I tried to keep my shoulders from violently shaking.

I knew what she meant. I knew how it seemed. But, I did care; I cared so much it drove me insane.

"I messed up," I whispered, still facing away from her. I wasn't even sure she could hear my defeated voice. "I'm sorry."

"I told you about my brother's friend. I told you I didn't want to let myself down again. To feel so empty. I know we would've been fine if I didn't tell you to stop last night, but the point is that, I thought you knew I wanted you to. I thought you understood. All the times you listened to me and made me feel like I mattered, like I wasn't just anyone, but you didn't last night."

I couldn't tell if she was looking at my back, as I sat with my head pointed at my lap. A tear collected in the corner of my eye. I could've stopped this, I could've been different, but now . . . I was losing her.

"Can't we just go back to how it was?" I asked, practically begging. A tear streamed down my cheek. I couldn't turn back around to face her. "You'll never be just anyone. I know I scared you and hurt you, but that's not me." It was me. I could've lived over and over again and still never deserved her, but I wanted to deserve her.

I turned around, folding my leg underneath me, to see she was staring right at me.

"No." She shook her head and pushed herself up straighter. A mellow, sad song streamed from the speakers. A soft voice sang about being a creep and a loser. "I should've answered you today, because I wanted to explain, but I didn't know how. I just can't forget what happened." She glanced out her circular window lined in half heart shapes before looking back at me. "I don't want to."

I bit down on my lip, looking away from her again. My chest heaved. I made myself stand up and take two steps toward the door. I stared at one final quote on her wall: *Some moments have no reason, some mean everything, and they are the same in the end.*

"I don't want this to be over," I said, as I hovered by the door. I spun to face her, wanting nothing more than to walk back over to her, wrap her in my arms, position her head in the space between my chin and chest, and protect her. Only, I was the one she needed protecting from.

She sat on the edge of her bed and stared back. Her eyes were red and veiny, salt on her face—a look of being all cried out.

"It has to be," she said.

I tried to steady my lower lip from quivering as I turned the cool, brass doorknob.

"But I love you," I whispered, biting down on the inside of my mouth. I had no idea if it was true.

She didn't look shocked. Just sat still, waiting for me to leave, and she said, "I don't think either of us really knows what that means."

TWENTY

I texted Lace for the next couple of days. She answered, but it was obvious she didn't want to talk to me. She just said things like: She was fine, just busy. She had a lot of school-work. She was working on new paintings. Basically, all bullshit answers that were code for, "You're the last person on earth I want to talk to."

I was even more distracted than usual in school. Staring at my phone, waiting on an answer from her that I didn't even want. Staring out the window thinking about how I could've done something so horrible. Thinking about how I had done horrible things for years and it took this to make me realize it.

The bell for lunch rang. I left history class and walked in the opposite direction of the cafeteria. I couldn't eat much without feeling sick these last few days.

"Yo, Mase!" Dillon called from behind me. He jogged to catch up. "Where you going, dude?"

"I don't know, not really in the mood for lunch."

"Not in the mood for lunch?" he asked like he had to make sure he heard me right. "It's quesadillas today, you're going to skip out on that?"

I cracked a small smile. The cafeteria quesadillas were probably the most edible lunch option we had. "Think I'm just gonna go chill outside."

"Want me to come?" Dillon asked.

"Nah, man. I don't want to keep you from the chicken and cheese."

Dillon laughed. "I'll go grab some and meet you out by the baseball field."

I shrugged.

Dillon met me outside ten minutes later, carrying a tray loaded with enough quesadillas for the two of us (unless he was planning on eating all of them, but knowing Dillon, he brought me nourishment, too).

"So, what happened?" he asked. I was thankful he didn't bring the other guys out with him.

"Nothing happened, man," I said, breaking off a piece of one of the tortillas, strings of cheese stretching between my fingers.

"Mase, come on. I won't say anything to the other guys. You've been weird since the weekend. You never hit me back about hanging after Mark's party and you've barely said two words this week."

I shrugged my left shoulder, rolling the greasy cheese into a ball.

"You don't have to say anything," he said, leaning against one of the bleachers. "I know we're not supposed to talk about our feelings and shit." He smiled.

I laughed. "Thanks, man."

"No problem. Just remember, I'm not Chris."

"Believe me, I know."

Dillon always had my back, just like he did on the field. He was the same way as a friend. He did his best to protect me from what I could or couldn't see. But he was the one with the blind side when it came to me right now. He might not have been here, taking hits for me, supporting me, if he knew what I'd done—who I really was.

We sat in silence while Dillon ate most of the quesadillas. I didn't feel any better. I checked my phone. No new texts. I shut it off completely.

I LOOKED UP cutting and depression online again over the weekend. I Googled Prozac and antidepressants. I was now well versed in the language of mental health when less than two months ago I had no idea what mental health even was. There were a lot of generalizations on the web and a lot of "beware of suicide signals" sort of stuff, but I really didn't think Lace was suicidal—though I obviously couldn't know for sure—and that made me feel sicker.

Some of the articles I read seemed to be true for her. Especially the stuff I found that said people who suffered from depression and anxiety tended to be naturally more sensitive than other people. They felt deeper. I never knew we all had different temperaments and brain chemistry or whatever. Probably because I never bothered to think about it. I wished I could be there for her, but I screwed it up and now she didn't want me to be. I was an added cause of all her stress and disappointment. Another person who let her down. Like her brother, her friend, that guy, her parents . . . now me.

I pretty much shut myself away for the week. My friends seemed to think I was just bothered by the slow progress of my wrist and I definitely didn't feel the need to correct them. Lace humored me here and there for a few days. But on Sunday night, she finally texted what I had been waiting for—however much I didn't want to see it.

Lace: *I don't think we should talk anymore. It's just going to make it harder.*

Even though I saw it coming, my heart drummed against my chest. My labored breathing was the only sound I could hear, but the air wasn't reaching my lungs as I paced back and forth, gripping my phone.

Then, I threw my phone on the carpet and slammed my fist into the wall. My right fist. A pinging vibration went through my hand. The cast didn't protect me. The fiberglass split on the side of my palm. I screamed and clutched at it, collapsing on my bed, kicking my legs. The pain intensified even more after a few seconds, and it was like bursts of lava were coursing through my veins, my bones so brittle they could crumble inside my skin. I wanted to cut my arm off to make it stop throbbing.

My mom and dad both ran to my door, eyes wide and breathing heavy.

"What happened?" My mom examined me.

I buried my head in my mattress, gritting my teeth as tears of agony streamed out of my eyes.

My mom eased me up by my shoulders and took my cast in her hands, turning it over.

"Oh my gosh, Mason, you broke it." She tried to pinch the material back together.

My breath echoed inside my ears. I didn't say anything, until finally the searing slowed down. I swallowed hard, exhaling with difficulty. "It's not that bad," I said, still gasping.

"I hope you didn't injure it any more, son," my dad said from the doorway. "Need me to do anything, Teresa?" He realized this was a job for Mom, like most things were.

"Just get some ice," my mom said. "Here, lie down, sweetie." She grabbed an extra pillow and put my arm on top of it. "What did you do? You know these aren't that easy to break." She offered a smile. Then, she glanced at the wall behind me where there was a small black mark on the light blue paint. I didn't even do any damage to the wall, just let my stupid arm take all the impact.

"It's not a big deal." I swallowed again, finally able to breathe normal.

She pressed her lips in a tight line, then nodded. She learned over the years the only way to get me to tell her things was if she didn't hassle me. I was never going to tell her what happened with Lace, though. I couldn't tell anyone else. Even Chad looked at me with a worry and seriousness I'd never seen before, and up until now, he'd thought I could do no wrong. I tried not to think about the word *rape*, but it was written on the inside of my eyelids every time I tried to relax.

"Do you think you need to go to the hospital? We have Dr. Kalad in the morning, but if you think it can't wait . . ."

"It can wait." Not only did I deserve to suffer until morning, but I didn't want to do a damn thing that required leaving this bed.

"Did you feel any sort of snap or anything?" Mom asked, stroking the arm hair above my cast.

"No," I breathed. "My hand kind of vibrated. I don't know, it's hard to explain. It was probably just because of the wall."

"Okay." She nodded. "Good."

My dad came back with the icepack, handed it to my mom, patted me on the shoulder, and left again. My mom positioned it around the side of my wrist and hand. She kissed me on the cheek. "It's all going to be okay. You'll play again."

She didn't know how untrue that statement was. She smoothed my hair for a few minutes, as the cold of the ice set into my hand, giving a little relief to the stinging and burning. "It's all going to be okay," she repeated.

I shut my eyes and let her keep stroking my hair, feeling oddly comforted, which I didn't deserve. She kissed my temple again as I drifted to sleep, I heard the soft close of my bedroom door and let the exhaustion barrel over me like a whole offensive line.

TWENTY-ONE

L ace's car wasn't in the parking lot the next day when I went to Dr. Kalad, and she wasn't by the elevator or anywhere else. My chest constricted as I wondered if maybe she changed her appointment time so she would really never have to see me again. It didn't stop me from attempting more apologies, though. I was almost ready to accept her not talking to me anymore, but then I had an idea this morning, hoping this one last gesture would make her change her mind.

I found a card in our kitchen drawer. My mom kept cards for every occasion imaginable on the off chance that she ever needed one for a baby shower or bar mitzvah or something. But I found one dedicated to *thinking of you*. It had a rose on the front and inside it said:

Just to let you know,

I was thinking of you today.

I took a pair of scissors and cut it in half vertically. On the half that said: *Just to let, I was thinking,* I wrote: *Is it a cliché not to feel whole anymore? I'll keep the other half for you.* I put it in the envelope and mailed it to Lace on the way to Dr. Kalad (when my mom stopped for coffee—not like I was offering up our breakup to anyone else). I put the other half in my desk drawer. Inside it, I wrote: *For Lace.* I didn't even recognize myself anymore, and for once, I didn't think that was such a bad thing, but it was still too little too late. I deserved to feel this way.

Shooting pains had been firing through my wrist after my run-in with the wall last night. My wrist was constantly sore, but then it would suddenly feel like it was being put into an incinerator for a few seconds. And of course the point of going to the doctor today was so that he could test the tenderness of my arm to see if he could take the cast off and put me in a removable brace. I didn't have high hopes of that anymore. And not just because he said I'd probably have to be in the cast longer since the bones weren't knitting that fast.

The physician assistant, a girl in her twenties, cut my cast off with this weird saw-like machine that I definitely would've thought would slice through my flesh, but somehow it didn't. I glanced up at her, my eyes landing on her chest, then I quickly looked at the ground. I hated myself. Realizing my mind was still capable of going there crushed me even more than the feeling in my wrist.

Usually, I would've liked having the girl stand this close to me, but I couldn't even look at her. In fact, I couldn't wait for her to get away from me, like maybe she thought I could force her to have sex with me at any minute or something. My mom was in the room with us and the door was open to a busy office of doctors and patients, but still, I was messed up.

"How'd it crack?" the assistant asked.

"Huh?" I looked up again, not realizing I'd been focusing hard on the lines in the floor tiles.

"Your cast. It's cracked," she said over the buzzing of the saw as it vibrated against my arm and sent dust in the air. She sliced right through the football field Lace drew on my cast. That day we sat on the bench at the park and she opened up to me. I watched her the whole time she held my arm in her lap. The whole time she told me about what happened to her—how empty it left her. Now, I was empty, too.

I pressed my lips together before answering. "I hit it."

She nodded and didn't say anything else. I didn't see why it mattered. My bones weren't fractured anymore; the cast was just a precautionary thing. There was no way I re-broke my wrist. But I couldn't help dwelling on why it hurt more than usual right now.

My cast was finally off. Lace's artwork was severed just like my heart. It smelled like it'd been sitting in a sewer for the last month, and the inside of it was brown. My right arm was actually now smaller than my left, which made me want to cry—yeah, stupid. Usually, my right arm was noticeably bigger than my left because of all the time I spent throwing the football with it, but now, even if I got to play again at some point, I'd have to start all over. It was flaking like a rattlesnake shedding its skin, too.

I wiggled a few of my fingers and tried to turn my hand back and forth, but it wouldn't move. I grimaced and flipped my whole arm over.

"Mase," my mom said, watching me. "Just wait until he comes in to try and move it."

I exhaled. "Yeah."

I held on to my wrist with my left hand, like it was too weak to support itself.

The assistant told me I could wash my arm off with soap and then I'd get more X-rays with the cast off before seeing Dr. Kalad. As I rinsed it off in the sink, I noticed hints of purple and blue beneath the peeling skin. Was it normal for it to be bruised like that? My fingers looked kind of fat and swollen, too. As I scrubbed at my hand, intense aches radiated up my arm like I was bruised right into my bones.

I sat with my arm propped on the X-ray table as the machine lit up above me, thinking about how it had been exactly six weeks since I met Lace. How could so much happen in such a short time? How could my heart be breaking while my wrist was mending?

The X-ray technician moved the weighted vest from my chest and walked with me to the door when she looked at me and said, "Oh no, honey, are you okay?" She was an older lady, probably close to seventy.

I looked up at her, confused, then I realized I was crying again, for like the fourth time in the past week. I doubted I'd ever cried four times in my life. I didn't even cry when I broke my wrist and that shit hurt.

"You're going to get your strength back, don't you worry. These injuries just take time." The X-ray tech gave me a reassuring smile. I nodded and walked back toward the exam room. I leaned against the wall for a second, wiping underneath my eyes and taking a few deep breaths. I entered the room when I was sure I had gotten rid of all the tears. Dr. Kalad was already waiting.

He pressed on the inside of my wrist after greeting me and having me sit back on the exam table. Whatever he was doing didn't hurt; it just felt weird for my wrist to be unprotected again. Then, he turned it over and as soon as his fingers touched the bruised, swollen area, I sucked in air and pulled my arm back.

"That's strange," he said. "I don't usually see bruising this late in the healing process."

He leaned down and took a closer look at my arm.

"Julie said your cast was cracked when she took it off." He walked over to the sink where my disgusting, rotten cast was sitting on the counter. He picked it up and turned over the half with the crack in it, the half with Lace's football on it. "Oh," he said. "You could've called me with a crack like this. Sometimes it happens if there's a weak spot in it or swelling underneath. But you must've hit it hard. It's pretty big."

"Uh, yeah. Only happened late last night. That's what the bruise is from?"

"Probably," he said. I glanced at my mom, who was biting her fingernails.

He scratched his head before pushing his glasses farther up his nose and walking back over to me. "Actually, I'd like to test something. Can you stand up?"

I stepped down off the table, my heart rate picking up.

"He didn't do any more damage, did he?" my mom asked, sitting at the edge of her seat.

"Well, the good news is that the X-rays are still normal, but I'm wondering if I should look at something other than the bone now. Here, put both of your hands flat on the counter," Dr. Kalad instructed.

I leaned over the counter and placed my palms flat on the surface, trying to avoid putting any weight into my right hand. It wouldn't even sit flat without me having to lower the rest of my arm down to the counter's height.

"Now, move your left pinky out to the side and back without moving any other fingers."

I did it easily.

"Okay, try the right."

I tried for the same movement, but my pinky stayed glued to

the countertop. I kept trying, determined to make it move. Why wasn't it even budging?

Dr. Kalad sighed. "I'm going to need an MRI," he said. "I think the tendon in your hand might've ruptured when you hit it."

All the color must've drained straight out of my face. No. How could I be so stupid? My shoulders and legs started shaking, and I felt so heavy and hazy I thought I'd collapse.

All I wanted for weeks was to heal, and now it was like I was going out of my way to punish myself. Maybe this was what I deserved. My wrist didn't hurt nearly as much as the ache in my chest.

"Let me see when our technician is in this week," Dr. Kalad said. He walked over to his computer and tapped the screen, clicking the mouse a few times. "Okay, how about Wednesday morning?"

"Of course," my mom said, probably louder than she expected. "As soon as possible."

"All right, I'll schedule you for nine a.m. Wednesday." He typed something in before glancing back up at me. "I'm going to have you wear a removable brace until then. But don't take it off at all, even to sleep or shower. It makes more sense than putting you back in a cast before the MRI, but we need to keep it compressed."

I put my head down, biting my lip as hard as I could without drawing blood. It was the only way to keep the tears behind the surface—hidden where no one could see.

TWENTY-TWO

I showed up for my MRI on Wednesday morning, free of all metal like the doctor instructed—sweats were my friend again. I was given a binder to pick out the music I wanted playing during the half hour I'd be lying there. I scanned the choices; apparently I had to go with one artist, not a whole genre. Must've been some archaic radio type thing they used. My eyes landed on Nirvana, before I shut them tight and tried not to think of Lace. Of the first day I actually talked to her when my mom went into the gas station. When I looked at her face in the rearview mirror. When I saw her.

My mom kissed me on the cheek after the MRI technician called me in. "It'll be fine, sweetie," she said before sitting down to read her romance novel that she probably wouldn't be able to fully focus on.

I told the tech I'd listen to Nirvana during the exam. She then explained how the MRI worked and told me to try and be as still as possible for the next thirty minutes.

I was transported into the tunnel-like machine of bright lights and noise. The technician's voice came through the headphones, "Comfortable?"

It was hard to hear her over the jackhammer blaring of the machine. The Nirvana songs were barely audible either.

"I'm good," I said.

"Okay," she said. "We'll start in a couple minutes. Music volume good?"

"Could be louder."

She turned it up. It was still washed out by the MRI.

I shut my eyes. "Come As You Are" played as softly as ever through the headphones. Not everyone should come as they were. Especially not me. I squeezed my eyes tighter. "Ready?" the technician's voice came again.

"Yeah," I said. I just wanted to get this over with.

A half hour trapped being as still as possible, with music I could barely hear, music that of course reminded me of Lace—it was too much time alone with myself.

Finally I was transported out of the machine after what felt like hours. No more blaring in my head.

"We should have the results before your next appointment." The technician took the headphones, told me to feel better, and I was sent back to meet my mom in the waiting room.

I couldn't believe I still had to wait days to find out if my wrist was more screwed than I thought. And if it was, what would happen? Dr. Kalad never even said what he'd do if the tendon snapped, and I didn't think to ask.

I begged my mom to let me take the rest of the day off from school after the MRI. She felt so sorry for me that she agreed.

The rest of the day consisted of falling asleep on and off, the TV quiet in the background. It was almost 7 p.m. when I realized Lace never acknowledged my card. I figured she would've gotten it by Wednesday, especially since she lived one town over. Not that I expected her to talk to me anymore; I honestly wasn't sure what I expected. What I did know was that I hated myself more and more. My arm was still useless. I had to wait on MRI results, with no idea what they'd say. I didn't know how to act around my friends. I completely betrayed the one girl I ever cared about. All I wanted was to play football and not deal with the rest of the world. Not deal with myself.

ON THURSDAY NIGHT, I lay in my bed thinking about how no one ever really told us exactly what sexual assault meant. Sure, we'd gotten lectures at school about how if a girl was really drunk then she might not be able to consent. Even though no one seemed to take that seriously. And who would? If she was all over you, and you were drunk too, how were you supposed to be a decent person? People should've been. I should've been. We all shouldn't have thought it was so obvious—so black and white. That you were either a rapist or you weren't.

I'd always thought of rape as this monstrous thing that only scumbags did. Guys who either couldn't get laid and thought it was owed to them, or violent creeps. The type of people I couldn't relate to. It was like us guys spent our whole lives knowing not to rape girls, that it was some inherent trait you were born with, just like red hair or brown eyes. But no one ever told us how easy it was to cross that line without realizing you were doing it. Why didn't anyone tell me? It turned out those guys could be anyone—and that scared me.

I started thinking back on all my experiences with girls, realizing how often I'd pressured them and manipulated them. How they put a certain amount of trust in me, but they didn't want me to know that I hurt or upset them, because after everything, they still wanted me to like them. How fucked up was that?

One time I was at Mindy's house and she was asking me

questions about football, said she wanted me to teach her. I assumed she was just flirting or whatever. I started taking off her clothes and she said, "No, really. Will you teach me the rules?"

I said, "There are no rules, Mindy." Then I kissed her neck and slid her skirt up her thighs. She pushed me away and stared at me.

I stared back before smiling and kissing her again. She sighed, with annoyance, not excitement. And she gave in. There *were* rules.

Another time, I was at the bay at night with Emma Litsky. We were making out and I started moving things along. She said, "Stop, Mase, someone could come out here." I kept going anyway.

She pushed my hands away from her pants. I exhaled and sat up in the sand.

"Someone's uptight," I said. "Think you need another drink." I pulled the bottle of rum out that we had been drinking at the party before we ended up at the beach. She laughed and accepted it, taking a large swallow.

Within a half hour, she didn't care so much about anyone coming onto the beach anymore. She didn't care so much that my hands were down her pants. She didn't care so much that I was scum.

There were so many girls I promised calls, second dates, that I *liked* them. I thought it was their fault for not knowing better—that they should've. But it was me who should've known better. It was just me.

For a guy who was told repeatedly that I saw the whole field, that it was one of the things that made me such a great quarterback, I couldn't see myself at all. I had no idea what a terrible person I'd been all this time.

I was glad I was broken right now. Maybe I'd get a glimpse of what being broken really meant. How I broke other people down. Now I'd have to endure the pain to heal just like them—because of what I'd created, because of what I'd done.

I rummaged around in the back of my closet for the bottle of whiskey I kept on hand for parties. I had to switch my hiding spot when Mom found a bottle under my bed over the summer. I unscrewed the cap and chugged some, desperate for anything to drown out this nonstop noise in my head, more than the heavy metal in my headphones was capable of. I realized I had become one of those people I felt sorry for—drinking alone—but I didn't deserve anyone to feel sorry for me.

I sat down in front of my computer, scrolling through another article about self-mutilation. I chugged some more. I went to my Facebook page and deactivated my account, and then I did the same with Instagram and Twitter. I deleted the Snapchat app from my phone, chugging more and more whiskey.

I opened my desk drawer and picked up the half of the card I kept for myself. My teeth chattered as I stared at the slightly crooked edge. Then, a tear dripped off the end of my nose and splattered onto the thick cardstock.

I stuffed it back in my desk, turned my phone off, and turned the music volume on my headphones up. I lay back down in my bed, continuing to drink, spilling liquor on my pillow.

At some point in the night I passed out and woke up with a worse hangover than I'd had in months. Going to school was the last thing I wanted to do right now. A few tears ran down my cheeks as I stared at the ceiling. My mouth felt like it was stuffed with sand and dead grass. My throat was so dry; I wanted to drink all the water in the world. But that would've required moving. I needed something to make this awful headache go away.

The whiskey bottle was on the ground next to my bed, still half full, and I figured, what the hell? It was the only real cure for hangovers, anyway. I took a few sips, fighting the urge to puke. Then, I poured the rest into my Gatorade sport bottle.

Chris stopped me at my locker after third period. "Yo, dude." The whiskey was almost gone now. "I've barely seen you in weeks, man. And what the hell happened to your social media? Did you get hacked or something?"

I hadn't talked to Chris much in two weeks, especially not outside of school. And I wasn't about to tell him I got drunk last night, cried, and decided to cut myself off from the world. That I didn't want to obsessively look at Lace's profile and get a million selfie Snapchats from girls in our grade. I didn't want them to "like" my photos or re-tweet my tweets. I didn't want anyone's attention—I was the last person who deserved it.

After the day by the baseball field with Dillon, I sat with my friends silently at lunch. I answered their texts with one or two words. They just steered clear of me, thinking I couldn't deal with the fact that I was still in injury mode. Thinking that I was still with Lace and that the reason I wasn't hanging around was because I'd become a loser who revolved around his girlfriend. Thinking I was busy in bed with her. God, it made me sick.

"Let's hang tomorrow," Chris said, when I didn't answer.

"Sure, whatever." I stumbled as I tried to get my math book from the back of my locker.

Chris grabbed my arm to steady me. "Dude, you kind of reek of Jack. Are you seriously drunk right now?"

"It's Friday, Chrissie. Basically counts as the weekend." I slid down against my locker and sat back for support, trying to laugh it off, trying not to give myself away. Suddenly, the thought of moving was beyond comprehension. I couldn't even pick up my books.

"Speaking of weekend. You going to party tomorrow night?"

I hadn't been to a party since Mark's house. My friends could hardly believe whoever I had become. I didn't know who I was anymore either.

"Doubtful," I said, shutting my eyes and continuing to rest my head on the cold metal of my locker.

"Dude, you're lame these days," Chris said. "Even if you are so cool you drink at school." He laughed, mocking me. "This girl has you whipped."

I snapped my eyes open to look at him. "Screw you, man. You don't know what you're talking about." Damn, I would've been a lot more convincing if I wasn't practically slurring.

Chris laughed again and leaned against the locker next to mine. The halls were thinning out now that fourth period was approaching. "Even Garrett still hangs out and the kid revolves his life around Vicky." He snorted again. "But I guess Vicky is a little different than your girlfriend, huh?"

"We fucking broke up!" I threw my left hand in the air. Chris stared back at me, opening his mouth, then shutting it again. He glanced sideways then straightened up and backed away from me.

"Man, you're about to be seriously busted." Chris lowered his voice and jerked his head down the hallway where Principal Banks walked toward us. Most of the kids were now in class since there was about ten seconds left until the bell. "Later, man, I'm not trying to get suspended." Chris turned down a side hallway. I stared after him. Why didn't he help me?

"Mr. Vance, shouldn't you be in class?" Principal Banks asked, standing a few feet away from me. I was about to say the bell hadn't rung yet, but then the piercing sound filled the hall.

Shit.

"I'm on my way, just had a leg cramp, sir."

He stepped closer to me and his nose twitched. Dammit. He was about to figure me out. He took another half step in my direction.

"Mason!" he snapped. "You can't come in here smelling like an Irish pub!" He was yelling, but worry lines were streaked across his forehead.

"Ah, but I'm not Irish, Mr. Banks." I pointed my finger at him like I had won some sort of argument. I was exhausted.

"Mason, get up!" He raised his voice.

I stumbled to my feet, clutching my right arm like I had been doing for days. Bile rose up in my throat and I gulped it back down, shutting my eyes tight. Banks stood with his arms crossed.

"What's going on with you?" he said as I got my feet beneath me.

"Won't happen again. Just a misunderstanding," I slurred, leaning against my locker as everything blurred.

He shook his head and let out a long sigh. "Clearly this isn't the best time to discuss it." He started walking ahead of me. "My office, now."

I followed him down the hall, trying to get my eyes to focus.

"This is really disappointing, Mason." He raised his voice again and let out another exhale as he turned the doorknob.

"Sorry, sir." Even I could hear the sloppy sound in my voice, but I couldn't get it to be normal.

"Sit and wait." He pointed to the bench outside his office and slammed the door behind him.

I might've fallen asleep on the bench outside the principal's office, because next thing I knew my mom was tapping me. I opened my eyes to see her green eyes staring back at me like frozen glaciers. A vein bulged on the side of her temple and a lump in her throat was bobbing beneath the surface of her neck like it was trying to decide whether to scream or cry.

She shoved me in her car. At least I didn't feel drunk anymore, just hungry and thirsty.

"Mom, can we get McDonald's or something?" I asked as I fastened my seat belt.

"Mason! What the hell has gotten into you?" She hadn't started the car. I glanced in the back seat, hoping there was a water bottle.

"I'm sorry, Mom," I said, shrinking down in my seat.

"Why! Why would you drink at school?" she shouted.

"Because I'm messed up." I put my head in my hands and felt the tears coming. "I just didn't want to think anymore."

"Because you can't play football, Mason? Is that really such a big deal right now? You're going to play again. You can walk—you didn't get paralyzed out there. Stop feeling so sorry for yourself!"

"It's a huge deal." I took a shaky inhale and willed myself not to cry in front of my mom, especially because she was being harsher on me than she'd ever really been before. "I feel lost." I wanted to tell her it wasn't about football, not really. I wanted her to understand, but I knew she never would. She'd hate me.

She stared at me in silence for a few minutes. Then she shut her eyes and pressed her fingertips to her temples, sucking air in through her nose. I tried desperately not to let the tears escape.

She let her breath out before opening her eyes and saying, "You are going to be just fine." She gripped the steering wheel. "You have your whole life."

I couldn't hold it together anymore. I burst out crying, so hard I was practically convulsing. Tears and snot dripped down my face and I thought my chest was going to explode. Once I started, I couldn't stop. I wasn't looking at Mom, but I heard her start crying, too, undoubtedly having no clue what to do with me since I had never done this in my life. She unfastened her seat belt and pulled me toward her, kissing my head over and over.

"Baby, calm down, shhh," she muttered and took deep breaths. "Shhh, Mason. You're okay."

Finally, after what felt like an eternity, I was able to catch my breath and wipe my face. My mom had put a box of tissues in my lap. I cleaned myself up and glanced at her, swallowing hard. The lines on her forehead were like earthquakes stretching across the ground. Wrinkles extended like spider legs from the corners of her eyes. We sat in silence for a while as I finished calming down.

"Let's get you home to bed," she said, squeezing my hand tight, before finally turning the ignition.

TWENTY-THREE

My appointment with Dr. Kalad, to read my MRI report, was on Monday morning. I had another day of suspension after this for my drunken incident, so it worked out. But I didn't know what to expect anymore. I had thought there was no way to do damage to my bone since it was mending together, but I didn't think about the tendons and ligaments around it. I just couldn't believe this was happening.

"It looks like what I thought," Dr. Kalad said. "The tendon in your hand ruptured when you hit it the other day. And I hate to say this, but you're going to need surgery to repair it."

My mom gasped—actually gasped—like this didn't feel dramatic enough.

I stared at his eyes beneath his glasses and pushed my lips together so tight it felt like pliers were pinching them shut. It was the only way to keep from having a total meltdown. I quickly looked at my lap, blinking a few times, while I gripped my shirt in my left hand.

"When?" I asked, still focusing on my legs, trying to show no emotion. Trying not to show that my insides felt like they were being deposited into a wood chipper—tearing every last piece of me apart.

"We'll want to get you in within a week or two if we can. It's going to be really uncomfortable, just to warn you, because even though your bone is healed now, everything around your wrist is frozen. You need to start physical therapy, but you won't be able to right after the surgery, so it's going to be a painful process once you're ready."

I shut my eyes, my neck still bent downward. "But it can still heal?"

I opened my eyes and stared at his shiny, laced black shoes.

"Of course," Dr. Kalad said. "As I said from the start, it might not be the same. But you could still get plenty of mobility back."

I finally raised my eyes to see him sitting at his computer, clicking the keys. He pushed his glasses up his nose. "So, I operate on Tuesdays and Thursdays at the North Shore Hospital. How about next Tuesday? Just a bit more than a week from now. We can get this going."

My chest shuddered as I exhaled. "Sure, what else am I gonna do?"

I WAS IN a shitty mood when I returned to school from suspension on Wednesday. I also had to serve detention every day until Christmas break (or actually, when I checked out early for Christmas break for surgery).

I'd texted the guys to tell them about my impending operation. Dillon was concerned for me, of course, asking if I needed anything. Chris might've been secretly enjoying it, but I tried not to talk to him since he left me drunk at my locker almost a week ago, too afraid I'd lose it.

He'd texted me later that day, not even to ask about how much trouble I'd gotten in. He just said: *You seriously broke up with the chick? I called that one, didn't I?*

I'd nearly crunched the screen of my phone and didn't bother answering him, ignoring his requests to hang out over the weekend. I'd only texted him on Monday to tell him about the surgery.

But now, here I was sitting with the guys at lunch on Wednesday, wishing I were anywhere else.

"So are you ever going to tell us why you broke up with the chick?" Chris said.

"Her name's Lace," I said, clenching my fist under the table.

"How could we forget Mase and Lace?" Freddy kidded, still killing the unoriginal joke from before Mark's party. It was annoying then and it was just too much now.

"Yeah, whatever," Chris said, waving his hand at the air.

Dillon stared at me and gave a half smile. After my outburst last week Chris told them all about Lace and me. They'd each texted me, and all I'd said was it didn't work out. End of story.

"Yeah, Vancey," Freddy said. "Why'd it end? Gave up on trying to get her into bed?" His damn high-pitched laugh made my ears feel like they were bleeding.

Garrett punched him in the shoulder but didn't say anything. He kept eating barbecue chips.

"Look," I said, gritting my teeth. "That's not what it was about. We never had sex. It just didn't work out, okay?"

"Ah," Freddy said, nudging Dillon. "So guess that is why it didn't 'work out.'" He made air quotes and laughed again.

Dillon squinted and shook his head at him.

"No." I stared at Freddy hard, until the smile disappeared from his face. He looked away and took a loud gulp of water. It took a lot for Freddy to stop joking around and get serious, so when he did, you knew he was uncomfortable.

Chris snorted. "What a prude, damn."

"Don't fucking say that," I snapped. I pushed my tray to the side and gripped the table, feeling like I was on a trial where I desperately had to prove my innocence. It wasn't like I could tell any of them what happened, so why did I care if they had it all wrong anyway?

"What's with you, man?" Dillon asked. "Calm down."

"Nothing. Just forget it."

"Oh come on, just tell us what happened, Miss Vance." Chris wiggled his eyebrows, but I didn't think it was funny.

"You're a fucking asshole, Chris," I said, my lip twitching.

I stared at him as I gripped my fork, the metal cutting into my palm. He tried to figure out if I was actually being serious, and when he saw that I was, he planted his hands on the table and stared back at me, his mouth twisting into a smile.

"At least I never had a fat bitch of a girlfriend who wouldn't even fuck me."

I stood up so fast, my chair clattered to the ground. I shoved past the side of the table, knocking over two iced teas. Ice cubes and sticky liquid sloshed over the floor. I grabbed Chris by the collar of his shirt with only my right fingers, ignoring the pain in my hand. I pulled back my left arm and let my fist connect with his smug, freckly face. His sandy-colored hair flopped as he stumbled back, tripped over a chair behind him, and fell to the ground. I continued to stare at him, fuming, even as his eye was swelling in front of me.

The cafeteria was suddenly so silent a coin toss could've been heard. I glanced around, and basically everyone's eyes were on me. Mindy was a few tables over. She looked like she didn't recognize me, like she was afraid.

"Seriously?" Chris finally said as he stood up, touching his finger to his eye. He was so quiet, I barely heard him.

None of my friends said anything, just stared at me along with everyone else. I glanced at the teachers' table where the senior English teacher, Mrs. Coyle, was already standing up and making her way toward me. I grabbed my sweatshirt and headed out the door, hoping she wouldn't follow me. I shook out my left hand, which felt like it was just run over by a tractor. Sharp, crushing pains radiated from my fingers to my forearm. Hopefully I didn't break that one, too. Wouldn't that be something to break one wrist after the other?

I burst through the door to the empty hallway, still hoping I'd lose Mrs. Coyle, and I turned down the hall for my locker. There were twenty minutes left of lunch. None of my friends came out after me, not that I expected them to; I'd put them in an awkward situation. I couldn't believe I punched my best friend since Pre-K in the face. The guy I played peewee football with after both of us had to persuade our moms to sign the permission slip. The guy I called right after I lost my virginity to Brianna Headley. The guy I snuck my first beer with from the fridge while my dad was out. The guy I thought I could always count on. The guy was a douchebag . . . and we weren't the same people anymore. The guy I hated with every muscle in my body right now.

The sound of high heels clicking the tile got closer to where I sat against my locker.

"Mason," Mrs. Coyle said, looking down at me. "I think we need to pay Principal Banks a visit."

I stood up without argument and followed her to his office. My first day back from suspension probably could've gone smoother. Just pile the detention on.

TWENTY-FOUR

My wrist (and the fact that I punched Chris) was basically the only thing that kept me from obsessing over Lace like I had been for almost three weeks. I still hadn't heard from her. She said she didn't want to talk anymore, but I had hoped that didn't mean like ever. Apparently, it did. I was still surprised she never answered my card. I couldn't bring myself to look at the half I kept after I cried on it when I was drunk. It just made me feel worse about what I'd done. I found myself crying or short of breath sometimes while I was sitting at my desk doing homework or watching TV in the den. I'd pull Dove close and breathe as deeply as I could into her fur.

I tried some of my football visualization techniques whenever I started freaking out. Like before a game, I'd visualize doing everything right—throwing perfect passes, making handoffs, running the ball in. Now I simply visualized myself happy—letting go of what I did—forgetting it, but learning from it. I visualized myself having normal conversations with my friends about sports, video games, food—stupid stuff where I couldn't be disrespectful and hurt other peoples' feelings. I visualized cheering Chad on at lacrosse games without checking all the girls out in the stands. I pictured a real life ahead of me, hoping it would be one I'd want to live. It calmed me down a little, but I still couldn't get over it.

It was a couple days after I got the news about surgery, and I was driving with my mom to pick up dinner from an Asian takeout place. My chest tightened as I thought about Lace again. I wanted to tell her about my surgery, talk to her about how I felt, but I didn't have her to talk to anymore and that killed me. My mom glanced over at me every few seconds as I gripped the fabric of my shirt around my heart.

"You okay, hon?" she asked as I looked out the passenger window, taking deep breaths.

"I don't think I am," I admitted. "Mom, I don't know what's happening to me."

She pulled over to the side of the road and put the car in park. "What's going on, Mase?"

"I just—" I took another breath.

"Mason, what is it? You're scaring me." She paused. "Are you worried about the surgery? It's a routine operation."

I shook my head, my throat too tight to speak. I wasn't worried about the actual procedure, just what came after, and I had a while to see how that would unfold.

"It's Chris, isn't it?" She sighed. "You can apologize to him, you know. I didn't want to get in the middle of your fight, but his mother is pretty upset. Maybe you should—"

"That's not it."

"Oh." She slumped down a bit over the steering wheel, shutting her eyes. "Then, what? Lace?"

I gave one small nod. "Kind of."

"She's not pregnant, is she?" She choked on the last word.

"No," I said, my eyes widening. Of course that was what she

thought. "It's not that."

"Mase, talk to me." Mom touched my shoulder.

"I can't!" I whipped around to face her.

Her shoulders jerked as she pulled her hand away, and a tear fell down her face. She stared at me.

I didn't want to admit to her what was going on, but I needed a way to lift this giant weight from my body. I looked back out the passenger window, remembering that Lace saw a therapist, which was how I met her. She said it helped and that she'd made progress from where she was a year ago. Or maybe she said that the antidepressants were what helped. Either way, I had to do something.

"I—I can't talk to you, Mom. But I think I should talk to someone else," I said, finally, raising my eyes to meet hers.

Her chest rose and fell, her forehead creased, and another tear trailed down her cheek. "Promise me you're okay," she said. "Promise it's not something I *should* know."

"I promise," I said, taking another deep breath. "I just need . . . something."

"I'm going to look up psychologists under our insurance," she said. She squeezed my knee before putting the car back in drive.

TWENTY-FIVE

The therapist my mom found had an opening for Friday afternoon, and I was already second-guessing my decision. Why was Mason Vance seeing a shrink? Who the hell was I? I'd be starting physical therapy after my surgery, and now I was going to psychotherapy, too? Not even seventeen and completely falling apart.

Her name was Dr. Hagen and she invited me into her office after greeting me in the waiting room. At least I was the only person sitting there. I kept glancing around like I would be found out. God, if my friends saw me here they'd have a field day. I tried not to think about everyone else, to try and let this doctor help even though I had the feeling she would spew a lot of bullshit. I didn't know what to do anymore.

She already had me fill out an online form after my mom booked the appointment. All the questions were about my anxieties, depression, alcohol usage; you know, anything that could point to me being unstable. I didn't know how truthful to be with my answers either. She probably saw all sorts of stuff with other people, but I wasn't supposed to talk about my feelings and fears. One question on the form asked: *What brings you to therapy today?* I wrote: *Overwhelmed.*

"How are you today, Mason?" Dr. Hagen asked after staring at me over her glasses for a minute. I ran my fingers along the top of my wrist brace a few times and shifted on the sofa that had way too many throw pillows on it.

"Okay," I said, looking around the office. It seemed normal enough, just books, typical flower art on the walls, some armchairs, but I still couldn't help feeling like I was in some bizarre other world.

"What can I do for you?" she asked with a neutral expression.

I shifted again and rubbed at the back of my neck.

"Your mother said you haven't been yourself lately," she continued, skimming the printed form I'd filled out online.

"She probably thinks that's a good thing," I said under my breath, but loud enough for her to hear. Joking was the only thing I had left right now.

"Why do you think that?" she asked, taking me more seriously than I meant her to, but the stereotype about shrinks dissecting every last thing you said must've been true.

"Because I'm not a good person," I said, figuring I may as well get to the point.

She wrote something in her notebook before saying, "Usually, if someone isn't a good person, they wouldn't know enough to say it about themselves. So, I'm guessing, and correct me if I'm wrong, you aren't proud of your behavior. But the way it's affecting you shows that you care."

I nodded, not sure if I even understood her.

"Was there something that happened that you wanted to discuss?" She leaned back in her armchair and tucked her pen through the bun on top of her head. "You wrote that you were feeling overwhelmed." She waved her hand at the notebook and papers in her lap.

"Yes." I swallowed and looked out the tiny window at the far end of the room.

"Everything you tell me is totally confidential, you know that, right?"

I nodded again and took a deep breath. "I—" I paused. "I don't really know how to explain it."

She folded her hands over her legs. "Your mom mentioned your wrist on the phone. Is that what has you stressed?"

I shook my head once. "Kind of. Like, it's made me upset and stuff, but something happened recently."

"Can you try to tell me what it was?" She leaned forward. "I know it's odd to trust a stranger, so we can talk about whatever you'd like."

I didn't say anything.

"It seems like you want to talk about it, though." She continued to stare at me. I ground my teeth back and forth. "Did someone do something to you?"

I shook my head again. "I did something to someone." I glanced down at my lap.

She made an "hmm" sound. I knew she wanted me to keep going. I took a deep breath.

"My girlfriend . . ." I started. "Uh, ex-girlfriend, she, uh . . ." My mind went blank and I couldn't get the words out. What happened between us? "I hurt her . . . like actually. I don't even know." I paused and looked up at her. "I'm not sure."

She raised her eyebrow, but otherwise kept her expression neutral. I wondered how much training it took for psychologists to perfect that indifferent stare.

"You hit her?" she asked.

"No," I said, my left hand shooting up like a stop sign. I must've sucked at explaining if that was what she thought. "I'd never do that."

She nodded and pulled the pen from her bun, about to write more notes.

"That wasn't what I meant," I said. "Okay, I've never had a girlfriend before. And honestly I never really even liked girls—for their personalities anyway." I took another breath, wanting to get it all out as quickly as possible. "I've slept with a lot of girls, I don't even know how many, but none of them ever meant anything to me, which I feel really guilty about now. And like, that's weird for me when I never felt guilty before. But anyway, I met this girl a couple months ago and she was different." I paused and tried to gauge how Dr. Hagen was taking this, but as expected, her expression was blank.

"So," I continued. "We started hanging out a lot, like going on dates, everything, but we never hooked up."

"Hooked up as in slept together?" Dr. Hagen cut in.

"Yeah, but like we didn't even do anything. We kissed, but even that happened a while after we'd been hanging out. And like, she told me she struggled with depression. I saw that she had scars on her arm—that she made herself. And I saw she had antidepressants in her medicine cabinet. And it all really freaked me out, but I liked her." I shrugged.

"So what did you mean when you said you hurt her?" she asked after a minute, when I stopped talking. I forgot I was supposed to keep going with this story, or maybe I just stopped wanting to.

"This one night, she came to my friend's party with me. We'd never drank together or anything, and looking back I really shouldn't have asked her to, but I just wanted us both to let loose and have fun together. I guess that was stupid of me because she also told me about this one night she got drunk—that she did something she regretted and felt like she wasn't herself or something. I wasn't even planning on us hooking up, I got that she wasn't ready, but I don't know. My friends were giving me shit, I was drunk, and I really liked her. I didn't want to be completely changed especially with everything going on with my wrist." I ran my hand through my hair and stared at the wall. I had been looking pretty much everywhere other than at Dr. Hagen this whole time.

She didn't interrupt me. I kind of wished she'd decide I could be done talking, but I didn't give her a clear enough idea about what happened.

"So, yeah," I said. "We were both drunk and we left the party and we started hooking up. I was excited obviously; I had been dreaming of that since the day I met her, so I got kind of carried away. I didn't notice that she kept telling me to stop, or maybe I did, but I wasn't processing it." I paused, deciding not to admit that I didn't know whether I wasn't processing it or just didn't care. "I honestly don't know." I put my head down in my lap and grabbed my hair. My voice came out muffled between my knees. "I kept going, taking her clothes off, you know, all that, and then she hit me, finally snapping me out of it and I just—I couldn't believe what happened. She broke up with me right after."

I sat back up and shook my head, taking in a ragged breath. I shut my eyes tight, feeling like my heart was on a trampoline. A drop of moisture collected in the corner of my eye, so I squeezed it tighter. It wasn't even that I was overwhelmingly sad, I just felt uncomfortable, but also relieved. And once I finally opened my eyes and looked at Dr. Hagen, I was totally embarrassed. I just gave a fifty-year-old woman the play-by-play on my sex life.

"That must've been difficult," she said. "Having to reassess yourself that way."

"It's just, no girl ever really said no to me before. Or like, if they did then I stopped, and didn't talk to them anymore. Which must make me a huge jerk, right? And I started thinking about all the times I kind of pressured girls into it. Like maybe they did say no at first, but I kept persuading them until they gave in. I'd promise them things, tell them what they wanted to hear. And I just feel so awful about it now."

She tapped the pen against her lip. "I'm glad you're realizing all this," she said. But something flashed across her face other than indifference. The way she narrowed her eyes, the twitch of her lips—she looked like she was disgusted with me. I couldn't tell if I was making it up in my head because it was how I felt about myself or if it was actually there on her face. "Some people never realize how much they hurt people. Some people don't even care."

"I care," I said, like I needed to convince her I wasn't scum.

"Good." She gave a tight smile. "Don't be too hard on yourself, though. You can't erase what you did, you can only learn from it at this point."

I nodded. I wished she could tell me a way to erase it. How was I ever supposed to feel like I wasn't a piece of garbage because of this?

"What's her name?" she asked.

I glanced at the window again. "Lace," I whispered.

She wrote it down in her notes. "Have you talked to her since?"

"We texted a little. She doesn't want to talk to me." I kept staring at the trees outside the building.

"You have to understand it must be hard for her," she said.

"You both have to work your feelings out."

I looked at her again. "I miss her." I hardly recognized my choked up voice.

Her neutral expression was now full of sympathy and understanding. "You mentioned your friends before, how they influence your behavior," she said.

"Yeah." I was thankful she drew the attention away from Lace's feelings. Just thinking about how sad she was made me want to bury my head and never see light again.

"I know with teenage boys there's this whole competitive nature and it's not cool to talk about feelings. I also know that you guys will turn a blind eye even if one of your friends is doing something wrong. But you should start to think about how you can help each other be the best versions of yourselves. There's no harm in joking, but there is when the joking is harmful. You see?"

I looked down. She was right. I acted like a dick to impress my friends. They weren't the only reason, but I fed off their worship. And even someone as decent as Dillon wouldn't try to get any of us to stop being us. He'd call us out for being assholes, but never actually do anything about it . . . why did it have to be that way?

"I punched my best friend the other day," I said.

She leaned back. "How come?"

"He said some shit about Lace. But he doesn't know what happened. None of my friends do." I shrugged. "And I can't tell them," I said, looking back at her. "Some of them only care about looking cool. And like, they kind of all worshipped me before. I know they were just screwing around when they gave me shit about having a girlfriend, but I let it make me feel like I was less cool, less myself or something. And then, I guess I learned who I really was . . . what I did to Lace . . ." I trailed off and swiped a tear away that hadn't fallen.

"Peer pressure is toxic," Dr. Hagen said. "People do things you never would've thought them capable of when influenced by others. The way people can get inside each other's heads is very interesting."

Like the way I got into all those girls' heads. Thinking what they needed was convincing rather than an actual decent guy.

"Do you want to work it out with your friend?" she asked.

"I don't really know." I pursed my lips. "I just—I don't want to be like this anymore."

She nodded and kept staring at me. "There's always room for growth."

I THOUGHT ABOUT what Dr. Hagen said for the rest of the night. I told her I'd let her know about making a follow-up appointment. I already felt better for the first time in a while as the night went on.

I considered texting Lace tonight. The appointment made me wonder if she was making progress on working things out, too. Maybe she wasn't so sad anymore and didn't think I was such a scumbag. Also, my birthday was on Sunday, so I thought maybe that meant I'd get a free pass to talk to her or something.

It wasn't like I was going to ask for any more chances. I knew we weren't together, but after everything she told me, I wanted to know she was okay, I wanted her to know she could trust me if she ever needed to. I probably didn't mean it when I said I loved her. She was right—how the hell would I know what love was? Still, we didn't need to be together if she wanted someone to talk to.

It didn't feel like I'd ever be okay after what happened, and

I definitely wasn't who I used to be, but I just wanted to let it go—I wanted permission to let it go. Like, if I could be a better person, maybe it'd make up for it somehow.

I went for it and texted Lace.

Me: *Hey*

Lace: *Hey*

My heart pounded against my chest. I didn't think she'd answer.

Me: *How was your week?*

What I actually wanted to write was: *Do you miss me? Did you break up with me because you think I'm a bad person? Why do I still think about you all the time?*

Lace: *Okay I guess. You?*

Me: *Ok too.*

It wasn't okay. I wanted to tell her about my ruptured tendon, the MRI, that I'd be getting surgery in a few days. That I punched my best friend. But she wasn't mine to tell.

Me: *It's my birthday on Sunday.*

Lace: *I know. Any plans?*

Was she hinting that she wanted to have plans with me or was she just being nice? I was the one who texted her, after all.

Me: *Yea, but none I want.*

Lace: *What do you want?*

She was giving me an opening, to at least be honest after all this time, but I couldn't take it.

Me: *Nothing I deserve*

Me: *I'm glad ur ok.*

Lace: *Happy birthday, Mason.*

TWENTY-SIX

My birthday wasn't happy or unhappy. It was more like mediocre. I went to my favorite restaurant, which was this amazing steakhouse, Bryant & Cooper, with my parents and Chad. I was going out with my friends after dinner to a bar on Port Boulevard—one that couldn't care less if you were twenty-one. I didn't tell my parents where we were going, just that my friends wanted to take me to celebrate. They said I deserved to celebrate my birthday—just not too much—and told me to be home by eleven.

The steak was awesome. The mashed potatoes were awesome. The chocolate cake was awesome. Hell, even the asparagus was awesome. I was stuffed when Garrett picked me up. I wore the new smart watch that Mom and Dad got me as a gift. The inside of the band was engraved: *You have all the time in the world.*

It was nice that they tried to make me feel better about going in for surgery in two days. I wondered if they were worried about the procedure, because they'd been acting weirdly calm. Maybe they just didn't want to show it. They also probably wanted me to feel better about Lace, though. They didn't know what went on between us, but the fact that a girl affected me at all probably made them respect me more and realize I had a soul. Plus, you were supposed to make your kid's birthday special.

"So, we've got to find Vance a hot chick to hook up with now that he's single again," Freddy said as we sat in a booth at the back of the bar. Since when did I need my friends' help finding girls? Maybe they needed me to be their leader again and show them all was right in the universe. Already, no one was acknowledging the awkward fact that Chris wasn't here. He hadn't missed one of my birthdays since I was seven years old. He texted me this morning: *HBD*.

Wasn't exactly heartfelt. I didn't reply.

"What did that relationship last? All of five minutes?" Garrett joked. At least he wasn't afraid to mess around after I decked Chris.

"It's okay, I need a break from girls," I said.

"Yeah right," Freddy said. "That's the last thing you need."

"Yeah, come on, Mason, you need a girl more than ever. You can't even jerk off with that deformed wrist." Garrett pointed at my brace, cracking up. Dillon and Freddy laughed along with him.

I cracked a smile. If Chris had said that I probably would've been pissed, but I had to loosen up. Even after putting them all in a weird spot, caught between Chris's and my drama, my friends were still here for me and wanted my birthday to be cool.

"I've got lefty skills," I said, and we all laughed harder.

"Hopefully that surgery doesn't mess you up for good," Freddy said.

I pursed my lips. I'd played off the surgery to my friends just like I'd played off the severity of my fracture. They didn't question me when I told them that plenty of people snapped tendons because they couldn't move them for so long and they got too tight. The doctor actually did say it wasn't totally uncommon, but I left out the detail that it occurred when I slammed my cast into the wall because I betrayed the person I cared most about.

"What about that girl?" Freddy pointed behind him to a girl who was at least twenty, wearing tight jeans and a sweater that showed her whole stomach. She must have missed the memo that it was December 17th and below freezing. She also looked a lot like Mindy; I bet Chris would've pointed her out if he were here, too.

She glanced over at our table and whispered to her two friends. They turned around to look at us, too. The girl made eye contact with me before whispering something else.

I looked away from her and shook my head. "I told you, I need a break."

"Dude, don't be lame," Dillon said. Even Dillon was joining in now? Maybe he saw how down I was and thought this was what I needed. That I was happiest when I had random girls hanging all over me. Not anymore.

"I'll make it easy for you," Freddy said as he hopped up from the table and walked over to the girl. Even though I felt her look over every so often, she was now laughing and twirling her hair as she talked to her friends. In a matter of seconds, Freddy had them pulling their barstools over to our table.

"Like I was saying," Freddy went on, apparently in the middle of a conversation. "This is the birthday boy, Mason, and he also happens to have just broken up with his girlfriend." He jutted his lower lip out, like this news should've devastated the nearly shirtless girl and it was her duty to make it up to me.

"Sorry to hear that," she said in a voice that suggested she wasn't sorry at all.

"Thanks." I nodded. Okay, she was hot and she was already

into me and it was my birthday. All great reasons to let what happened with Lace go already and get back to my old self, just with less of the assholishness. If she liked me, then I wasn't taking advantage, right? Ugh, all I wanted was to shut my brain off for five minutes.

"I'm Tiffany." She leaned forward, letting her boobs topple a little bit more out of her non-existent sweater. She inched her chair toward me. "What happened to your wrist, birthday boy?"

"I broke it playing football."

Freddy kicked me under the table, which I knew meant, "What the hell is your problem? Where is the *real* Mason Vance game?"

I shrugged.

"He's getting surgery in two days," Freddy chimed in again. "Maybe you should make his last night out memorable." He nudged Garrett, who laughed with him but shook his head.

I glanced at them sideways. "You guys are assholes."

Tiffany looked back and forth between my friends and me. Then she flipped her hair over her shoulder and stood up. "Want to come to the bar with me to get a proper birthday shot?"

"Sure." I shrugged and stood up, too, which seemed to satisfy my friends. Really, I just wanted to get away from them for a few minutes and Tiffany seemed to realize that. Garrett smacked my ass under the table. I held my middle finger up behind my back and heard Tiffany's two friends giggling.

"You don't seem like you're having a very fun birthday," Tiffany said, once we were alone at the bar. "Anything I can do to help?" She smiled and put her hand on my shoulder. Her breath reeked of liquor. No wonder I couldn't hide the fact that I drank half a bottle of whiskey at school.

"Not really. Thanks, though, you seem nice."

She moved in closer so our hips touched, and she put her hand around the back of my neck, running her fingers through my hair. "Are you sure, Mason? You don't have to be so serious, you know."

I swallowed hard. Why was she throwing herself at me? I was a jerk, my friends were jerks. She was drunk, that was why. She leaned in and waited for me to kiss her. I shut my eyes for a second, taking a deep breath, then I decided, what the hell?

I tried not to think about how she wasn't sober. How maybe this wasn't a coherent decision for her. I tried to tell myself I could kiss her without walking that dangerous line I walked with Lace a few weeks ago. And I deserved a birthday kiss, right? Our lips locked and I slid my hand down to her waist, shaking as it hovered over her bare skin, afraid she was going to smack it away and scream at me to stop.

As our tongues met, she tasted like whiskey, peanuts, and vomit. Magical. Still, I kissed her for a few minutes, trying desperately to enjoy what I used to enjoy so much, but it was no use. She rested her hand on my belt buckle and I backed away. "So, how about those drinks?" I asked.

Tiffany was all over me for the next hour. She kept putting her hand on the inside of my thigh and trying to turn me toward her to kiss her again. I continued to reject her as nicely as I could. She even asked if I wanted to come over when we were leaving the bar. Not like I'd be up for that anytime soon, if ever. Freddy had no problem going home with one of her friends, though. At least that'd be one thing my friends could talk about at school tomorrow instead of what a wuss I was. Actually I barely even saw them at school the last few days because I told them to just sit with Chris at lunch, and in our other classes, while I did my own thing.

Tiffany put her number in my phone and texted herself so

she had mine, too, but I wasn't going to hang out with her again. I was already an asshole for giving her the impression I was interested—just like always.

I was buzzed by the time I got home. My friends gave me shit for not going home with her—well, they were just joking around, but Garrett and Dillon said Freddy was going to pull ahead of me when he may as well have been a virgin. That obviously wasn't true, but compared to me everyone may as well have been. They were still pleased that we made out and she groped me all night, which was kind of funny when I stopped to think about it. Lace was right—what was that good for? My therapist was right, too (I couldn't believe I used the phrase "my therapist"), but what was with the desperate need to seem cool for my friends? Especially when what they thought was cool didn't match up to what I thought was anymore.

I told them that my parents would've been pissed if I didn't come home, especially since this was our last week of school and we had finals tomorrow. I had to take my remaining two finals in one day to get them out of the way before surgery. I already took two last week—probably scoring solid Cs on just about everything. And I still had detention every day that I was able to go to school before break for my whiskey stunt. I'd have more after break for my punching Chris stunt. My friends agreed those were valid points, but they still called me a pussy—whatever.

I found myself texting Lace before I realized what I was doing. She never texted me *happy birthday* again, even though she already wished me one on Friday.

Me: *U awake?*

It was only ten thirty. My parents would've been furious if I stayed out past eleven, birthday or not.

Lace: *Happy birthday*

Me: *u don't have to say that*

Lace: *I was going to text you at 11:59, so I'd be the last person to wish you a happy birthday. I've never cared about being first, people seem to overlook the significance of being last.*

My mouth felt like it was stuffed with cotton, hard to swallow. I enabled my social media again the day before my birthday because I must've wanted all the birthday wishes. Maybe I thought it'd make me feel better or something, but so many people wrote on my Facebook and texted me at midnight. They all wanted to wish me a happy birthday right at the start of it, hoping to be first. It was so predictable. And she was different, and even more, she still cared about me. Tears brimmed in my eyes, but I refused to let them spill over, feeling like such a pansy—my friends were right. I took a shaky sip of water from the glass on my nightstand.

Me: *Ur a pretty awesome person*

I stood up and took off my shirt and jeans, then lay in bed in my boxers, staring at my phone. She was typing.

Lace: *Is it weird to miss you even though it'd be easier not to?*

Me: *Is it weird to love u even tho it'd be easier not to?*

I sent it without giving myself the chance to regret it.
She answered instantly.

Lace: *Do what's easy.*

Me: *U told me once easy isn't as rewarding. No pain, no gain, right? So what if I don't want to?*

She didn't answer. The beer put me to sleep pretty quickly, and I didn't really care that she didn't answer. Maybe, deep down, I thought I'd eventually get over her or that in some parallel universe we'd get back together. I didn't know which one I was hoping for.

TWENTY-SEVEN

It was time to head to the hospital on Tuesday morning. My legs bounced and jiggled for the whole car ride, which was only like seven minutes from my house.

My mom and dad both came with me. Chad had come in my room to wake me up before he'd left for school. He'd flopped in my bed under the covers and patted my head like I was Dove.

"Good luck, Mase," he said.

"Thanks, bro."

"Just remember when you get home, Mom will have like thousands of Christmas cookies made."

I smiled and rubbed my eyes. "Thanks, Chad. Don't fail your finals today." I noogied his hair with my left hand.

"Do my best. See you later!"

Now I was lying in a hospital bed after filling out tons of paperwork, getting weighed, having my vitals checked, and of course, changing into a really mortifying hospital gown.

Dr. Kalad came in to walk me through the surgery beforehand. His voice was more soothing than usual, and he wore a shower cap thing and an all blue outfit that looked like it was made of plastic and paper.

He drew a large black X on my left arm before describing the operation. I didn't get why, but then realized it was seriously so he didn't cut the wrong arm open. My eyes widened and my breathing came shallower. He mostly explained the procedure to my parents, like they were the ones who needed to be put at ease when I literally just had my left arm marked as a no-go.

Then a nurse came to take me to the operating room. My mom and dad both kissed my head, told me I'd be fine. My mom's worry lines were creased pretty deep, though. She tried.

The nurse wheeled me down the hall in my rolling bed to the operating room; antiseptic wafted into my nostrils as we reached the door.

"Okay, let's get you on the table," she said, helping me off the hospital bed. My ass was definitely being flashed to all the doctors in the room.

The anesthesiologist came to my side once I was positioned on the table.

"Hello, Mason," he said in the most hypnotizing voice I'd ever heard. "I'm Dr. Fagan. Have you ever been under anesthesia before?"

"For my wisdom teeth," I said. My heart raced while I lay on the metal table underneath the harsh, bright lights. Dr. Kalad was preparing an abundance of tools to the left of us.

"Great, great," Dr. Fagan said. "You won't feel anything. And I'm going to be here the whole time to monitor you, okay?" This had to be like the easiest guy to trust while you were being cut open.

I nodded.

"Okay, as soon as the doctor is ready, we're going to get started. Do you have any questions for me?" His gray eyes looked right into mine.

"I don't think so."

Dr. Fagan smiled.

"Okay, Mason," Dr. Kalad said, coming to my side. Two other doctors or nurses crowded around me, too. This must've been what it felt like to be dying, all these faces circling above you, shining in bright lights. "This is Dr. Spiella and Dr. Randall. We're all going to be here to make sure everything goes just right."

"Okay." My voice was hardly loud enough to hear. My heart started to race.

"Mason, focus on my eyes," Dr. Kalad said. "You're going to be just fine. Take a deep breath."

I did, shutting my eyes to calm down. I opened them and looked back up at Dr. Kalad after a few seconds, ready to get this over with.

"Are you ready to get started? It'll feel like no time at all before you're awake and that tendon is fixed up." Dr. Kalad smiled down at me.

"Yes, just like going to sleep for a little while, Mason," Dr. Fagan said.

I nodded, trying to get my heart rate under control. Racing beeps sounded from the heart monitor I was hooked up to. I swallowed, having trouble getting moisture in my throat.

"Okay," Dr. Fagan said. "Now I'm going to have you count down from ten, okay? Whenever you're ready."

I shut my eyes, the machine still beeping in the background, and began to count. "*Ten . . . nine . . . eight . . .*"

I didn't remember everything going dark or fading away, but next thing I knew, I was in a different room, back in a hospital bed, and my wrist was taped up in a splint.

"Hi, Mason," a nurse said, walking over to me. "Do you need some water, sweetie?"

I nodded when I realized my mouth wasn't about to form words. I opened and shut my eyes, my whole head spinning and woozy, like it could float away any minute.

The nurse handed me a miniature cup of water then said something about taking me back to a room. Her voice sounded far away. She was at my side, unlatching the locks on the bed wheels.

Then, I was back in the room I'd been in before my surgery. My mom and dad were sitting in chairs, just behind a curtain.

My mom stood up and kissed my cheek as the nurse wheeled my bed back into place.

"Hey, baby. How do you feel?" Mom asked.

"Tired," I whispered.

The nurse set ginger ale and graham crackers down on a tray in front of me. "Might be a good idea to have some sugar," she said. "Dr. Kalad will come check on you shortly."

My mom opened the package of graham crackers and broke off a piece, holding it up to my lips. I shook my head. "Too tired," I said.

"Just take a minute, hon. You'll be okay."

My dad smiled at me from his chair. "Hard part's over, Mase."

I pushed myself up farther and tried to focus my eyes. Dr. Kalad arrived at my room and peeked around the corner of the curtain.

"Hey, how you feeling?" he asked. His shower cap was gone now and his brown hair was tousled and damp.

"Waking up," I said.

He chuckled. "So," he said, glancing around the room at each of us. "The surgery went beautifully. Take a few days to rest and we'll meet again in a week? Day after Christmas?"

"Definitely," my mom said, exhaling a long breath. "Thank you so much."

I nodded. "Thanks."

"You'll probably be able to start physical therapy a few days after, right after I get the stitches out and the incision is healed. Good news, right?" he asked, smiling.

I had spent months wondering when I could move my wrist again, when I could start making progress toward football, and right now I didn't have the energy to care, wacked off anesthesia and desperately wanting my bed.

"All right, everyone," Dr. Kalad said. "Have a wonderful Christmas. Rest up, Mason. And please, don't hesitate to call if you have any concerns."

My mom and dad each shook Dr. Kalad's hand and wished him a Merry Christmas. Then, I got to go home.

AFTER A MUCH-NEEDED nap, I spent the rest of the night with Chad, watching horror Christmas movies that my mom begged us to turn off. She had to retreat to her room with headphones and a book to drown out killer Santas. We had Dove wrapped under a blanket in the middle of us and I felt like I was ten years old again.

Chad happily blew off studying for his last finals and essays to lift my spirits and gorge on snowflake and angel shaped cookies. He was jealous I got to miss the rest of school before Christmas and I offered to break his wrist for him—joking, of course.

I didn't think I could actually feel happy the same day I had surgery and with everything else that had happened the past few weeks, but I did. I really did. Chad knew exactly what I needed, which was to not talk about Lace (or Chris), not be a jerk, and just hang out—carefree even though I was swimming with cares.

TWENTY-EIGHT

It was finally Christmas break, my favorite time of year—other than summer and football season of course. Okay, so it was my third favorite time of year. And, okay, I technically checked out for Christmas break early to recover from my surgery.

My parents really spoiled Chad and me on Christmas. They always went overboard with gifts, but this year it seemed like even more than usual. I'd already gotten a glimpse of their pity with the watch they gave me for my birthday a week ago.

They got us tons of sports shirts, signed posters, video games, a new Xbox. They even got us all a brand-new, enormous TV for the living room. It was cool being with my family for the day. Mom cooked a big dinner and we all watched *Elf* and *How the Grinch Stole Christmas* before that (more my mom's type of movies). I was glad we didn't have any family coming in and that we didn't travel anywhere else. I could sit on the couch in my sweatpants all day and not have to shower.

I had been recovering from my surgery pretty well. The doctor said I'd be sore and groggy, but for the most part I didn't feel much different. I was back on the prescription bottle of pills, and my wrist was now in a temporary splint instead of a brace or cast. But, other than that, my arm was immobile, it hurt a little, and I couldn't play football or train. Same as before. At least now I was one step closer to physical therapy.

I could tell my mom had been worried about me. She asked a few times this week about scheduling another appointment with the psychologist. She kissed my cheeks way too many times and massaged the arches of my feet while we watched Christmas movies. I understood why she was cautious or whatever, and I was sure she felt bad that I had to go through surgery, but I really had been feeling better lately about Lace. So, all I wanted was to relax over this break.

Chad and I ate popcorn and Mom's Christmas cookies, while watching more lame holiday movies all night. Usually Chris came over on Christmas night. He didn't have much family. He was an only child and pretty much became a staple of our holidays at some point during the day. It kind of sucked not having him here. Neither of us tried talking to each other after he "wished" me a happy birthday. I'd barely been in school since I punched him, so avoiding him was pretty easy. I didn't think I could have him in my life anymore if he was going to be such an ass, but it didn't stop me from missing his "You'll shoot your eye out, kid" impression during *A Christmas Story.*

"You could invite him over," Chad said like he was reading my mind. He had Dove, the world's largest lapdog, on his legs.

"I think I'm done with him, honestly," I said, glancing back at the TV. I hadn't really admitted it to myself, and especially not the other guys. I didn't know how they'd deal with our group being forever destroyed, but how could Chris and I go back to the way it was?

Chad stared at me as he scratched behind Dove's ears. "He's practically like our other brother."

I squinted. I hadn't realized that even my brother missed Chris, the jerk. That everyone around me wanted me to make up with him. That maybe they all secretly thought I was the one in the wrong for punching him. I felt a little bad seeing his swollen purple eye in school (plus the constant reminder from my own bruised knuckles). But then I remembered all the shit he'd said, including the night at Mark's party, and I didn't feel so bad.

"Don't worry about it, man," I said to Chad, shaking Chris from my head. "Anyway, what's new with you lately?"

I realized I hadn't asked Chad anything about his life and I kind of sucked in the brother department. Maybe he would've been better off with Chris as a brother, after all. Ever since I opened up to Chad about what happened with Lace, he'd just been trying to make me laugh and occasionally ask if I was okay. But I never returned the favor with his life and his problems. I only thought about myself and how I was grateful for how Chad made *me* feel.

"What about that girl? Aurora, right?" I said when Chad didn't answer.

"Yeah." He sighed. "We made out at the movies again, but I don't know . . ." He looked at me like he wanted to ask something and I might've known what it was: *Is it still okay after what happened with you?*

"Cool, man," I said, scratching the back of my neck. "Do you like her?"

"I think so." He shrugged.

"Well, you're only fourteen so like, no rush, right?" I tried to smile.

He nodded. I couldn't give him advice anymore . . . after everything. I was a fraud. He realized the change in me and it must've made him just as nervous and confused as it made me.

"Weren't you fourteen, when, you know . . ." he said in a near whisper.

I coughed. "Thirteen," I said, biting my lip and looking back at the TV.

"Thirteen?" he repeated, his voice going up.

I thought about Brianna Headley—the girl I lost my virginity to. How I joked with my friends about her last name being evidence of her "readiness." She asked me if I wanted to hang out again the day after we slept together and I said, "What would we have left to do?" I totally blew her off and got worshipped by all my friends; I tried my luck with every other girl.

I really hadn't turned out to be any less of a dick. I had barely even bothered answering any of the girls who still texted me. The only one who never texted me was Lace, and I felt guilty that she was the only girl I ever cared about, and the one I ended up treating worse than all of them. Well, maybe not worse, but definitely not any better.

Then, as if she'd read my mind, my phone vibrated with a text.

Lace: *Merry Christmas*

Me: *u too, did u have a good day?*

"Is it Chris?" Chad asked, staring over my shoulder.

"Uh, no. It's Lace."

"You still talk?" he asked, an edge of accusation in his voice.

"Not really, but sometimes." I shrugged.

Lace: *It was nice. So, remember I told you how my paintings are going to be displayed at this place in the city on the 30th if you wanted to come? It was a while ago and it's not a big deal, but if you still want to . . .*

"So, you're like friends or something?" Chad asked, shoveling a handful of popcorn into his mouth and letting a few pieces drop for beggar Dove.

I barely heard him. A smile spread across my face, my eyes still on my phone screen. She wanted me there. She wanted me in her life again. I tried not to get my hopes up in case I was reading too much into it, but it didn't work—they were way up.

Me: *I wouldn't miss it.*

I looked up at Chad, who stared at me without blinking. "Yeah," I said. "I guess we're friends."

TWENTY-NINE

My first follow-up with Dr. Kalad after the surgery was on Tuesday morning. He'd said it would probably only take a little more than a week for me to start physical therapy. So, today might've been the day I'd get the news.

"How's it been holding up?" he asked.

"Feels okay. Was just painful for the first few days."

He stood on my right and examined the stitches. "This actually looks totally healed," he said. "I'm going to take the stitches out now."

Damn. I was healing quickly for once?

He took a small pair of scissors down from one of the medical cabinets and ripped them out of the paper packaging. Then he wiped my hand and wrist with alcohol before cutting through each stitch and sliding them out of the side of my palm. He wiped it down with antiseptic again and put ointment on the incision. Then, he started flexing my wrist back and forth.

I cringed when he stretched it too far.

"Looks pretty good," he said. "No bruising. Bones are strong and aligned from X-rays. Now comes the hard part."

"You mean the past two and a half months weren't the hard part?" I hoped he was joking or it was just an expression or something.

He chuckled. "Physical therapy is going to be painful. It would've been even if you didn't have the surgery because your arm has been frozen for so many weeks. But your therapist will help you ease into it. It's exciting that you finally get to move it, isn't it?"

Did he really expect me to be excited? Maybe if he handed me a football I would be.

"I'm not even gonna ask about football again," I said.

He laughed again. "Give it a few weeks in PT. You healed pretty quick from the surgery, so we'll see what happens."

I STARTED PT a few days later on Friday. My physical therapist was this massive guy named Sid. Like of course, when I was at my most fragile, I had to be paired up with a guy who could kick my ass when I was my toughest. Not that he was really trying to kick my ass or anything, but that is sure as hell what it felt like.

My wrist dangled from my arm like some sort of overcooked spaghetti noodle. Sid said he'd go easy to start, stretching my wrist from side to side. But it felt like my wrist was wrapped around itself like a pretzel when it was only moved a half a centimeter to the left. I was getting seriously anxious about if I'd be able to play football again. I couldn't believe I didn't know that my wrist would be completely frozen in place. No matter how much the doctor or anyone else told me it would be, I didn't expect it to look and feel like this. It didn't seem natural for it not to move at all.

I tried to hold back from talking to Sid about football since Dr. Kalad kept crushing my spirits at the mention of it. But I couldn't contain myself.

"Do you think I'll be able to play again?" I asked him as he worked warming cream into my wrist like he was trying to start a fire.

"I think so, man," he said. "Plenty of athletes at the professional level still play after breaks and surgeries."

I exhaled. "That's what I thought. My doctor keeps saying he doesn't know, though."

"Yeah, you can't know for sure unfortunately. Sometimes it just doesn't heal like you expect it to. And I mean, football is a *rough* sport. That makes it harder."

He was right. If I played any other sport people probably wouldn't have been as hesitant to give me good news. I put my head down, trying to hide the pain across my face as Sid did some "light" stretching on my wrist.

My chest shook as I breathed out. This was only the beginning. I could handle the pain. I could keep fighting for what was important.

THIRTY

I asked Chad if he wanted to come with me to Lace's art show in the city. Not because I was trying to make up for being a sucky brother, even though I should've been, but because I needed moral support. I wouldn't have dared ask any of my friends to come with me, even if they weren't as big of assholes as Chris.

We took the train to Penn Station in the afternoon. The gallery thing didn't start until six, but the train ride was about forty-five minutes from Manhasset to the city, then we had to figure out how the hell to get to the gallery once we were actually in the city. The only times I ever came to the city were with my mom and dad for like fancy dinners or my mom's favorite— Broadway shows. I'd suffered through more of those than I was proud to admit. I also came with my friends a few times because we found out about a couple bars near NYU that were lenient with IDs, but from the address Lace sent me, it didn't seem like it was near any of them.

The city was packed with an insane amount of tourists, all flocking to Rockefeller Center to check out the giant Christmas tree before they took it down for the year. Plus, everyone was gathering in Times Square to watch the ball drop tomorrow night. People were already staked out at their spots more than twenty-four hours in advance. Chad and me couldn't walk more than two feet without someone shoving into us. I got a little jittery when anyone came near my wrist. I had a thick supportive brace and I tucked my arm inside my jacket against my chest, but I wished I had a little space to move around the sidewalk without being sent back to the ER.

I always forgot that I lived just a few miles from the most popular tourist destination in America, but hardly ever visited. It was strange watching everyone take pictures of buildings and billboards and every window decked out in Christmas lights, and . . . pigeons. It was dirty and smelled like piss, but greatest city in the world, right?

We finally got to the place just after six. It was kind of crowded, but still a break from what was going on in the city outside. And it wasn't so crowded that I couldn't spot Lace right away. She was over near the set-up bar talking to some guy in his fifties, even though everyone else here looked younger. Like it was encouraged to be between twenty and thirty or something.

She wore tight, fake leather black leggings, laced up boots with studs on them, a loose, low-cut T-shirt, and a short gray jacket. But what I noticed first was that she had dyed her hair. It was dark brown, still just past her chin. All her heavy eye makeup was applied, just like I remembered. She spotted me after the guy shook her hand and walked away, and she made her way toward me. She didn't smile or anything even though I felt myself smiling wide. I hadn't realized how much I missed her.

She stopped in front of me, like she wasn't sure what to do, then she said, "Hey."

I reached in for a hesitant, awkward hug, but feeling her hand on my back was worth it.

"Thanks for coming," she said, as we went back to standing

a couple feet away from each other.

"You changed your hair," I said.

"Oh, yeah." She laughed, with no smile, her cheeks pinkening. "Like a month ago." Right after she stopped talking to me.

Chad had disappeared to get snacks and a drink without my realizing it. He came back over, biting into a sandwich.

"Hey, Lace," he said with his mouth full. Yeah, we definitely didn't belong in a classy art gallery.

She smiled at him. "Thanks for coming, Chad," she said. "I'm sure this isn't your first choice of places to be."

He laughed. "I'm fourteen, what else have I got to do?"

She smiled wider and ruffled his hair. They had only met that one time and it was like they were part of some secret club. She was hardly comfortable with anyone, but here she was joking with my little brother. The person I cared about most. Watching them interact made my chest ache even more.

"So, you can walk around if you want, my paintings are kind of spread out, but you'll see them," she said to both of us. "I have to meet some other people, apparently talk to them about the paintings if they want to buy them, but I'll find you in a little bit? We can catch up?"

I nodded so hard that my brain might've rattled, like there wasn't anything better in the whole world than the idea of Lace sitting next to me again. Was I pathetic? I didn't care. We stared at each other for another minute; she smiled, then walked back toward the other end of the room.

"Seems like it went well," Chad said with a mouthful of who knew what. "I mean, she obviously still likes you, right?"

"You think?" I asked.

"Well, she invited you here. She wants to catch up with you.

All good signs." He started choking from stuffing his face. I laughed, patting him on the back.

"Since when did you start giving me girl advice?" I asked, still smiling.

"Since you stopped giving it to me."

He was joking, well, maybe he was. I still felt shitty about it, though.

"Yeah," I said. "To be honest, I'm lost in that department these days. Just don't feel pressured by your friends or anything. You shouldn't try to do stuff if you're not gonna keep talking to the girl."

He nodded. It might've been stupid advice, because I had never known a fourteen-year-old guy who wasn't ready to have sex, or ones who actually thought about their feelings rather than their . . . well, you know. But look where that got me. What would my life have been like if it hadn't been practically all I thought about the last few years? Maybe I would've been even better at football; not much ever distracted me from that, but it did when I broke my wrist. The one moment where distractions mattered most. If I hadn't been looking at Sharon Martin, planning my night out, maybe none of this would've happened. Maybe if I hadn't obsessed over girls so much, I would've had other interests and known what the hell I wanted to do with my life if football didn't work out.

"Yeah, I mean, none of my friends have done it yet. I can't believe you were thirteen." Chad shook his head like he had given this a lot of thought lately. I used to think it was a good example and I was someone to be looked up to and worshipped for all the girls I'd gotten, but as I glanced back across the room and saw Lace smoothing her hands over her dark hair and shifting from foot to foot, as a woman talked to her, I knew that it wasn't right. She mattered.

"I'm kind of ashamed of it now," I said, looking back at Chad. "But it's not like I can do anything about it."

Chad shrugged. "You could start with her." He pointed at Lace.

I nodded, staring at her a few seconds longer. "Anyway, let's be sophisticated and check out the art, shall we?" I said in a horrible, British accent. He laughed and followed me to the nearest painting.

We walked around for a couple minutes, looking at the displayed pieces. I spent a lot of time cocking my head to the side, like I was analyzing something without knowing why or what it was. There were a decent amount of nature paintings, flowers and trees and stuff, some cool images of people. I saw one of Lace's paintings as we made our way around. It was this really awesome black and white piece of a skeleton that kind of looked 3D. Out of the ones I had seen so far, hers were definitely a different type of art—they were dark and haunting. Not every painting here was cheerful and flowery, but they weren't as creepy as Lace's. It made sense a lot of people here were younger because I couldn't picture a set of grandparents coming in and purchasing Lace's skulls and dark forests.

There were some abstracts and city landscapes, buildings and trains. Even a painting or two of obese naked ladies. There was no real theme going on. I was probably biased, but Lace's made me feel something, more than a picture of a bus or flower could.

We stopped at another one of hers. I read the description beneath. It was called *No*. And the blurb under the title said: *It is human to feel important when we have power over another, but wanting that sort of importance—is not human.*

I furrowed my eyebrows, trying to figure out what that meant. I remembered all the complex conversations we used to have, how many of them I never understood.

I glanced up at the painting and it took a minute for me to realize what the image was. It was a girl lying in the grass, beside a bench, with a look on her face that was a mix between sadness and fear. It was similar to that painting on her Instagram page that I spent a lot of time looking at.

In this one, there was a man above her, and you couldn't see his face. He hovered over her, only his back visible. His hands gripped her thighs, her dress pushed up to her hips. He was raping her.

My whole body began to shake. I was sweating and freezing at the same time. Sour bile rose up in my throat and it was really hard to breathe. I turned away from the painting, about to hyperventilate. I hunched over, my left hand on my knee. Chad touched my arm as I dry heaved.

"You okay?" he asked.

Tears stung at my eyes. I tried to swallow, but no air was coming, everything was dry and suffocating. Why would she paint that? Why would she invite me here to see that? I stood up straight and walked out of the gallery, past all the people who looked like nothing other than moving blurs now. Leaning against the side of the building, I tried to breathe deeply, letting the sharp, icy air into my lungs.

Chad came out behind me and rested his hand on my shoulder.

"Can you believe that?" I asked, my left hand tightening into a fist as I straightened up. I tried not to show the shame washing over my whole body.

He shrugged. "It's a really good painting."

"Are you serious?" I choked on a sob, wiping my mouth with the back of my hand. I sniffled hard, shuddering. Then, I shut my eyes and leaned my head against the bricks of the building.

"Why don't you just ask her about it?" Chad tried to pull me by my elbow back toward the door.

"How can I talk to her now? That painting is about me! She doesn't forgive me, she never will. Jesus, Chad, she thinks I raped her!" I banged my head against the bricks again, grabbing my hair with my left hand.

"Mase," Chad said, lowering his voice, glancing over his shoulder like he was nervous people would hear. "I don't think she means it like that. Maybe it's really just a painting. I mean, her other stuff is similar to it."

"It's never that simple with her." I snorted, pulling my right arm closer to my chest. Maybe I had built her up in my head so much all this time and just wanted to talk to her because I felt guilty. Maybe I didn't love her, let alone like her at all. Maybe after all this time and all these headaches and tears, I had no idea who she was. It was like she wanted to make me suffer.

I went back in a few minutes after Chad. I sat down in a chair by the bar and stared at Lace from across the room, gritting my teeth. I wanted nothing more than to leave, but I'd wait and say goodbye. I even texted Mindy while I was outside and asked if she wanted to hang out later tonight. Yeah, it was a jackass move, but I was so pissed. Pissed at Lace, but pissed that I felt so ashamed. I knew I didn't have the right to be annoyed, but that night with Lace nearly ruined me. She had to process what happened in her own way. I knew she hadn't wanted to talk to me anymore, that I hurt her too badly. But why did she have to display that painting for not just any random person to see—but for me to see? I swiped a tear hanging on the end of my eyelashes.

Lace walked over to Chad and me, smiling. Maybe she had just sold a painting, because I was sure I didn't look inviting. I was sure I didn't look the least bit happy. Chad got up to go to the bathroom.

"Are you okay?" she asked, sitting down beside me. The mellow jazz music was louder than ever in my ears.

"Your stuff is really good," I said, running my hand down the back of my head.

She stared at me, confused, probably by my blatant lack of enthusiasm.

"How could you do that to me?" I turned to look at her.

Her lower lip quivered. "What do you mean?"

"Are you trying to tell me what a scumbag you think I am in some creative, passive aggressive way? Because you could've just told me that. No one forced you to invite me tonight," I said, leaning closer to her.

A few beads of sweat collected between her eyebrows, and she swallowed hard.

"I don't know what you mean, Mason," she whispered. "Why are you mad at me?"

I laughed. "Whatever, Lace."

She actually looked confused, like she couldn't figure out why I'd be angry. Either she was a really good actress or a freaking sociopath.

"My painting?" she finally asked, her eyes glossy. She opened her mouth then shut it again. Chad returned to the table. I picked up both of our coats and stood up. "The one you're talking about . . . it's not about you," she said, her voice getting quieter. "It's a metaphor," she continued, like she didn't know why she bothered to explain. "About all guys, even all people, how sometimes humans act the least human, whether they're aware of it or not. That's why he doesn't have a face."

I laughed, knowing she, of all people, understood that she

just described me—and that night—perfectly. For once, I didn't care about her metaphors and explanations, especially when those metaphors were based on the worst part of myself. It was about me. She knew that—she thought about *everything*.

"See you later, Lace." I turned and pulled Chad with me until we were outside.

We stayed quiet on the way home. I was so mad, but I didn't even know who I was mad at. I had a pretty good idea that it was myself, especially as I drove to Mindy's house to pick her up.

We drove to the park and climbed up the ladder to the slide on the jungle gym. She giggled as she slid down the tunnel slide a couple times, strategically flashing what was underneath her skirt.

"How are you not freezing?" I asked as she made her way back up the ladder. My voice had no life left in it. This was the last place I wanted to be, and yet, here I was.

"You could warm me up." Mindy shrugged and patted the space next to her at the top of the slide, smiling. I didn't smile back. How many times was I going to keep treating her like shit? I never apologized to her after Mark's party . . . not that it would've carried a single bit of credit since I kept doing all the same stuff. I'd always be the same.

I walked over and kneeled in front of her. I kissed her hard, shaking so much I thought I'd drop dead as she leaned back and pulled me on top of her. I glanced behind her to where that bench was, where I did what I did to Lace, but the jungle gym blocked it from my view. My left hand barely worked as I moved Mindy's skirt up her thighs. I couldn't stop picturing her crying and telling me to stop.

I pulled back.

"What's wrong, Mase?" Mindy asked.

"Are you okay?" I said.

She smiled and kept kissing me. But she didn't say she was okay. She didn't say *this* was okay. My hand rested limply on her leg. Why was I doing this?

I shook my head and kissed her again, unbuckling my belt. I was breathing so heavy, and not in a good way. My eyes were shut out of pure fear and hatred.

I tried to keep my hands and the rest of my body at a distance even though we were as close as two people could possibly be. I shook and bit my lip, ready for it to be over.

I dropped her off at her house and I got even madder after I texted my friends to brag, if only because it wasn't the least bit enjoyable.

Me: *Guess who just christened the tube slide at MJ Davies park?*

Freddy: *Haha! Surprised it took u so long*

Garrett: *Yea, u sure that hasn't been checked off ur list? Or was it just the tire swing?*

I shut my eyes and shook my head. I was an asshole. I may as well at least make sure everyone else knew it.

I continued to prove that and get madder at myself as I called Tiffany, the girl from my birthday, and asked if she was doing anything. I was just plain sick of being me when I went to meet her at the bar in town and followed her back to her apartment.

"Do you want something to drink?" she asked, pulling her sweater off and exposing a tight, see-through tank top.

"I'm good. We don't have to talk," I said, walking toward her and pushing her up against the wall. I backed away quickly at the thumping sound of her body connecting with the sheetrock. "Shit, did I hurt you?"

"You'll have to do a lot more than that to hurt me." She smiled and kissed me again.

Don't worry, I would.

I didn't know what I was hoping for anymore, but I couldn't forget. I couldn't step outside of my brain. I couldn't be this despicable person I was trying to prove I was. Tiffany and I made out in her bed, which smelled like another dude's cologne.

When she took her shirt off and moved her hands to my waistband, I couldn't stand it anymore. I couldn't see the image of any more girls' crying faces on the inside of my eyelids.

"I gotta go, sorry." I grabbed my shoes and rushed out the door. I had to get out of there before I had the world's biggest meltdown. I wanted to puke my intestines out by the end of this night, and I was totally sober, which I really didn't want to be.

I went home and flopped into my bed without even taking my shoes off. I lay on my back and fucking cried. I covered my face with a pillow to mask the sounds of my sobs.

It was almost 1 a.m. by now, after my ridiculous and vile night, when Lace texted me.

Lace: *I don't want to . . . but I miss you . . .*

I didn't answer. I fell asleep, tangled in my sheets, tears streaking my face.

THIRTY-ONE

I t was a new year, and shit still sucked. I never thought I'd be glad about going back to school, but this break wasn't all it was cracked up to be, and as long as I couldn't pass the football, I wanted time to keep passing.

Since Chris and I still weren't speaking, I sat alone at lunch the first week back. I brought my SAT book with me and started working on the practice tests. I also started writing down ideas for my application essay. I had like four months to come up with something, but I didn't want to scramble to find a topic over the summer before early admission apps were due. I had seen firsthand how fast time could go this year. I wasn't sure how much my application mattered if the coaches would get me in anyway (assuming football was on the table), but having work to do and feeling like I was accomplishing something was a solid distraction.

My friends probably liked not having to deal with Chris's and my fallout over the break; now it was back to reality. I still felt bad for putting them in the middle, so I told them to keep sitting with him instead of me. I'd be fine.

I glanced up after finishing a practice test for the math section. Chris stared right back at me. Garrett turned to face me, too, giving a head nod. Him, Freddy, and Dillon begged me to "stop being a chick" and make up with Chris. Well, actually, just Freddy said that. Garrett and Dillon wanted me to apologize too, so we could all hang out, but they knew it wouldn't be easy after everything he'd said the last couple months. Garrett said he thought Chris was more jealous of me than ever, which was stupid since I was at my lowest. Chris legit took my spot on the football field for a little while and then still acted like an ass.

Mindy sat down across from me. "I've never seen you with so many books before," she said.

"Gotta get a head start on this whole college-future thing."

Chris still glared at me from behind her.

She turned around to see who I was looking at, but she was nice enough not to say anything about it.

"Impressive," she finally said. I wasn't sure if she was talking about me studying, or me still not talking to Chris, or Chris's eye (which still had hints of yellow around it a month later, so that was kind of impressive). "What're you writing your application essay on?"

"Not sure yet, you?"

I caught Chris's eye again before glancing back at Mindy.

"I'll probably just write about the volunteer work I did in Costa Rica last summer. I know, cliché," Mindy said.

I smiled a little. Avoiding clichés always made me think of Lace.

"It's too bad we can't write about the stuff that actually affects us, right?" She raised her eyebrow. I shifted as she kept staring at me, feeling like she saw too much of me. I didn't even know what she was talking about or hinting at, or if she even was.

"Like me?" I asked.

She shrugged.

"I'm really sorry about everything," I blurted. I had wanted to apologize to her so many times over the last month—for snapping at her at Mark's party, for sending her naked picture to my friends, for hooking up with her over and over and treating her like she wasn't even a real person.

But I did it again just a few days ago. I wasn't exactly dripping with sincerity.

"Like?" she said, running her hands through her silk straight deep-brown hair.

"For over break," I said, looking down at my books. "For the whole last year."

She shrugged again. "Nothing new."

I shut my eyes. Exactly. That was what people expected of me and I wanted them to expect something better now.

I bet Mindy would forget all about me once she was in college. We'd probably say a quick hi to each other while we were home during breaks; she'd be living a life totally separate from this school and me. I hoped I didn't impact her or any other girl as much as I thought I did. They'd all be fine and move on. I wished I could go around individually apologizing to all of them, but I didn't even know who some of them were, plus that seemed a little dramatic. I couldn't have mattered to anyone that much.

"Well, good luck, Mase," Mindy said, standing up and pointing at my books again. "I'm sure you'll figure it out."

I looked down at the papers in front of me. I should've figured it out already.

I picked up my phone to text Lace. I never answered her the

night of her art showing. I couldn't leave things like this.

Me: *Hey, wanna do something sometime?*

She didn't answer for another week until she finally said: *sure.*

THIRTY-TWO

We made plans on Saturday to meet up at a park near Lace's house and go for a walk together through the trails.

I stopped to get her coffee at Starbucks, remembering that the couple times we had gone together she ordered a soy latte. And, it was the end of January and freezing, so I got myself the biggest size hot chocolate.

She was there already, sitting in her car when I pulled up beside her. We looked at each other through our frosted windows for a few seconds. I swallowed hard and took a deep, steadying breath.

I got out after putting my gloves on and handed her the coffee.

"Thanks," she said, smiling. I still had to get used to her brown hair. Even though she wore a winter hat, the color showing at the bottom wasn't the Lace I'd come to know.

"Not the best idea to do something outside, I guess," I said, stuffing my left hand in the pocket of my coat.

"We can just sit in the car if you want." She shrugged, taking a sip of coffee.

"Sure."

I opened the driver side back up and she walked around to get in the passenger side. My breath caught when I realized this was like that night so many nights ago. We sat in front of the bay and Lace opened up to me. I shut my eyes, picturing the waterfront and the look on her face as she exposed herself. I'd been afraid and uncertain, only certain of how much I liked her. So much had changed since then.

I turned the ignition and put the heat on high as Lace shut the door behind her.

"So, what've you been up to?" I asked, pushing memories from my head and focusing on today. I took my gloves off and turned to face her.

"Nothing new, really. How's your wrist healing?"

The conversation felt forced. I wondered if you could ever salvage the special relationship you had with someone once it was gone and reduced to meaningless small talk. If you could ever be someone to them in the present, and not just memories of what they used to know.

"I had to have surgery," I said, only realizing now that I never told her that.

"Oh wow," she said, bringing her fingertips to cover her lips, her eyes widened. "Are you okay?"

My lips twitched up to the side. "Yeah, my tendon snapped after the bone healed because it was so tight for so long." I left out the part where I punched the wall because I hated myself for what I did to her. "It's getting better now, though. I'm in physical therapy and I don't wear the brace anymore, at least." I held up my arm as proof.

"It's so weird," she said, staring out the windshield.

I squinted. "What is?"

"Healing a bone." She turned to face me. "Like, first you have to immobilize it for months so that the bone actually knits together. Then, you risk the tendon snapping while that's happening and you have to heal that. You get the cast and brace off when that's all healed, but now all the ligaments and muscles around it are damaged. So, then you have to go to therapy to heal those, too. And the thing that ends up staying damaged isn't actually the thing you hurt in the first place. Plus, through all that pain and time spent to fix it, it'll probably never be the same. It's like the healing never ends."

I stared at her without blinking. I almost wanted to smile, because the small talk was over. But I couldn't smile because what she said was depressing. Not only about my wrist—but the metaphor.

"I'm starting to think healing is part of life. Nothing will ever feel perfect," I said.

She turned away from me and looked out the window again. A pile of crunchy dead leaves fluttered across the grass outside. "I've always had trouble accepting that."

I nodded even though she wasn't looking at me.

Then she said, "And now, anyone who sees you will never know you broke your wrist. There's no sign anything was ever wrong."

I held my wrist out to her to show her the thin scar that ran along the outside of my palm, up past the knobby bone of my wrist, where they made the incision for surgery. It was healed now, not red and scabby anymore—fading, but it'd always be there. She traced her freezing fingers along the edge of it.

We sat in this car months ago and she said she was fractured, too, only it couldn't be seen on an X-ray. People who didn't know her would never know anything was wrong either, but everyone had scars, whether visible or not. Maybe we all had fractures that couldn't be seen on X-rays, and maybe they'd never fully heal, but we learned to live with them. Or maybe we healed them just to let new ones form. The fractures constantly changing as our lives changed.

She pulled her fingers away from my hand and took another sip of her latte before setting it down in the cup holder. She reached into the pocket of her coat and rummaged for something. Finally, she pulled it out and held it up to me. It was the half of the card I sent her two months ago.

I stared, but didn't take it. Why was she giving it back to me?

"That was for you," I said, trying not to let the disappointment creep into my voice.

"I'm not as into halves these days," she said, still holding the card up.

"Why?" I asked, slowly reaching for it.

My eyes went to her neck where her half necklaces hung, but I couldn't tell if she was wearing one with her coat zipped up. I glanced back at the card.

"Because it doesn't really matter whether things are half or whole. It's like you said, nothing is ever perfect and whole doesn't need to mean perfection. Even halves are never perfect halves," she said. "Maybe it's about perspective."

"I'm not sure I get it." I kept my eyes on the card. I opened it to see my horrible lefty handwriting. The words I wrote when I was completely heartbroken, drowning in how much I hated myself.

"I think I wanted you to make me whole," she said. "Even if I knew that wasn't realistic or possible. I just thought, maybe, you'd make me better or something."

"I wanted to," I whispered. I knew what she meant, but I wanted to make her better at the time, too. And I wanted her to make me better. Little did she know that she did help me improve, even if it was only after everything shattered.

"I know you never meant to hurt me," she said. "I don't think I ever told you that."

I glanced up to meet her eyes, still fiddling with the corners of the card. I pressed my lips together to prevent the dry, lumpy feeling in my throat from escaping as a sob.

I handed the card back to her. "Keep it."

She took it and put it back in her pocket. We both continued to stare at each other.

"You have the prettiest eyes," I finally said.

She bit her lip, suppressing a smile. "I'm not even going to say it."

"It's not a pickup line," I said. She shook her head and we both laughed.

I leaned over and hugged her. She wrapped her arms around my neck and we stayed like that for a few minutes, like the comfort we needed was found in each other. I had no idea where we stood anymore, but that was fine. For the first time, it felt like things would be okay.

THIRTY-THREE

I was out for a run, something I had been doing at least four days a week since my physical therapist told me it'd be okay to do cardio. I took Dove with me some days, figuring she could use the exercise just as much as me, especially since Doritos and Cheez-Its were some of her main food groups. But, on the days she was peacefully asleep on the couch, I was a sucker and felt too bad to wake her up. Today was one of those days.

I was never much of a runner before I hurt my wrist, but something about it calmed me now. Usually I just stuck to jogging to warm up, and tons of sprints and agility for training. But now a nice long, five-mile run felt easy and it let me put everything out of my mind for a little while. It was just me, the road, and the ice-cold air on my face.

After my runs, I usually finished with core work, legs, and whatever upper body I could manage. My personal football coach during the off-season told me not to do anything overly physical yet, but he didn't really specify what was *too physical*. Obviously, I didn't want to screw up my wrist again, but I had more confidence now that I was getting back to my cardio and core shape quickly. It was still no indication of how throwing the football would go, but everything was connected. If my legs were strong and my abs and back were strong, it could only help.

I had been in top football shape back in October when everything changed, and even though it wasn't like I turned into a fat ass or anything, I got weaker throughout the winter. My right arm was only just starting to get back to the same size as my left and I still had to work to get it bigger . . . stronger.

My indoor coach wouldn't let me come in to try training until my wrist was, as he put it, "in the best shape it's ever been in." I usually didn't start spring training until March anyway, but that was when I had played football until November or December. And when I still worked out all year long—when I didn't have a broken bone. So, I wanted to get back and face the moment of truth. Would I still be able to do it?

The air pierced my lungs like the point of a knife; I couldn't believe it would be February in two days. This year was passing me by and it wasn't turning out anything like I originally thought. Just as I was rounding the corner back into my neighborhood, my phone buzzed in my pocket.

Chris: *Can we meet up?*

I went inside the house, huffing and out of breath, trying to decide if I should bother. Honestly, I had kind of written him off. It was hard, he'd been my best friend since before I could even remember having a best friend, but that didn't mean it was okay for him to act the way he had. He didn't say he was sorry. I'd lose it if he wanted to meet up just to act like an ass again. But I doubted he would've texted if that was the case. So, when I got out of the shower, I told him I'd meet him at the diner in town for dinner.

We sat silently as we waited for our food. We'd spent the last ten minutes staring off into space or at the TV on the wall. Coverage played on the Super Bowl, which was in three days.

I wondered if that was why Chris wanted to make things right. He'd already missed my birthday and Christmas. He probably couldn't stand the idea of missing out on another occasion with my friends and me.

We had a tradition of gathering at my house and eating more than anyone ever should each year during the Super Bowl, and we had our own pool for it. When we were younger, the pool was for food, but we had since upgraded to real money. Last year, we were big enough assholes to determine a clear-cut loser and declare that they had to go on a date with a girl the rest of the group decided on. Dillon came in last and followed through with the bet. He went out with Cindy Peters—I could be more of an asshole and say we picked her because she was heavy, had frizzy hair, and carried a Harry Potter backpack.

Dillon didn't want to do it. He tried to get out of it a bunch of times. I knew he felt bad because he was a lot nicer than the rest of us. Why didn't he stand up to us? We all gave him serious shit when he admitted he kissed her good night, too. The whole thing actually made me sick now, especially when I thought about how Cindy tried to say hi to Dillon in the cafeteria the next day, like she thought they were dating and he liked her, and he totally ignored her. I could tell he wanted to be nice, let her down easy, but with me and my friends passing judgment on everyone, he decided it was better to look cool. It really killed me that even Dillon, who hated being an asshole, was just like the rest of us, influenced the same way. I buried the memory back where it belonged.

"Look," Chris finally said, snapping me out of the god-awful memory. "You know I'm sorry." He fiddled with the straw of his chocolate shake.

"I do?" I looked behind me to see if the waitress would be bringing my grilled cheese and onion rings anytime soon. So far, this didn't sound like a real apology, even if I should've been apologizing, too.

"Come on, Mason," Chris said. "Can't we just move on? The guys are about to disown us. We're being pussies."

I snorted and shook my head. "No, we can't. I'm sick of this stuff. You insulted Lace. You treat girls like shit. It's just—it's not cool anymore."

"You're preaching to me about how to treat girls?" he asked, leaning back. It was obvious he didn't want to start anything more, but he had every right to call me out.

I exhaled. "I know, you're right."

He raised his eyebrows like he couldn't believe I actually acknowledged it and wasn't full of rage.

"Just to be clear," he said, tracing the drops of water on his glass. "I don't believe a lot of the things I say, I just do it because it's what we all do."

"Yeah, I did the same thing." I took a sip of water. "But it's not right. And I realized something."

The waitress rounded the corner with our food. Chris had been leaning in like I was about to say something earth-shattering, but he sat back and smiled at her. We said some thank yous, pretending we weren't just arguing with each other.

"Spit it out," he said after she walked away.

I stared at the ceiling and combed my hand through my hair, trying to figure out how to say what I was about to say. I ran my tongue across my teeth, my hand behind my head, before turning back to face him. He had his elbows propped on the table again, leaning toward me, waiting.

I took a deep breath. "The only people who can stop guys from saying such vulgar shit about girls like they're not even real people—is other guys." I shrugged. I had been thinking about it a lot after the day I saw Lace's painting. It may have stemmed from me, but it was about all of us, even the ones who didn't do anything. That was the point. It wasn't just about what we actually *did*, but the things we said, and the things we stood by and let happen. I had to speak up when I knew things weren't right. Garrett and Dillon did it sometimes, but they had to do it more. We had to stop acting like things were no big deal, like it was all in good fun. It wasn't.

Chris let it sink in while dunking a fry in ketchup, but he didn't put it in his mouth. "Jesus, you have changed," he said, keeping his eyes on his plate.

I rolled an onion ring between my fingers.

"The worst part is that if you had always thought like this, we would've, too. I've always been jealous of you and figured I should just do whatever you do." He chewed some of his coleslaw. "I knew you changed, but I figured it wouldn't last, so I just kept acting like you didn't."

"Then I guess I've been a shitty example. To everyone." I stared at the wall.

"Everything just seems so easy for you, man," Chris said. He took a huge bite of his burger. Then he added with his mouth full, "Girls like you better. You're better looking. You're insane at football, and you still have all this fun like you don't even have to work hard."

"I work harder than you think," I said into my grilled cheese.

"I know, I know." He put his hands up like he was presenting a white flag. "But you must see what I mean. Like, you broke your wrist when it wasn't even senior year and you met the one girl you've ever given a shit about at the freaking doctor's office!"

"What does that have to do with anything?"

"Even when something shitty finally happens to you, it's like you turn it into gold."

I shook a glob of ketchup into the side of my red, greasy basket of fried onions, letting his words sink in for a minute. I swirled one around before popping it into my mouth. I never thought about it like that, like breaking my wrist and going to Dr. Kalad's office where I met Lace was somehow fate. That I found the one person who could force me to see myself clearly when I thought I was at my lowest. I kept chewing, crinkling the paper inside the onion ring basket. I didn't turn it into gold, though.

Chris sat, eating his burger, staring at me.

"It's not like I planned it. And you said yourself that I've changed, but the problem is, why did I ever have to change so much? It's too little too late. I might not even be able to play football anymore, man." I rested my right elbow on the table and flexed my hand back and forth. I still barely had fifty percent mobility.

Chris's eyes widened and he sat up straighter, before glancing at the scar on my palm and the way my wrist was limited to small movements. I had gone months without letting any of my friends know that there was even a shred of doubt. Well, there was a lot more than a shred.

"And you know," I said, not wanting to give him the chance to spew some "you'll be fine" lines, "it's too little too late for Lace, too."

I didn't know if that was true. Lace and I had been talking since we hung out last week, but I didn't know where it was going, if it was even going anywhere. Either way, as long as I was with her, I wasn't sure I'd be able to move on from what happened.

"No way," Chris said, shaking his head. "You told Garrett you and her were friends now. I don't know why you broke up, but she seems to think better of you than you think of yourself."

I looked up at him, scratching my finger against the oily grilled cheese bread. Maybe I had written Chris off too quickly. He might've been a better guy than I gave him credit for. He didn't even ask why we broke up and I wasn't sure I'd ever tell him.

"And, man," he added, "you're Mason Vance. You'll always find a way to play football."

I kept staring at my food before looking up at him again. I wasn't sure he was right, but I nodded anyway. "I'm sorry I wrecked your face," I said, a slow smile forming on my lips.

"I had it coming for a while." He smiled back, touching his fingers to his healed eye. "And since you're a changed man now, you might be proud to know that I didn't take any girls up on their pity offers to nurse me back to health. Just Hayley." He smiled again. "I like her. Have for months."

I wasn't ready to give up on our friendship yet, just like I wasn't ready to let go of Lace. I didn't know where we stood, but for now that would have to be enough. Maybe just like his faded black eye and my healing wrist, the past could be diminished until it was no longer seen. Things wouldn't be the same, but that was what happened. There'd always be healing to be done and things to overcome. It didn't mean the pain never existed, but it'd go away or at least become tolerable.

"Now quit being a fat ass and give me some damn onion rings," Chris said, pulling my basket toward him. We kept smiling at each other like a couple of saps.

I laughed and grabbed his burger, taking a huge bite.

"Dick," he said, laughing, too.

THIRTY-FOUR

My physical therapy appointments were three times a week, and my wrist was definitely improving. When I first started, the damn thing wouldn't move a fraction in any direction. It was scary how stiff it was. My physical therapist, Sid, still almost brought me to tears every time I was in here, but I was getting used to it and I didn't care if he had to rip my wrist apart to force it to move, I'd do whatever it took.

Sid said I might get the mobility back to ninety percent. I thought he meant within a couple weeks, but he meant, like, permanently. That didn't sound good to me and I hoped on every quarterback to ever play the game that if I worked hard enough, I'd get the full one hundred.

I did my exercises at home twice a day, and Sid definitely held up his end of the recovery process by proving to me that I didn't have a high pain threshold like I'd thought. I bit down on my lip so hard the other day while he twisted my wrist that I had a sore in my mouth now. Even the ice and e-stim at the end of each session kind of sucked. I didn't want an icepack on my hand in freaken February when there was enough of a freeze outside. I was such a wimp.

Sid sat down, waiting for me to finish my exercises, so he could work on me. First I started with the arm bike, which was a new exercise he had me doing lately, and it was also pointless. It didn't hurt or stretch my wrist at all, it just made my shoulders tired. Which was depressing because I was obviously a lot weaker now. I used to do the arm bike all the time with almost maximum resistance; bench-pressed over two hundred, weighted pull-ups, dips, push-ups. Basically whatever anyone else saw as punishment was in my training regimen. I died a little bit every time I set foot in this room.

After the bike, I had to rotate my wrist back and forth, up and down, over and under. I did curls, *modified* push-ups (what a joke), and all of this was with a *five-pound* weight.

"Never thought you'd see the day where you'd be curling a five-pound dumbbell, huh?" Sid laughed. It was funny, but not that funny. My demise was pathetic.

"Seriously. I was up to fifties before I broke it." I didn't want to brag or anything, but I may as well since I was down forty-five pounds and might never curl a fifty-pound weight again. I technically could've curled a heavier weight, the five-pounder was just for my wrist. It wasn't like my bicep totally vanished. But I had to get my wrist strength back to work up to the exercises I did for my arms before.

"Wow, fifty is pretty good. You know where you want to play in college yet?"

A smile formed on my lips and I looked up at him before setting the weight down. He said "want" and "yet" as in something that *would* still happen.

I sat down in the chair next to his desk and he rolled another chair up in front of me. He took hold of my arm and massaged warming cream into my wrist.

"I don't know," I said, staring down at my arm. "I met a bunch of coaches at two different football camps I went to over the summer. Definitely somewhere big." I had never been one of those guys who put all his hopes and dreams on one school. To be honest, I had no idea where I wanted to go to college. Probably somewhere like LSU, Miami, FSU, Notre Dame . . . Stanford maybe? I didn't even have any idea what state I wanted.

"What camps did you go to?" Sid asked as he bent my wrist. I cringed. No talk of football and college could distract from the pain he inflicted. I was surprised my wrist hadn't just snapped off in the couple weeks I'd been coming here.

"Um, one in Houston." I twisted my sweatpants and bit down on my shirt. Sid pushed on my wrist harder. I took a ragged breath in. "And one in Tampa," I said through the fabric of my shirt.

"Good places to get recognition. It must be tough around here where football isn't that big. Guess you're a big fish in a little pond, huh?" He whipped my wrist back and forth like it was a gummy worm, rather than a limb attached to a human being.

He wasn't the first person to say that, and it was all the more reason I was freaked out by my healing progress. I'd seen how good some of the other guys were—especially in the south, but I knew if I got my playing abilities back that I could hang with them.

"Yeah, it would be if I didn't go to the camps. I've gone for three summers in a row. I'm expecting calls or emails in another month once coaches are allowed to hit me up." I exhaled a whoosh of air like talking for a few seconds was the most difficult thing in the world, and at the moment, it was.

"Good. Congrats, man." He took his hand away for a second and looked over his shoulder. The PT room was empty today. I swallowed, enjoying the chance to relax for a minute. Then, Sid picked my arm up again and twisted it in opposite directions. This had to be classified as child abuse. "I'm not supposed to tell you this . . ." Sid said.

"Huh?" The pain was too excruciating to process much else.

He put my wrist down again and I panted like I'd just run ten miles.

"I met the Stanford coach's brother around the New Year, and I told him I just started working on you." He took more cream out and kneaded his fingers into the side of my scar, like the world's worst massage. My eyes watered.

"Really? He lives here?"

"He was visiting family for the holidays and looked me up to work on his shoulder. Small world, right?" He bent my wrist back. I squeezed my left pointer finger and thumb together, my nail digging into my skin. "Anyway," he said, ignoring my agony, "he said his brother knows about you from one of those camps. I guess he helps him out with special teams or something. But, yeah, the coach was at the camp and wasn't allowed to talk to you yet."

Oh yeah, I had forgotten all about that. I was only going into sophomore year when I saw his name on the list of attending coaches.

"He's going to send you a letter in the spring," he said. "But please don't tell anyone I told you that."

"Really?" I said, only momentarily forgetting how badly his manipulations and contortions hurt. Stanford sounded kind of awesome, even if I would totally flounder academically. Maybe that was what I needed to figure out what else I could ever be good at.

"Yeah, I told him since you were so young that you'd probably be able to bounce back from this and be ready to go hard by the summer." He stopped to roll up his shirtsleeves. "Push back against my hand." He pushed down with so much resistance it was nearly impossible to move his gigantic hand. Even if I was still in killer shape, Sid could own me.

"You really think so?" I asked through gritted teeth, as I struggled against his hand.

"I do, man. No one can know for sure, but if you work hard, why not? You feel like you've made progress the last few weeks?"

"I think so," I said, even though my wrist currently felt like smoke was coming out of it.

"I feel like your injury happened at the perfect time," Sid said.

"I was thinking that a few months ago, I just didn't fully realize it because we still had a couple games left. And no doctor guaranteed I'd be able to play again. Then, the damn surgery."

He held my wrist and pushed it all the way to the left. Through the sharp pain, I noticed it moved a little farther than it did last time I was here. "Timing is everything, isn't it?" he asked, pulling it another millimeter.

I smiled, despite the agony, and thought about the oldest saying in sports, one I saw much differently now: *No pain, no gain.* Things were better when they weren't easy.

THIRTY-FIVE

For the rest of the winter, I basically didn't do anything other than study for my SATs, work on my college applications, run, and train (minus the actual football). I spent time with my parents and Chad, occasionally the other guys, and I kept in touch with Lace once in a while. We hadn't hung out again since that day at the park, but we texted sometimes. I liked having her to talk to, even though we both had our own lives and we weren't necessarily a big part of each other's anymore.

It was almost March. The weather was kind of in that odd stage where it'd be freezing one day, then randomly warm the next. We'd get a six-inch snowstorm just to be sweating in our scarves and hats the next day. (Not that I'd ever be caught dead in a scarf.)

Lace and I made plans again on one of the weirdly warm days. I didn't really have expectations anymore. It wasn't like my feelings for her were erased, but they weren't that strong either. I didn't feel guilty any longer; I didn't feel the need to watch the way I acted. I was a better person now—she was one of the reasons. I still had progress to make, but that was what life was. No one changed overnight.

We went to dinner together, and afterward, we walked down near the bay, but not all the way to the water (it wasn't *that* warm). The sky was clear and open, tons of stars scattered above.

"So, I applied to a few colleges in Florida for next year," Lace said, walking a few feet away from me, kicking at the sand with her boots.

"Really? So you want to leave here I guess?"

"For now." She picked up a rock and flung it at the water. I couldn't tell if it skipped in the dark. "What's next year look like for you?"

"Who knows?" I put my hands in my pockets and we turned to face each other. "I have my first practice session on Sunday. Can't believe it's been almost five months since I've picked up a football."

"Are you nervous?" She took a step closer to me.

I could just make out her eyes on the dark beach, shining under the moonlight.

I nodded.

She nodded, too, staring back.

I walked to my mom's car and pulled a blanket from the trunk. I laid it down on the sand near the tall, grassy dunes. I gestured for her to come sit with me. She hesitated for a second, picking one foot up but letting it hover above the ground. Then she shrugged and came over.

She sat beside me, a few feet away. It was kind of cold, but the winter was definitely thawing out. The night air was manageable, perfect for hanging at the beach, looking at the stars.

We lay back on the blanket and gazed up at the sky, not saying anything. I wondered if she thought the stars looked just as perfect and far away as I did, like they couldn't possibly exist in real life.

I reached for her hand, both of us still quiet. Her fingers twitched and she let out a breath. I pulled my hand away, but then she took hold of it and laced her fingers through mine.

"I know we're both going in different directions, and maybe soon these last few months will feel like they happened a million years ago, but I like knowing you," she said, talking into the air above her.

"I like knowing you, too." I squeezed her hand a little harder. "You'll never know what a difference you made to me."

She didn't say anything. We both continued to stare at the sky.

"It's so nice out here," she finally said.

I nodded even though she couldn't see me.

"You know, I can see why people say things like: you're a star, or you'll be a star. Shoot for the stars. Superstar." I turned to look at her as she kept talking, her face lit in the starlight. "Because really, who wouldn't want to be like a star?" She pointed at the sky. "Shining and untouchable, way out there . . . away from here. But no one ever really will be a star. We're just stuck here beneath them, reminded that there's so much more."

She turned, propping herself up on her elbow, and looked at me. I stared back, the heaviness in my chest—one I remembered all too well—returned.

"But maybe we don't need to be stars," she said, shrugging one shoulder. "Maybe this is enough."

"Maybe," I said, staring at her bright green eyes.

She turned onto her back again and looked up, or maybe she shut her eyes, I couldn't tell.

"Maybe," she repeated to herself.

"But the thing with stars," I said, still looking at her.

She turned her head to glance at me.

"You have to look up to see them, especially when it's dark."

Her eyes were locked on mine, and she smiled. "I like that cliché."

I leaned in closer to her. A bright, copper star shined off the necklace she wore. I didn't notice it before, but the way she was lying pushed it to the base of her neck, above the zipper of her coat. It wasn't a half. It was a full star. A star. I reached over and took it between my fingers.

"It's whole," I said.

She looked at me out of the corner of her eye and kept smiling. "Yeah," she said. "Today anyway, but that's a start."

And it was. A shooting star cascaded across the sky, but I didn't feel the need to wish for anything.

THIRTY-SIX

My coach at the indoor facility finally had me come in for an evaluation. I was excited to get back on the field, but, honestly, totally nervous. I was still lost in hope, expectations that I'd be able to pick up right where I left off five months ago. My wrist was in a lot of pain when I did certain exercises—even everyday things—and my physical therapist and Dr. Kalad, and basically everyone else, told me not to expect to play like nothing had ever happened, that it would take time. I was okay with it taking time, I'd gotten pretty used to waiting. But I hoped time was all it took—that I wasn't done forever.

My trainer, Gus, a boulder of a man who never made the cut for the Jets a few years back, greeted me with a ridiculous slap on the back. I warmed up on the bike, then did sprints and agility work. I was there for almost forty minutes without so much as touching a football. I could've easily done this stuff on my own. I was pretty much in the best cardio shape of my life right now since it had been my main focus the last couple months.

Finally, at the end of our session, only ten minutes to go, Gus tossed me the ball. I caught it with just my left hand, a smile spreading over my face. I had almost given up hope for the day, like maybe he called me here under the guise of playing football but just wanted to torture me instead.

"All right, Vance," he shouted in that voice that sounded like he swallowed a bunch of jagged glass and muscles. I really missed this guy, even if he did take his failed NFL career out on unsuspecting teenage boys. "Let's see what you got. Just some easy passes."

He headed down to the opposite end of the turf. I peeled my sweaty, gray long-sleeved T-shirt off, feeling the draft of the indoor building against my bare arms. My short-sleeved Manhasset High shirt clung to my chest in a pool of sweat. I jogged down to the end zone and took a few deep breaths as Gus waited for me at the thirty-yard line. The last time I was in this position, I got slammed into and everything changed. I shut my eyes and exhaled.

"You can do this," I whispered to myself. I took another deep breath.

I dropped back a few steps, planted, and released the ball, expecting a perfect spiral to sail right into Gus's barrel chest. Not only did the ball go nowhere near his outstretched arms, but it didn't even make it to him. It hit the brick wall next to the turf and bounced onto the green, artificial grass.

"Fuck," I muttered, even more nervous than before. I tried to force the image of the guy from Syosset High slamming me, and the snap of my wrist out of my head. I tried to forget the X-ray and MRI machines grumbling and flashing above me. The weighted vest. The way my pinky wouldn't move when Dr. Kalad realized I needed surgery. The anesthesia that knocked me out while they cut my arm open. I tried to tell myself it had been months and even though I was working out and gaining my strength back, it would take a few times to get my perfect motion back. I could do this. I had already been through so much.

Gus picked up the ball and threw it back to me. I reached out with my right hand and dropped it before I even got a grip around it, once I felt my arm sear. "Shit," I shouted, grasping my wrist.

"Maybe we're rushing this thing, Vance," Gus said, coming toward me. "If it's still this tender . . ."

"No! No!" I was afraid he was about to take the ball away and send me home. "My wrist is healed. It's obviously going to hurt when I haven't even touched a ball in months! My physical therapist said it was okay to play!"

My heartbeat quickened and my breath came in rasps. I was about to keep rambling and shouting across the field, but Gus held his arms up like he surrendered. "A few more, kid. You gotta ease into this."

I let out a long breath and swallowed hard, wiping my forehead with the collar of my sweaty shirt. Gus walked back downfield.

I picked the ball up again, determined to get the pass right this time. "Come on," I breathed, then went through my motion. This time when I released the ball, it soared right into Gus's arms.

"Thank God," I whispered to myself, trying to ignore the sharp pang in my wrist. "See, man. Just rusty!" I called across the field.

"Did you really think you wouldn't be able to throw anymore?" he asked, only now realizing how relieved I was. He started cackling that low, raspy laugh. "You need to relax over there, Vance. The season is months away!"

I laughed too and rolled my shoulders out. Maybe he was right. Now I couldn't stop laughing—not like psychotic laughter, but nervous, bubbling laughs. I could really play football. I didn't want to celebrate too soon because I still had to catch the ball and tackle and everything, and my right wrist didn't feel up for that anytime soon. I wasn't off the hook yet. I didn't know when I would be. But the first step was underway.

I KEPT TRAINING for the rest of the month, making slow progress. My wrist throbbed every time I caught the ball, but my passes were already almost back to where they were before I broke my wrist, the only difference being that I was crazy sore now. My shoulder and elbow felt like they were on fire every day for the past couple weeks. I soaked in ice baths a few times, which was total torture, but it really helped my muscles. I went through enough bottles of Icy Hot to keep them in business. And I popped a couple Tylenol before every training session. I also had one of the trainers at the facility wrap my wrist before I played.

Coaches were allowed to talk to me now and I already had a stack of almost fifty letters on the table in the foyer. I got bombarded with emails. And, just like Sid predicted, the Stanford coach called me.

I had a visit planned for the end of May. I researched their programs—beyond the football program—shocking, right? The thing was, I loved football. I might've lost myself along the way, the better I got at it, but I felt like I found it all over again and like I found a new reason to love it. The journalism program at Stanford looked interesting. If playing didn't work out, maybe I could write about it or be a sportscaster. But, for now, I'd stick to improving as much as I could (and maybe strive for higher than a C average in school).

Lace and I didn't talk as much as we used to. She got accepted to transfer to a school in Florida in the fall. We understood how much we liked each other and she was still more important to me than she'd probably ever know, but we both had other things going on in our lives. We made plans to hang out over the summer, but there was no pressure anymore. I'd miss her a lot when she moved . . . she knew that.

I had my last session at the indoor facility before starting Long Island spring training camp. Both of my parents and Chad came to watch me, sitting on the small bleachers outside the field and training area. We all planned to celebrate my recovery with ample amounts of pizza afterward.

Gus finished up with some other kid doing agility work in the weight room next to the field. I picked up the ball and walked to the opposite end of the building, jumping around to stay warm. I caught my mom's eye and waved. She smiled back and looked like she was seeing me for the first time.

Chad shouted, "Vance sucks!"

My mom tapped the back of his head.

"You realize your name is Vance, too?" I shouted back across the field.

"Damn," he said.

I laughed and shook my head, tossing the ball in the air a few times. Gus jogged to the other end, clapping.

"All right, Vance," he said. "Let's make good things happen."

I took some deep breaths, gripping the ball between my hands. I shut my eyes for a few seconds, feeling the roughness of the stitches beneath my fingertips. I inhaled the smell of turf rubber and exhaled my nerves. The fluorescent lights slammed into my eyes as I opened them.

No one knew what was going to happen in this life. Sometimes, you had to let go of who you were to become who you were supposed to be. Sometimes you had to smash your own heart apart to know how to put the pieces back together, and maybe some of them would never fit just right, but they'd still be part of the full picture. Sometimes you had to break in half to become whole.

I dropped back, planted, and released the ball.

ACKNOWLEDGEMENTS

First, I'd like to thank *you*, the reader. Your connection with my work means everything.

I'd like to thank those who played a role in helping me develop my craft, and encouraging me to keep writing, especially at Tulane University and Sarah Lawrence College.

Thank you to my developmental editors who helped me take this manuscript to the next level in its early stages, Emily Hainsworth and Lauren Craft.

Thank you to my critique partners for all of their attention to detail and vital suggestions, Kris Black and Lissa Johnston. I have really enjoyed our meetings.

Thank you to my good friend Alicia Neuner for being a trusted beta reader. Thank you to Kirsten Moore for her keen eye. Thank you to betas Cheri-lee Fisher and Devin Green for input in the final stages of this book.

Thank you to Murphy Rae for this amazing cover. Thank you to Alyssa Garcia for the interior formatting. Thank you to Emily Lawrence for proofreading.

Thank you to my family for always believing in my writing abilities. Jen and Mike, thank you for the encouragement. Mom and Dad, thank you for all of your continued support and belief in me.

Yes, I'm going to thank animals. My cat Licorice was with me through a few years of this book, and so was Oscar, bringing me comfort and blocking my keyboard. Now it's up to my giant-headed staffy, Bernie, who *really* blocks my keyboard. The companionship makes writing a little less lonely.

Finally, thank you to Pat, who doesn't understand what goes

on in my head, and that's probably for the best, but he always supports and believes in me—also thanks to him for assistance on the football references.

ABOUT THE AUTHOR

Shay Siegel is from Long Island, New York. She is a Tulane University graduate and former member of the women's tennis team. She has an MFA in Writing from Sarah Lawrence College. Shay currently lives in Charleston, South Carolina with her boyfriend, Pat, and their giant-headed rescue dog, Bernie. *Fractured* is her debut novel.

Website: www.shaysiegel.com

Instagram: @shaysiegelauthor

Facebook: @shaysiegelwriter

Made in the USA
Coppell, TX
08 July 2022